Dedicated to all the work Circles of which I've been part,
and particularly to the good folks of Broadneck, 1983-1985:

Carol Bartlett
Skip Booth
Suzanne Campos
Chris Cassaw (RIP)
Ann Gardiner-Cobb
Lou Nash (RIP)
Kate Purcell
All the Substitutes, Pages and Volunteers

Thank you, one and all.

Other Books by Don Sakers

Dance for the Ivory Madonna*
The Leaves of October*
A Voice in Every Wind *
Weaving the Web of Days *
Curse of the Zwilling
The SF Book of Days
Act Well Your Part
Lucky in Love

<u>Forthcoming</u>
Hunt for the Dymalon Cygnet*

* = Scattered Worlds series

And though we shall be parted by a galaxy or more,
Yet ever in each others' hearts we'll stay.
And you shall live out your life, and I shall live out mine,
Until arrives some distant dire day,
When troubles gather all about and I am sore beset,
And for your help and succor I must pray.
Then winging as my token, to call you to my side,
Shall a rose from Old Terra come your way.

from *Queen Orabella IV* (opera)

1
Rose
[CIRCLE]
Year 511 of the Sardinian League

"Jedrek nor Talin?"

"That's him. He'll be with you in just a bit. Can you wait?"

"Very well."

The exchange reaches Jedrek distantly; he pays no attention. It is only words from an unreal world—reality is the universe within the three-centimeter marble he clutches between his palms.

Images swirl past him, endless linkages of thoughts and ideas. To his left, ten million designs for low-grav habitat modules dance intricate gavottes; to his right, a thousand equations quiver in ranked arrays. And before him, a maze of billions of documents stretches away to grey infinity.

He holds to his purpose and follows his quarry like a hunter pushing through thickest underbrush.

Gotcha. And following that, the experience of a powerful *aha!* Out of ten trillion bits of data, myriad techniques, he has managed to locate exactly what he needs. The answer sets itself into his forebrain and he lets the marble slip from between his palms.

The office and the world return, and as always Jedrek feels a tinge of regret.

He closes his eyes. "Denys, I've got it. It's simple. The Empire synthesized dellsite beams under a grav field curved to match the loadbearing struc—who are *you?*" The presence of a visitor penetrates to him and he snaps his eyes open to look at the new person.

A slender woman, light-haired and pale-skinned, many centimeters taller than Jedrek or even Denys. Over a bony frame she wears brown coveralls, the general-issue utilitarian style of work clothing for Humans throughout the Galaxy. Above her left breast is a geometrical design involving a tight spiral and a number of ovals.

Jedrek's eyes widen. An Independent Trader, here in his office—?

"I be Trader Raalhord, out from Independent Trade Ship *LaMancha*." She offers the quick hand-signal greeting of the Traders; when Jedrek returns it she smiles.

"Jedrek nor Talin, once out from Independent Trade Ship *Franklin*. This be Denys Archet, partner me." Even after so many years, Jedrek slips easily back into Trader pidgin. He cocks his head. "Trader Raalhord, surely *LaMancha* be not interested in space settlements to buy?"

"Quite not. This business be more mundane. Two days past rendezvoused we with *Akbar*; when *Akbar* captain hear we come toward Borshall, he ask we bear you a delivery. I here only to drop off package."

"Thank you. Surely you stay for meal?"

"No, truly must be on way. *LaMancha* two kiloparsecs away be, and back must me go, me cargo to supervise."

"At least let me give you chit for payment to cover." Jedrek reaches for his crediplate. Trader Raalhord's hand on his arm arrests his gesture.

"No payment. Profit with you be, Jedrek nor Talin."

"As with you, Trader Raalhord."

She places a package in his arms, a cylinder about a meter long and a few centimeters around. The outside is marked with his name and a few of his better-known ident codes; it also bears the warnings INERT ATMOSPHERE and DO NOT VACUUM STORE.

She kisses his hand, bows, and leaves the office. As the door slides shut behind her, Denys leans back in his chair and puts his feet up on his desk. "No payment. Since when do you get free favors from the Independent Traders? You know what they'd charge us professionally for that few hundred cubic centimeters of shipping volume?"

"The Library has a long history of helping out the Traders. When I left there I hitched a ride with *Franklin* and stayed on a few years. They take care of their own." Jedrek frowns. Very few people would think to send him a package through the Traders. Who...?

One way to find out.

"Hand me your knife, Denys."

"Did you forget yours again?"

Jedrek shrugs. "Old habits. I never carried one until I moved here." He takes the stylus-sized instrument from Denys, dials for minimum dispersion and moderate power, and touches a contact. A red beam slices cleanly through the end of the cylinder.

Outer wrapping peels away and the office ventilation system steps up to rid the air of a sudden argon buildup. The contents of the package lay exposed in his hands, shedding a bit of perfume.

Yellow and velvety and perfect in aspect, he holds a single longstemmed rose.

Roses grow on many Human worlds, but he doesn't need a tenday's work with a superb biochem lab to trace the origin of this flower—only a handful of people would send him a rose, and it can only have come from one planet.

"I don't get it. Some admirer?"

"It's from Earth, Denys. A rose from Old Terra."

"So?"

Jedrek's eyes go to his own screen, to the plans that wait patiently. Blast, why did this have to happen now?

"Denys, listen to me." Jedrek takes a deep breath. "I swear to you, this is very serious. I have to leave—I don't know how long I'll be gone, I don't even know when I'll be able to contact you."

Denys' feet hit the floor. "You're kidding. In the middle of a project? *This* project?"

"I know how much Terexta Trojan Two means to the firm."

"It's *you* the firm needs. Your access to Imperial technology gives us an advantage that no other planning corporation can beat."

Jedrek looks away. "I know you'll be needing me, for a dozen problems like the one I just solved. But I *have* to go. I'll try to anticipate what I can before I leave, and I'll dump as much data as possible from my marble to the puter, but it's going to be—"

"What?" Denys stands up. "You can't leave, not after we've worked to get Archetalin Enterprises flying...."

"The firm isn't going to fail—we've taken it that far together. While I'm gone, control will revert to you... and if you want to buy me out, I'll let you do it at half the market value." He meets Denys' eyes. "With any luck, I won't be gone more than a year."

Denys puts his hand on Jedrek's chin, his azure eyes burning into Jedrek's hazel. "Can you tell me what's going on?"

Jedrek nods. "When I worked at the Library—when our Circle broke up and we all went our own ways—we made a pact. If any of us got into trouble that we couldn't handle, we would send a message to the others." He holds up the rose. "This is the message."

"No other information? How do you even know who sent it, or where in the Galaxy it came from?"

"No other information can only mean that it came from Terra herself. I've got to make my way there, and I've got to hurry."

"And I suppose you'll fly yourself there in your personal starship?" Denys' tone is derisive; he seldom has anything nice to say for Jedrek's piloting ability. There is little nice to say.

"I know better than that. Even if I were the Galaxy's best pilot I wouldn't want to venture though the Transgeled alone. No, there has to be a Trader ship headed in that direction soon; I'll just hop a ride and keep transferring until I get to Terra."

Denys shakes his head. "You're a fool. I don't know why I put up with you." He waves at the office. "And you expect me to keep all this together while you're gone? Alone?"

"You can do it." For an instant the thought of inviting Denys along crosses his mind—Jedrek pushes it away at once. "I realize how much I'm asking. Believe me."

"Oddly enough, I do." Again Denys shakes his head. "I'm going to miss you."

"Don't."

"All right, run off to Terra. But first make sure you've put down all the details of that grav-field shaping technique. And...and please hurry back." A sigh. "When do you leave?"

"I have to check on Trader ships. No sooner than two days. As quickly as possible after that."

Eyes closed, brows raised, Denys whispers, "We have work to do, then."

❈

Borshall falls behind at many times lightspeed, blue and white on the tachyscope. Jedrek glances at the Independent Trader shuttle pilot next to him, then back at the viewscreen. As quick as that, Borshall is invisible, its sun a star among many, identifiable only by the radial velocity assigned it by the boat's puter.

Ahead lies Trader ship *Narmer,* then step after step of transfers as quick shuttle boats outpace the slow-moving Trader Ships. And finally, more than a third of the way around the Galaxy, Earth.

Who is calling for help?

Why?

And...why, Jedrek asks himself, is he answering?

He sighs and closes his eyes. The days to come will not be peaceful; he'll be happy for any rest he can get now.

❈

LOOKING FOR SPACE?
Look no further!

Whether you're interested in a family vacation getaway module in the Spanshorran Rings, or a permanent habitat for two million, Archetalin Enterprises is the company for you.

Using long-lost technology from the Terran Empire, we provide superior construction at a price that leaves our competitors in total eclipse.

We also provide repair and renovation services for existing settlements and habitats, including expansion options.

With offices on Borshall, Terexta, and Sedante, we are fully licensed in all systems in the Sardinian League, and accept payment in all League currencies.

For a free consultation, contact *consult@archetalin.bor* on BorshallNet or *archetalin@borshall.biz* on LeagueComm.

❀

2
Terraformer
[CIRCLE]
Year 11 after the breakup of the Circle

Jedrek sits in his tiny cabin and rolls his data marble between his palms. The marble has a lot to say about the Transgeled, little of it good and none of it up-to-date. The Imperial Catalog of Planets is over thirty-five hundred years old; it passes the bounds of possibility that any worlds in such an unstable area remain as they were under the Empire.

The Independent Traders maintain files on every world they deal with; those files are concerned only with trading data, however, and as a matter of custom Trader Ships do not swap files very often. In addition, some of the lesser worlds go a century of so between Trader contacts. In a hundred years of revolutions and wars and political upsets, everything changes.

Jedrek sighs and looks around the tiny cabin, a transient's room in a shuttle racing to meet Independent Trade Ship *Alexander*. Set in the wall, as in every room built during Imperial times, is a full-size term with a display screen about half a meter square. Currently, that term links him to the ship's puter and all the data stored therein, plus an ultrawave hookup to the mother Trade Ship...if there are enough channels to spare.

Four millennia ago, that term would have given complete access to Imperial Centcom—and thence to any ultrawave transceiver in the Galaxy. A user would have been able to search the Grand Library on Terra and any of a myriad planetary databanks.

Gone, all gone. The marble between his palms, the few others like it, and the data packages stored in the Solar System—these are the only remnants of the Grand Library and all Imperial knowledge. And even these data go further out of date with each passing year.

With a savage gesture he returns the marble to its sealed

pouch at his hip. Twenty years of his life spent serving the Grand Library...what more can it expect of him?

The wall-term calls for attention, and Jedrek hits the comm key. The shuttle pilot's gaunt face appears in the holoscreen. "Jedrek, communication we have from Trader Ship *Odegaard*."

"Be Shrev Loudin still *Odegaard* Captain?"

"Yes. She greetings sends to you."

No sense wondering how the Captain of Odegaard found out that he was aboard. If the unofficial gossip network of the Independent Traders could ever be harnessed, it could very well act as the nucleus of a new Empire.

"Captain Loudin asks can we stop at *Odegaard* on way past."

"I think no. I want catch *Alexander* still in Otred system."

"*Odegaard* scheduled port-of-call in Trimenoorlen Hegemony. Be only twelve parsecs away from next *Alexander* stop. Two days from now. Be okay?"

One thing that hasn't changed in thirty-five hundred years was the position of the stars...Jedrek touches his marble and smiles. From Trimenoor it is only a kiloparsec to the main trade lane passing out of the Transgeled and into more civilized areas around Geled. And from there to Terra is only a shuttle's hop.

Besides, it would be good to see the Captain and crew of *Odegaard* again. Jedrek served time in the ship years ago—no doubt some of his repairs still functioned in the craft, would function long after he was dead.

"Okay, we meet *Odegaard*. Be your trade schedule disrupted?"

"Cargoes me be traded on *Odegaard* as easy as on *Alexander*. Crew votes for *Odegaard*."

Jedrek shrugs. "Call me one hour before arrive, please?"

"Okay yes." The pilot's image winks out.

Odegaard. Finally, something he knows and can count on in all the shifting changes of the Transgeled. It isn't until now, with a lost security is restored, that he realizes how much he craved it.

A security that will have to sustain him for the rest of the trip.

❄

The shuttle comes out of tachyon phase into a war. A few ships are idly hurling missiles and laser beams back and forth; the shuttle pilot gives full power to her defense screens and makes a series of tricky maneuvers, then ducks back into translight speed for a microsecond.

"Worry not," the pilot says over her shoulder to Jedrek. "Always war these parts. You learn: get used to it." She touches the controls and frowns. "I jump too far a bit. Ten minutes to *Odegaard*. *Odegaard* in high orbit that planet."

On the screen is a bluewhite crescent. Jedrek reads position from the naviputer display, then reaches into his pouch and cups his palm around the marble.

He finds the planet's Imperial listing without difficulty:

CELSIUS. Mars-type planet, third in its system. Discovered in TE 64 and terraformed over the next twenty years under an Imperial Council grant. Celsius obtained its name from the overwhelming coincidence that the length of its sidereal year (17,724,305 and 5/18 standard seconds) was exactly 5/9 of the Terran sidereal year....

Why was the coincidence "overwhelming"? What, in the first place, was so coincidental about the inconvenient fraction 5/9? And why did all this lead to the name "Celsius"? The hyperlinks are missing—the poor marble holds only a tenth of the Grand Library's data, and after Jedrek finished stuffing it with technical information, there was no space left for most of the Galactic Anglich Dictionary Database. The resultant dead ends have bothered him ever since.

Nor is the mystery made any clearer when the marble goes on to tell him that Celsius' chief cities in Imperial Days were named Tepid, Boiling and Absolute Zero....

"*Odegaard* coming up."

The suns are cut by Celsius' limb; against glaring sunset there is the movement of shadows, and Jedrek peers closely, straining to see a shadowy shape—

As the shuttle moves into eclipse, shadows suddenly come alive with a million faerie lights. Girders, odd-shaped life pods, the starlike gleam of ports, and over it all the indistinct pearly haze of a defense screen at lowest power...this is Independent Trade Ship *Odegaard.*

Jedrek's pilot takes her shuttle planetward of the large ship, moving in a predetermined course toward an assigned docking berth. Jedrek turns from screen to screen, his head spinning with the beauty of the ship as it sweeps past against the stars. Five kilometers long, holding perhaps a quarter-million crewmembers, *Odegaard* has tripped the starways unceasingly since the time of the Empire. Millennia and generations passed, age after age of people who knew only this ship, ignorant of the change of politicoeconomic systems, ignorant of the decline of technology, ignorant in some ways of even the powers of their long-dead sires who had built the ship. The Independent Traders know but one life, and that is to trade—and if in trading they manage to stitch together the remnants of a once-Galactic society, well, they spare little time or concern for that.

The shuttle spins, viewscreens track against stars and planet and ship—and then *Odegaard* engulfs them in a durasteel-and-dellsite womb.

Disembark from your ship, turn to the left, and sooner or later you'll reach a startrippers bar. It is a universal custom of Humanity. On planets, the establishment might be kilometers from the spaceport in an appropriately seedy portion of town; on board *Odegaard* it is a twenty-five-meter cubical volume just down a dimly lit hallway from the main docking bays.

Returning Traders always stop in for a drink or jolt when their missions are completed—for visitors it is *de rigueur* to be seen at the bar. Jedrek is accompanied by six of the shuttle's crew...the rest will follow after securing the boat. He doesn't worry about his luggage. *Odegaard's* central puter, which routes thousands of packages daily, can handle his three small bags without supervision.

When he enters the bar, a fight is in progress. The bartender has switched off grav for the spectacle; the two combatants float in mid-chamber, grappling and shouting drunkenly. Jedrek pushes his way to the bar, hands it his crediplate, and taps for a package of skyhitabs. Breaking the seal, he pops two of the tabs into his mouth. Seconds later, the jolt hits him and he leans back to watch the fight in a much more receptive mood. Barehanded wrestling, rules as old as the race...they are getting along quite nicely.

In a matter of minutes, a winner emerges. The loser presents his front to the victor, turns his head aside, exposing the neck. The winner bows his head, kisses the losers forehead, and then the two separate. Grav cycles to normal, and the patrons turn to their own pursuits.

"Jedrek nor Talin?"

The speaker is a Trader; she wears a complicated set of jewelry and symbolic markings revealing to the practiced observer her exact station aboard *Odegaard*.

"Yes?"

"To *Odegaard* be welcome. Captain her compliments sends. She want to see you outside." The woman leads him out of the bar and through a door. On the other side, in an unused storage chamber, stands *Odegaard's* Captain.

Shrev Loudin is tall and thin, and wears her fiery orange hair short and spiky. Her jewelry is elaborate, and rank tattoos start on her left cheek and train halfway down her left forearm.

"Shrev." They embrace.

"What you be doing with yourself, Jedrek?"

"I to Borshall went and be now respectable." He grins. "Now be designing settlements."

"And you back come to us. We trade just about anything— but not much market for space settlements in this part the Galaxy. Not much profit for you."

"No, I be on way to Terra. Not back to Trading." He glances around the room. "Can we somewhere more cozy go, for drink and talk?"

"I be sorry, Jedrek. The Mistress asks see you. She learn you be coming, she convince us change course so take you aboard."

"The Mistress? Who be that, new Astrogator?" On a Trade Ship, the Astrogator is often held in reverence approaching that of a priest or priestess.

"No. She has own ship. You must ask her."

Whomever she is, this Mistress must be a very powerful woman. Independent Traders are loath to change course, to alter in any way their ships' orbits around the Galactic Core. "Take me to her."

"Follow."

Half a kilometer away, Shrev stops Jedrek at an airlock door; viewscreens about him show a ship cradled between girders of *Odegaard*. On any other scale it would be a staggering vessel: fully a hundred meters long, marked with the designs of the Trader ship and...is it possible?...the six globes of the Terran Empire.

Jedrek suppresses a chill. It must be some kind of relic. He touches his marble, its surface cool against his palm. The Imperial Ship Registry reports no vessel with this configuration.

The airlock inner door opens. Shrev motions Jedrek in. "She want see you alone."

As he crosses through the airlock, there is the slightest change in pressure and gravity. The inner door opens and a mechanical voice greets him. "Welcome to Independent Starship *Worldsaver*. Please follow the indicator light." A bright dot of green forms in the air in front of him; he walks after it. Only a few steps later a door opens and he enters a banquet room.

A dinner is set out on a table done up in the most sumptuous style of the Late Empire. Behind the table, behind food and gleaming serving dishes, behind decanters of varicolored liquids, sits a short, chubby woman with long ebony hair and the darkest possible eyes.

Jedrek cannot not resist stepping forward. Time has not been kind to her, and she's gained more than a few kilograms, but there is no chance of not recognizing her. Cilehe.

On the table before her, in a white vase, is a single red rose.

❂

"So you be Independent Trader now?"

"Not really." She sips the sweet wine made on board *Odegaard*. "Please, speak Standard. I'm not a Trader."

"Oh, right. You're 'the Mistress.' What does that mean? How did you manage to get a Trade Ship to change course?"

"Simple. I own about forty per cent of *Odegaard*."

Jedrek coughs. Forty per cent...! "Excuse me, Honored Sayyid. I don't know if I am fit to dine at your table. Where did you get *that* kind of money?"

"It's a long story. After we all broke up, I spent a year or so hopping about near Terra. Then I decided to head away. You'd hitched rides with the Traders; I thought I might as well follow."

"You were chasing after me?"

She blushes. "Not at all. I didn't know that much about the rest of the Galaxy, you know. Best to go in someone else's tracks, I thought."

"Go ahead."

"Well, it must've been sometime around '76 that I hooked up with *Odegaard*. You must have just finished hitching with the ship."

Jedrek thought back, mentally adding tendays and months, converting from Sardinian League dates. "About a year after, probably."

"Soon we passed through the Epsilon Dentanna system. No, don't go for your marble, I'll fill you in. The one habitable world is Trworgyn, oversize moon of a gas giant. It was terraformed and settled late in the Empire. A greenhouse-effect atmosphere kept temperatures bearable. But they hadn't taken care of themselves. Over the millennia much of the atmosphere had leaked off, and there were no Imperial Navy ships around to fine-tune their ecology. To top it off, a century earlier they'd been in a war with some neighboring world or other—I never did get the details straight—and chain reactions set off in the upper atmosphere were destroying the ozone layer. No defense against the gas giant's radiation belts."

From somewhere at her side, Cilehe produces a crystal marble that, but for the selection of information it carries, is twin to Jedrek's. "Do you remember all that work I did on plans for re-terraforming Luna?"

He remembers. One summer Cilehe spent hours every day with the Grand Library's master puter—she calculated every detail of her plan. It would have worked, too, if she'd ever gotten around to implementing it. A few comets here, repairs to a ring of mirrors there, a good deal of energy to hydrolyze the Lunar seas…and the decay that had been proceeding since the first Sack of Terra could be reversed. But Cilehe never made the effort.

Jedrek nods.

"It turned out that all I had to do was move a few decimal points and the calculations applied to Trworgyn. It took five years, with *Odegaard* doing most of the work, but Trworgyn was saved. I took in half the profits. I bought into *Odegaard* and when we stopped at Tep Kecor shipyards I had them refit this ship as *Worldsaver*."

"And you've been re-terraforming planets ever since?"

"Seven in the last three years. It gets easier with practice. And each world pays heavily. There are a lot of wars out here, and many times ecological weapons are used. The arrangement works to the benefit of *Odegaard,* the planets involved, and myself."

"It's a good thing you put all the Empire's terraforming data into your marble."

"Certainly is."

"Too bad the ship will have to get along without you for a while."

"Whyever?" She frowns, then her eyes shift to the rose. "Oh, *that.* Don't tell me you're taking it seriously?"

"Don't tell me you're *not?*"

"'Course not. Listen, Jedrek. Who could have sent it?" She ticks them off on her fingers. "It wasn't me, and it wasn't you. Sukoji? Can you imagine her getting into trouble and calling for help?"

"Of course not."

"Kedar, then? Kedar? He wouldn't ever get into a situation in which he might not come out on top. That leaves only Drisana."

"I'd already figured that out."

"And you want to answer this? She probably wants to have a reunion. To convince us all how wrong we were to leave the hallowed halls of Alexandria. I can do quite nicely without that, thank you."

Jedrek shakes his head. "Drisana needs help. I'm going to help her. Blast it, we were a Circle. Don't you remember the vows we took?"

"Do you think I care about those vows now? Have we kept them? Did *you* keep them, running off to New Sardinia or wherever you went?"

"Borshall."

"Did Sukoji keep her vows? Not even Kedar stayed. And now you want me to go back to keeping my word, keeping a promise made to a Circle that no longer exists?" She takes a breath and makes a show of calmly sipping more wine. Her hand is shaking.

He says nothing. Cilehe stares at him, looks away, then a tear trickles down her right cheek. "What are you staring at? I've found a life I'm happy with. Finally. Do you think I want to give it up and go chasing back to Terra with you? Think again."

Jedrek settles back in his chair. "Happy?" He raises an eyebrow.

"*Yes*, happy. A whole shipload of Independent Traders to do my bidding, worlds at my feet, a big ship to live in with every comfort I could wish…" Her voice catches.

"Do you have friends, Cilehe? Do you have anyone who means to you what our Circle once did? Or are you caught up in this big luxurious ship afraid to face the Galaxy or the people outside?"

For a moment he thinks she will throw a tantrum. Chancy, being this personal with someone he hasn't seen for eleven years. She might be a different person. But…but he knows the old Cilehe is still there.

She doesn't explode. She reaches for him, and he is there as she buries her face in his arm. For a long time neither speaks. Then she looks up into his eyes.

"It's not going to be the same," she says. "The Circle is broken forever, you know. We'll never get it back. No matter what Drisana thinks."

"I know that. I've known it since we broke up. You're going to have to learn it, deep down where it really means something. You're going to confront the pieces, else you'll never be free of it."

She nods.

"Good. I'll tell Shrev that we're leaving ship to connect with *Alexander*."

"No."

"I thought…"

"I am coming along. We can get to Terra a good deal

quicker in this ship." She forces a smile. "Are you still as terrible a pilot as you were?"

He ignores the question. "This is a wild area. We need protection. We'd better stay with the Traders."

"Never mind that. *Worldsaver* was a decommissioned Geledi Navy Destroyer, fitted with a power plant ten times over spec. Her lasers are powerful enough to bite neutronium. Her antigravs can drag small planetoids. And her defense screens can black out a planet. No one is going to bother *this* ship."

"Good. Let me get my luggage from *Odegaard*, then we can say our goodbyes and be gone."

"Goodbyes?" Cilehe brushes back her hair. "Yes, I guess I should tell Captain Loudin that I'm going away. I'm sure she'll appoint someone to manage my share of the cargo while I'm gone."

Cilehe gets up from the table and walks away. For a second Jedrek stares after her, then he too stands.

Before leaving the room, he notices that Cilehe's rose is beginning to droop. He pours the rest of his wine into the vase, then follows her.

❋

Ship's Log
Independent Trade Ship *Odegaard*

19 Feb 6481

PROPOSED: That *Odegaard* shall galactic orbit break. For time period ten years, *Odegaard* in local trade shall engage. Policy after ten years review shall be.

Odegaard shall trade strategy ally, with Mistress Cilehe Rev out from Independent Ship *Worldsaver*, Shareholder from *Odegaard*. Captain *Odegaard* shall Mistress Rev assist, with terraforming and associated trade, to profit of all.

Thus is the will of the Corporation.

VOTE:
   Captain Shrev Loudin: Yea
   Astrogator Edoli Cais: Yea
   First Officer Lirit Noma: Yea
   Pilot Ros Dekel: Yea
   Cargo Mate Ojal Sundari: Yea
   Crew Liaison Huela Taariq: Yea
   Shareholder Cilehe Rev: Yea
   Shareholder Helki Loudin: Yea
   Shareholder Winta Stas: Nay

3
Sting
[CIRCLE]
6484 CE

A very ancient verse gives the names of the worlds encountered on the last leg of the Geled-to-Terra run:
  Bluewhite Barebia, barns and barrows;
  Tethys teeming, seastones sing and sigh;
  Kell creeps, keeping careful clockwork;
  Tut triumphal, tombs and towers;
  Yonder Euphrates, Kentaurus crucial.
  Ship, swing silent, slide soilward;
  Manhome magnificent.
Of course, nowadays no one remembers that verse, still less the unprepossessing planet that occasioned it.

As *Worldsaver* swings through space and her naviputer picks out the beacons of the last five worlds, Jedrek reflects that things have changed since Terra ruled the Galaxy. Then, no ship would have been allowed within a kiloparsec of Sol without complete identification and verification from the TERRAD system. Now no one stops them, no authorities even care.

Inside the world of the data marble, it is as if the Empire never fell. And Jedrek has spent half his life in that world. The contrast is always with him, between the frozen past of the marble, and the decay and decline of the real present.

And he's never sure which one he prefers.

Fifteen light-seconds from Sol, Cilehe brings her ship out of tachyon phase. She shoots a smiling glance at Jedrek. "These antigravs will be tying space in knots as far out as Saturn," she brags.

"Just get us there."

Soon Earth is visible on the viewscreens. Jedrek compares it to similar views frozen in his marble, and sighs.

The Patalanian Sack of TE 381 did a good deal of damage,

much of it still visible. The Lagrange settlements, L4 and L5, LA and LB and all the others, working their way through the alphabet and several rows of punctuation symbols—they were blasted, wrecked, depopulated, their hulks simply never repaired. People might still live in those settlements—but if so they do not make themselves known to the mother planet.

Luna is a far more obvious catastrophe. Jedrek aches, comparing the ashen grey and black crescent on the viewscreen to images of a world once blue and alive. Most of Luna's seas are evaporated, her atmosphere a thin remnant hardly capable of kicking up a good dust storm, her legendary jewel cities now mostly dark. Whatever life remains on the Moon is a weak and degenerate remainder of her rich past.

"You use that thing too much," Cilehe says, gesturing to the marble between his palms. "It's not healthy to live so much in the past."

"It's such a tragedy, what Earth has become."

"It's not a tragedy. That happened a long time ago, Jedrek. Earth is the same planet its been all your life. It's my home world, and I like it that way it is." She meets his eyes. "You can't spend the rest of your life convincing the Galaxy how wonderful Earth is. The rest of the Galaxy doesn't care. The Empire isn't going to come back. Terra isn't going to be rebuilt."

"I know that."

"Do you?" She sighs. "Still, I do wish I'd gone ahead with re-terraforming Luna."

"It's still not too late."

Cilehe closes her eyes. "It is. I don't even know what I'm doing here. Look, there's the spaceport beacon; I've got to take this bird down."

Eisenhower Spaceport has a message for them. As soon as *Worldsaver's* puter transmits their postal identification codes, the message draws itself on their data screen: TOUCH DOWN AT THE SPACEPORT. YOU WILL BE CONTACTED. It is signed with the seal of the Grand Library.

"What do you think?" Jedrek asks.

"I just follow directions. Touchdown in five minutes."

Soon the four domes of New York are visible on the horizon. *Worldsaver*, directed by the spaceport traffic puters, spins down to a waiting berth. Jedrek closes his eyes for the final approach; he is willing to admit to anyone that he is not and never will be a confident pilot. When he looks again, Cilehe is shutting down the ship.

The Portmaster himself meets them, a dour red-faced man in an overstuffed business suit, with odd bits of gold braid here and there. Jedrek wonders if there are so few ships arriving at Eisenhower—or if the man has simply sized up *Worldsaver* and figures there is profit to be made.

When the Portmaster raises (ever so discreetly, of course) the matter of landing and berthing fees, Cilehe pays in something more valuable than the customary metals or drugs or offworld manufactured goods—Independent Trader chits, redeemable for merchandise from any Trade Ship.

The Portmaster is so delighted that he throws in personal baggage handling for no extra fee. Two heavy-browed semintelligent simis take their luggage and follow in their tracks. No mechanical autoservants for such rich customers, no. Gengineered monkeys are much higher-class. Jedrek tries to hide his amusement.

Eisenhower Spaceport will live forever, Jedrek knows that for sure. Among the Library's post-Empire holdings are the complete minutes of every (infrequent) meeting of the Terran Council. The Council's very first decision after the Empire's fall was to spare no expense in maintaining the Spaceport. A functioning, state-of-the-art Spaceport was the key to Terra's survival without Imperial support. For decades every surplus erg and Imperial Dollar on the planet had gone to refurbishing Eisenhower Spaceport. Borshallan sapient puters make the port totally self-repairing even in the event of an asteroid strike, all construction is of imperishable dellsite and not simply permaplastic, and the Port's defenses are better than in Imperial days. Eisenhower Port is practically immortal...and as long as it lives, so lives Earth.

Jedrek can't help shaking his head. The port was designed for literally millions of transients per day; the very corridors are large as whole buildings. For its job, Eisenhower is a model of design, a model that no other world has yet matched. And how many pass through it now? Ten thousand a year?

"You're brooding again. Stop it."

Their slideway reaches the main terminal, and Jedrek has no more time to brood.

There are only, he thinks, about a half million people on Terra today. In a hall built to hold twice that number, there is a respectable crowd of derelicts and hustlers, the usual folk found at any port on any world or settlement. Faces are blurred, bodies indistinct—Jedrek is sure he saw the exact same people on Borshall when he left. Do they migrate from planet to planet, like an unpleasant, unwashed circus troupe?

"Need a place to stay, mister?"

Jedrek looks for the source of the voice, lowers his eyes, and finds it.

A young Human male of indeterminate age (15? 17? 20?) stands next to him, all of 130 centimeters tall. The boy has very short dark hair, a serious expression, and eyes that seem perpetually in shadow, as if peering out from under an invisible rock. He wears black denim overalls with feet and torso bare; a shapeless black pseudoleather cap perches atop his head.

"Welcome to Terra, nobles. My name is Sting."

"Your name is nothing," Jedrek answers, with automatic hostility. He just wants to get away from the terminal and, preferably, into a warm bath. "We're being met, so we don't need your services."

"Excuse me, Honored Sayyid. I did not mean to interrupt." With alarming speed the boy dances away from Jedrek's reach. He gestures to the two simis, who stand confused, holding Jedrek and Cilehe's bags. "I see Rort gave you simis—they're conditioned not to leave the port. Wherever you're going, you'll need a taxi."

"Not interested. Nice try, lad, but go bother someone else."

"Bother *you*, Jedrek nor Talin." The boy turns up one of his palms. Traced in the surface of his skin is a series of fine metallic lines. They match those traced on Jedrek's and Cilehe's palms.

"Who are you?"

"Who I said. Sting's my name; apprentice at the Grand Library and part-time taxi driver."

Cilehe sighs. "What will Drisana think of next?" She stands back, hands on hips, inspecting Sting. "Can't say she's picked a winner this time. Still, what Drisana chooses to sleep with is no business of mine."

"Can't say you're that much of a winner yourself, tubs," Sting answers. In a second he is three meters away, waving. "Follow me. Sayyid Drisana sent me to pick you up along with the others."

Jedrek catches up; the simis have to trot. "Others?"

"Mesayyid Boratte and Yavam."

Oh, Sukoji and Kedar. "Where are they?"

"I'm taking you to them." Over his shoulder, at Cilehe, he throws a quick, "Step lively now, Sayyid Blubber."

Jedrek keeps his hand on Cilehe's arm as they follow the boy. Sting carried himself like a person either well-armed or not in need of weapons—Jedrek doesn't care to see if he lives up to his name.

Sting leads them past rows of autotaxis to a private skyboat marked with the seal of the Library. He relieves the simis of their burdens and sends them scurrying back to the port, then helps Jedrek and Cilehe into the boat.

The boy clicks off the autopilot and all at once the craft is airborne, swinging around obstacles on its antigravs as easily as a feather in the wind. Eisenhower's broad expanse of lined concrete falls away behind, and Sting flies the sixty kilometers to New York in somewhat less than two minutes.

The four geodesic domes of New York sparkle in midmorning sun; the skyboat's polarizers are not quite fast enough to catch the occasional dazzle from a dome facet. Figures race across the control panel; Sting swings across the Queens dome and Jedrek barely has time to throw up his arms before the boat submerges in the East River. A second later they break surface inside the Manhattan dome, and sail upward like a metallic flying fish.

In and out of the ancient towers of the city they fly. Now Jedrek relaxes, allowing himself the luxury of feeling at home after a long, confusing journey. New York is a familiar place, both through the marble and by personal experience. No Terran was unfamiliar with the vistas of what had once been the most important city in the Galaxy.

Atop the Plaza Complex, three hundred meters above Central Park, the skyboat touches down lightly on the surface of a still lake. Before they even reach the shore, hotel autoservants swarm over the boat, snatching luggage and making a flourish for their arrival.

"Someone else had better be paying for this," Cilehe mutters.

Sting looks ready for a quick retort; but by that time they have reached the shallows. There, amid flowers, trees and milling people, is the welcoming party.

Kedar Yavam stands just under one and three-quarters meters; broad-shouldered and substantially built, his narrow face topped with light brown hair that has thinned and faded since Jedrek saw him last. He wears a green and blue jumpsuit and carries his customary inhaler—in all the time Jedrek has known him that inhaler has been filled with nothing more than a mild narcotic.

Standing next to Kedar, Sukoji Boratte looks almost like a member of another species. Not only is she a full ten centimeters shorter, but she cannot mass half as much as Kedar even after a heavy meal. She is wrapped in a wispy cloak and her arms are ornamented with thousands of twinkling points of light. Sukoji's hair is a river of glowing ice, and when she steps into shadows her eyes glow like embers.

Kedar gives a tentative bow. "Welcome back, Cilehe. Jedrek."

For long moments there is no motion, only the distant dizzy feeling of years falling away, and then...Jedrek leaps over intervening water and has them both in his arms in the most sincere welcoming embrace he's ever given.

❁

Terra on the Cheap by Tunella Gennero
©6473 CE, Interstellar Publishing Group, Bosip

Eisenhower Spaceport

Over 90% of traffic to and from Terra passes through Eisenhower, earning the spaceport its nickname "Gateway to Terra." Regularly-scheduled tourist flights departing from Bosip and many other worlds are the best way to avoid variable landing and berthing fees. Be wary of pickpockets, con artists, and others who prey upon tourists.

Transportation

Aircabs to New York City are available in front of the main terminal. Be sure to use only cabs displaying a license from the Terran Tourist Board.

What to See and Do

Main Terminal: Believed to be the largest spaceport terminal in the Galaxy, the Main Terminal is an excellent example of Late Empire architecture. At its peak, the Main Terminal served five million transients per day. Don't miss the many local food vendors, which offer the chance to sample authentic Terran cuisine like Athan's Otdogs, the Madonna Bigmac, and Crottled Greeps. Wash it down with genuine Buckstar's coffee.

Grand Central Clock: The centerpiece of the Main Terminal was perhaps the most famous clock in the Terran Empire. relocated from Grand Central Station in New York, the clock's four faces are made from opal.

Hotels & Inns

Many fine hotels and inns are available in New York.

❀

4
Night on the Town
[CIRCLE]
6484 CE

The Astoria Restaurant hangs from the underside of the Manhattan dome like a spider perched in the center of a ceiling...only this spider is a kilometer above street level. Jedrek pulls his finest outfit from his suitcase for the evening, and is pleased to see that the others are also dressed in the relative finery of their worlds. Even Sting makes a concession to dignity, wearing an ornamental sash from shoulder to hip. As afternoon deepens into evening and city lights wink on one building at a time, they watch from their table and feast on a dinner of scrambeggs, fried chicken, and other typically Terran dishes.

It doesn't take long to catch up on the last eleven years. Sukoji fled Earth after the Circle broke up, but she didn't go far. The planet Aetor had recently purchased a Norn Twelve Thousand puter from Borshall, several metric tons of sapient machine that any programmer would give her leg to play with —Sukoji applied her Library experience to Aetor and in no time at all moved into the One Thousand, the social and political elite of the Aetorian League.

Kedar's story is similar in outline. He moved to Bosip and took a job teaching—when he found out that he loved working with children and that the government of his settlement didn't give him enough freedom, he moved to a newly-opened settlement and carried on a lucrative practice there.

"I was on Earth just two years ago," he says, "visiting with Drisana. I didn't notice anything that would have led to a crisis then. Whatever this is, it must have come up awfully suddenly."

Cilehe shoots a pointed glance at Sting. The boy sits at the foot of the large table, looking at them over folded hands. "I don't suppose you're willing to tell us what this is all about?"

"Sayyid Drisana will tell you when she is ready. Now that you're all here, I am to escort you to the Library tomorrow."

"And meanwhile, I guess you're relaying our conversation to her. Drisana was always a paranoid little snot, if you all remember."

Sting's shoulders tense, but he keeps his voice even. "Are you asking me if I'm squealing on you to Sayyid Drisana?"

"In a word, yes."

"Well, I'll tell you, Bibi Rev—for a price. I give nothing away free."

"Leave the child alone," Kedar says. "He's following instructions, and you won't tempt him into breaking his promises to Drisana. And don't blame her too much, Cilehe...after what she's been through, she can't help being a bit, well, wary." As he says this, Kedar looked at Jedrek; Jedrek looks away.

Sukoji speaks up. Sukoji the peacemaker, Sukoji the ever-naive. "What does it matter what Drisana wants? We'll find out tomorrow, and meanwhile we have a whole night to get reacquainted. Jedrek, tell me about your business. Designing settlements seems so complicated—do you and your partner work alone?"

Her eyes meet his, and he smiles inwardly. No, he reminds himself, Sukoji is not naive—she just uses that pose as a convenience. Aware of Cilehe's tension and Kedar's usual self-righteous attempts at fairness, he realizes that his reply will be the deciding factor in whether this dinner turns into a shouting match or a friendly bit of nostalgia.

Sukoji...Cilehe, poised...Kedar, somewhat unsure...and Sting, elbows on the table, silver-laced palms steepled as if ready to strike.

What the venus, he is curious himself about what Drisana wants.

"It is a difficult task, but we have the help of one of Borshall's best puters. Of course, a Norn costs too much, we have to get by with a Svarth 2000, plus data I took from the Library. Denys and I make a good living, and our settlements are getting noticed. The last one we made was a high-grav beach motif. Everything went along fine until we had to stock it with fish. You've no idea how many chemical factors have to be matched before particular fish will survive. Acidity, salt content, aereation—finally we found it cheaper to mutate new varieties of fish."

He goes on, and when he fumbles, Kedar takes up the conversational ball. So they talk, through a few drinks and shots, then a staggering dessert of chocolate and flaming ice creams and fresh fruits.

Through the whole dinner Sting sits, relaxed, toying with a tiny glittering scrap. Jedrek finally recognizes it as a data flake not unlike his marble. What information, he wonders, did Drisana impress on that flake—psychprofiles and years of personal reminiscences about the Circle? Recommendations of how to deal with each one, with combinations, with all four at once?

Knowing that he will never find out, Jedrek shrugs and gives his full attention to the reunion.

They stay awake almost until dawn, talking. They relive old experiences, exhume long-forgotten inside jokes, and by the end of the night they are only too happy to go back to the Plaza and fall asleep in one enormous, luxurious sleep cocoon.

Sting, however, sleeps alone.

❋

The Astoria Restaurant
MENU

APPETIZERS

Macadamia crusted soft shell crab over cucumber salad
Gumbo of the evening
Scrambeggs with prosciutto cotto
Scallops with spinach and garlic butter
Cheese & fruit plate

SOUPS & SALADS

Udon and clam soup in ginger broth
Caesar salad with grana padana
Avocado cream soup with salicorni
Pear soup with calamari sticks

MAIN COURSES

Wok Fried Tofu
with stack of tomato, thai and wild rice

Char Sui Roasted Duckling
with watercress, basmati rice & snow peas, mushroom-tomato reduction

Colonel Sanders' Chicken
on cheesy stone ground grits, parsnip chips with carrot-cardamom curry

Seared New York Strip
with wild mushroom-port salut bread pudding

Truffle Sea Bass
grilled sea bass, truffle sauce, spinach and figs

Signature coffees & teas - ask your server

28% gratuity included

5
The Circle Reformed
[CIRCLE]
6484 CE

A vast sea covers the once-verdant land where the trees of the Mediterranean Forest had soared. Earth tolerates the sea—having neither the money nor the interest to reclaim the land, Earth has no choice.

On the southern shore of that great sea is an ancient city, so ancient that even the Library has only second- and thirdhand reconstructed images of its original form: Alexandria. And near the center of aged, nearly-abandoned Alexandria stands the marble edifice of the Grand Library, repository of all recorded knowledge of the greatest Empire in the history of Humankind.

The skyboat carrying Jedrek and his friends circles above the multitiered Library building, then dives. At the very last instant Sting pulls up and the craft's landing pads just barely scrape permaplastic on the landing terrace.

"Here we are," Sting announces.

"I would never have guessed." Cilehe undoes her safety straps and is out of the boat before Sting. The lad shrugs and gestures to the others to follow her.

As Jedrek steps out onto the roof of the Grand Library, he takes a deep breath of sea-scented air. The fragrance stirs memories. He can hardly blame Cilehe for strolling decisively toward the obsidian main entrance as if she were part owner—this building was home to them all, they were totally familiar with all its corridors and halls and rooms. With the aid of his marble, he could walk blindfolded through the Octagon Palace on Laxus or any other completely unfamiliar building without missing a step—but here he doesn't need the marble, long experience has engraved every square meter on his memory.

They enter the Library.

Around the domed and arched entrance hall are millions of exhibition books, from hand-painted codices to printed sheets of papyrus and vellum, to microfilms and fiches, Late Empire permaplastic bookfilm cards, and puter chips and disks by the thousands. In other galleries are nonprint materials: an almost-complete selection of musical productions, video recordings going back to the very beginnings of cinema, including a mint set of *Captain Video* television programs retrieved from a hundred fifty lightyears away by a pre-Imperial scouting mission.

All this is simply display, unnecessary for the Library's true function. Jedrek lets his gaze sweep the walls of the Main Hall, then it comes to rest in the center, where the real heart and brain of the Library resides: a clear sphere of delicate crystal, just a little over twenty centimeters in diameter. The sphere is supported in a zero-grav field a meter above the floor; it is girdled with its own small antigravs and a troop of autoservants follow it wherever it goes to ensure is safety.

This is the most important part of the Library. A much larger version of the individual data marbles, this data package holds all the approximately ten-to-the-sixtieth bits of data in the Grand Library, perfectly organized and available to the touch of hands.

Jedrek's palms itch; he can hardly resist the temptation and reaches out to caress the sphere one more time.

Sting's hand is around his wrist. "Don't."

"I know how to handle this sphere. I'm not going to damage it, kid."

"Nevertheless, I don't want you to disturb its orientation or programming. That's a very delicate piece of equipment."

From the corner of his eye Jedrek sees Cilehe fuming. He holds out his palm to Sting. "Look, friend, silver lines the same as yours." Jedrek puts out his hand and touches the lad's right palm. There is a tingle like that preceding datafeed, a tickle in the nerves, a faintly-sexual shiver.

"Sting, you may allow any of these people full access to the sphere. We have no need to fear that they will harm it."

Jedrek spins, the datasphere forgotten. In an archway across the room, her long red-brown hair alive with electric highlights, Drisana Hardel stands with hands on hips.

If the word "Librarian" has any meaning at all, it refers to Drisana. Short and slight, she wears her dark, curly hair short. Her face, composed of lines and planes, falls naturally into a serious, studious expression.

Her dress is comfortable and utilitarian, jumpsuit coveralls and pseudoleather sandals. A datapad hangs from her belt along with a stylus and bookreader. Above all is her manner. At ten centimeters over a meter and a half, she can never be physically imposing—she makes up for it with strictly controlled facial expressions and a sparsity of movement that is impressive in person, and even more so on the holoscreen, her preferred method of interaction.

"Good of you all to come," she continues without losing a beat. As she steps into the Hall Jedrek sees her silver flute hanging at her side like a medieval warrior's short sword. "I've been at my wit's end for the last four tendays."

Sting takes a few steps and turns, standing slightly in front of and to the right of his mistress, hands poised. Jedrek feels the others move behind him, and he is suddenly aware of the invisible line that draws itself across the Hall: Drisana and Sting on one side, himself and the rest on the other.

Drisana stops, crosses her arms, and taps a foot. She lets her features slide into a look of weariness. "Don't tell me we're going to waste time with this kind of foolishness. I don't have time for it, really I don't. Forget the past. I don't need your memories and your resentments from years ago—I need your abilities. And you're the only ones I could call upon." She delivers the last sentence with such a pitiful face that Jedrek, who knows her tricks, is almost convinced.

It is Kedar who steps across the line and, in crossing it, annihilates it. He strides past Sting without deigning to notice the boy and gives an arm to Drisana; she buries her head on his shoulder.

Another minute, and they are all gathered about her. She hugs Sukoji, gives Cilehe a kiss, and barely nods at Jedrek. Then she shakes her head.

"You'll all want refreshment."

"Not really," Kedar answers. "We ate at the hotel."

"That was an hour ago. Besides, it's lunchtime here. And I have a long story to tell you."

"I was wondering when you'd get to that," Cilehe says. "Why did you call us back?"

Drisana holds up a finger, signalling Cilehe to wait a second. She purses her lips and whistles a quick tune. Autoservants drag in chairs; another tune, and there are refreshments. She motions to them to be seated. They form a circle around the datasphere.

Except for Sting's presence, this could be one of their regular sessions years ago, Jedrek thinks. With data screens and terms before them, and hands placed on the sphere, they would be ready to deal with the business of the Library again, taking care of problems too complex for the search puters to solve.

Drisana stands over the sphere, her hair falling over her shoulders and covering her full bosom. She whistles two notes; the room darkens until there is only one pearly light on the sphere.

Reaching to the right, Drisana places her hand palm-down on a term pad. Her left hand she rests on the surface of the datasphere, almost cradling it as an eagle holds its prey.

A holographic image of the Galaxy appears, swimming in the air around them, filling the entire room and spilling over its boundaries. Not today's Galaxy, but the Milky Way as it was at the height of the Empire. All twelve thousand Human planets and hundreds of thousands of settlements are charted, along with political boundaries, Imperial lifeguard stations and ultrawave relays. The major known Nonhuman planets are identified, along with Human and Nonhuman trade routes.

"We know this," Jedrek says, unimpressed by the illusion. The same map is repeated in his marble—it is a useful starting point for all sorts of inquiries.

"Pay attention," Drisana says calmly. Most of the Galaxy mutes, fading to skim milk. Only six bright green dots remain, forming two interlaced equilateral triangles around the center of the Galaxy...one at one-third diameter, one at two-thirds.

"The ultrawave relays," Drisana says, as if telling them something new. "Key to the Empire's internal communication. Each covers a circle roughly a third of a galactic diameter across, amplifying and retransmitting all ultrawave signals."

"We know." That must be Cilehe.

"Sting doesn't. And you haven't seen this next bit." The map blurs and shifts; in the near distance a clock appears, counting off years in the traditional Terran Common Era style.

There are incomplete sections, and many portions of the Galaxy fade out, leaving blank areas that indicates lack of data. Still, this historical summary must have taken years of puter time to create. Jedrek has to commend Drisana for it.

The clock reads 2757 CE. "This is when most of our transmitters went out, during the Triple Confederacy attacks on Terra. The Library is generally supposed to have gone off the air at this time, but we maintained sealed-beam links with thirty-two worlds, via relays."

4020 CE. "The plague called The Death more than decimated the Galaxy's population, and left the Library off the air for three years. In the confusion, Relay Gamma was destroyed, reducing our contacts to nine worlds."

4723 CE. "Relay Delta failed. We lost three of our outpost contacts, bringing us down to six contacts with the Galaxy."

5378 CE. "During the Geled-Natal war, Relay Beta was completely destroyed, and Library service was reduced to only one planet."

"Ancient history, Drisana." Cilehe frowns. "One world is all we've ever worked with. People who need us badly enough can always make their way to Eironea...or here to Terra, for that matter. "

The clock races ahead to the present. "What you don't know is that thirty-six days ago Relay Alpha failed. We are no longer in contact with Eironea."

"What's the problem? You still have walk-in patrons."

"The last was four years ago. He wanted me to go to Odonia with him. That's when I took on Sting and Betha Maitt as apprentices. But now it'll do no good."

For long moments of silence the Galaxy hangs suspended around them. Jedrek feels a lump in his throat, knows what she wants him to say...and knows that he will not.

Cilehe finally speaks. "So the Library is finally off the air. You're free of it now, Drisana, and you can start a new life."

"*This* is my life."

Sukoji tries being gentle. "We went through all that long ago, Dris. We all hoped it wouldn't come to this, but now it has. You'll just have to face reality." She reaches across the darkness; Drisana ignores the proffered hand.

"For eight days I did nothing but sit in my room, play my music, and weep. Then, out of a dream and music, it came to me—the promise we made when we broke up. I sent the roses, and the rest you know." Her voice catches. "I need you. Without you I don't stand a chance of repairing that relay. With your knowledge and your specialties, we might be able to do it."

Kedar attempts gentleness too. "Imperial machines are complex, none more so than the Relays. I've seen holos of them here—big black boxes with megabit explanations of every molecule. Even with the resources of the Library...I don't think we could."

"I..." Jedrek begins, and suddenly all eyes are on him. He swings his gaze around the Circle, strikes Drisana's face and feels the need in her eyes like a physical slap. This is no pretense, no game, no maneuver to get sympathy and force her own way. He only seldom saw the inner Drisana, as she seldom saw the inner Jedrek—but now one reaches out to the other, and he knows the decision is his to make.

He takes a deep breath. If only because he might someday want something as badly as she wants this....

"I think we might stand a chance. I...I'd be willing to try it, with the rest of you to help."

She reaches across the datasphere and their hands meet. There is a warm tingle and everything, for once and surprisingly, feels right.

❁

So You're Going To Geled...

(*Galactic Traveler*, April 6484 CE)

The most difficult adjustment for non-Geledi tourists is to the odd Geledi calendar. No matter what your local system, you are probably used to a Terran Standard calendar of 24-hour days. A year is 365 such days, arranged into 12 months of three tendays each, with five vacation days scattered throughout.

Geled is the only major Imperial splinter state to abandon the Terran Standard. The Geledi Standard Day last 22.4 hours; a year is 292 days (1.3467 Geled years is one Standard year). The year is divided into 16 months of 37 days each. Each month consists of six weeks (called *nyeedyeh*) of six days each, plus an additional day (Prahznyeh) at the end of the month.

The days of the Geledi week are Senkyeh, Mahnyeh, Tarehyeh, Vrenzyeh, Geletyeh, and Soobtayeh. The months of the Geledi year are Yeenvahr, Fyeevahr, Vyeesyahbr, Mahrt, Ahpryehl, Migh, Lyehyahbr, Iyon, Ilyul, Ahvgoost, Ossyahbr, Syeentyahbr, Ahktyahbr, Nahyahbr, Zeemyahbr, and Dyeekyahbr.

And just to make things more interesting, every so often there's a leap year, in which the 37th day of Zeemyahbr is dropped.

Tourists are advised to purchase conversion software for datapads and headsets. In addition, inexpensive Geledi timepieces are readily available at tourist shops and in spaceports—these usually run for a few centuries without adjustment, and make fine mementos and gifts once your trip is over.

❖

6
Ebettor
[GELED]
Geledi Year 3216

Irina Lerenko is careful to stow all her utensils before she leaves the galley—anything left lying about will likely be pitched out the airlock. It's happened before.

She reaches the Bridge ten minutes before her shift begins. Trying to be inconspicuous, she crouches in an alcove, closes her eyes and tries to force her muscles to relax. It doesn't work; the tightness across the back of her neck will surely be a full-fledged ache before her shift is over.

Of all ships, why was she posted to *Deathcry*? And as her first assignment! After six weeks, she is learning the routines of the ship...and she's learned the most important thing, for which no orientation lecture could prepare her, the reason no veterans ever put in for transfer, the reason that ship's nickname among the rest of the Fleet was *Deathcamp*: Captain Fedor Kassov is a madman.

She feels a presence, looks up to see the Captain in his polished dress uniform, every strand of braid impeccably in place, his thin mustache trimmed to the millimeter. She is aware of increased tension around the Bridge—even the other shift scurries to look busy.

"Time to get to work, Gunner," Kassov says to her, in a tone that makes it clear that she's been caught loafing. She pulls herself to her feet and makes her way quickly to the gun station, feeling high-ranking eyes boring into her.

Taking over command of a Bridge station, at least on *Deathcry*, is a meticulous procedure, requiring at least fifteen minutes except in combat, and gods help anyone who skips a step. Still, Irina rather likes taking over...it kept her busy for a while, and therefore less of a target for the wrath of the commander.

Kassov, of course, is exempt from takeover procedures;

indeed, he chats with the relieved second-in-command. Irina shakes her head and bends to her work.

"Attention crew." The Captain's voice rings like the wrath of the gods from speakers scattered through the ship. "We are due to make rendezvous with the Ebettor ship this watch. I expect *Deathcry* to be an example for the entire Geled Navy. I am sure that no one on board wants more complaints relayed to fleet headquarters."

Damn right. A communiqué from HQ will surely trigger one of Kassov's starship-fast mood changes, making the crew's lives miserable for weeks after.

"This meeting will be the first physical contact between Geled and the Ebettor Hegemony. I am to make certain that the crew is especially reminded not to make derogatory comments, in public or private, about the physical form of the Ebettor crew. Aliens are touchy about that sort of thing and the last thing I want is from my ship to be credited with an interracial incident."

Right. Irina has never seen any aliens, has never been trained for this sort of contact...but then, neither have most of the crew. Including Kassov.

"One hour before rendezvous, all stations will turn control over to the command station."

"But Captain..." the Navigator says.

"But nothing. I will take sole responsibility for this approach and rendezvous."

Then why, Irina wonders, is she so sure that *she* will be one of those blamed if anything goes wrong?

Kassov stares directly at her, and she straightens her back, hoping her face is impassive. Shipwide intercom clicks off. "The Ebettor will be wanting to see our Bridge, and I have orders to show them whatever they wish. So let's get some of this metalwork polished. We've still six hours until we come out of tachyon phase."

Irina forces her half-smile not to desert her lips. She's been over this ground before—Kassov doesn't allow autoservants on the bridge, even to clean…he claims they are a dangerous obstacle in combat. That leaves cleaning chores for nonessential personnel. And what can be less essential than a gunner in translight speed, when the chance of meeting another ship wavers between nil and zero?

Somehow it makes a distorted kind of sense. Sighing, Irina picks up a rag and some cleaning compound, and goes to work.

❊

Rendezvous made, Irina watches the odd-looking Ebettor ship on her screens closely. Her hands are poised over gun controls—not that it does any good, with all her panels slaved to Kassov's master controls.

As a small gig flies over from the alien ship, Irina frowns. Kassov is allowing the puter to track the gig with only two minor lasers and no missiles at all. In an attack, the milliseconds necessary for puter to tie in more weapons could prove fatal to *Deathcry*. When the gig is safely docked, she sighs with relief. It's now a matter for Security.

The Bridge's large holoscreen shows the interior of the docking bay, the curve of the alien gig just visible on the right edge of the screen. Irina can't take her eyes away as the gig opens. The image is being relayed live to home: all through the Geled states, audiences await their first sight of the Ebettor.

It's been nearly a century since the first ultrawave contact with the Ebettor. In that time, Many artists had imagined how the aliens would appear. Irina, along with the rest of the crew, has scanned all the representations—insectoids, ameboids, walking bilberry bushes; there is no agreement. Now the reality is here.

Dead to the rest of the world, she leans forward as the first alien steps from the gig. Even an attack from their mother ship could not make her take her eyes from that screen.

Nothing she scanned has prepared her for the reality. The awful truth is that they do not look alien enough. Paleskinned, unhealthily thin, they have the same bilateral symmetry and general head structure as Humans. There the resemblance ends.

The Ebettor are either too light for their height, or too tall for their weight. Their faces are totally functional, but the features are a wild distortion of the Human face. She is not sure how many fingers they have on each hand, but there are more than five, and all but the thumb are the same length. The arms are not in proportion to each other—one is longer and neither really fits the body. Luckily the legs seem normal enough under drapes of drab cloth…until she sees one bend in four places.

There are six Ebettor, each a pantographic copy of the others except for minor differences in the dull shades of their uniforms. They stand in two rows of three, and Irina has the absurd notion that they will all speak in unison.

They do.

The ship puter, having been programmed with the Ebettor language, has no trouble translating.

"We are instructed to speak with Captain Fedor Kassov of the Geled Navy Warship *Deathcry*. The named individual will now reply." Irina doesn't like the Ebettor language; it sounds too much like the scraping of bones one against another.

"This is Captain Kassov. Our Security people will accompany you to our Bridge, and then we may speak face-to-face." The puter translation of this speech into Ebettor makes Irina's skin tingle; right then she knows Kassov will learn to speak the Ebettor tongue if he can, only to make his crew more miserable.

"We are ordered to accompany Geled Navy Warship *Deathcry* to Ultrawave Relay Alpha. We are prepared to give such technical aid as is necessary and possible in order to repair and replace the defective piece of equipment. You will begin the mission at once."

Irina sees Kassov frown, senses how close the Captain is to exploding. "By the time you arrive at the Bridge, we will be under way."

This is going to be a bad week.

❄

At the start of the next shift, an Ebettor shows up at Irina's station. "I am instructed to learn your instruments."

She glances toward the Captain, who nods and looks away.

After an hour of practice, Irina realizes that the alien is ten times the gunner she will ever be. He—she?—handles the unfamiliar Human controls like a seasoned veteran. So far the Ebettor has only been allowed to compete against puter simulations, but just the same Irina knows that *Deathcry* would not stand a chance in a fight against an Ebettor ship.

"Where did you learn to fight so well? Did you go to a school?" The creature stares at her blankly (or is that simply its normal expression?) until the puter finishes a long translation; then it snarls and croaks in reply.

"Our skills come from our predecessors. They are fixed in us during natal development. It is a highly efficient method."

"I had to study for years, and then spend quite a bit of time practicing before I was allowed to have a live gun on a ship." She smiles ruefully. "I got to hate those puter simulations pretty thoroughly." A chuckle.

"Your computers are stupid." As if to prove a point, the Ebettor proceeds to wipe out every bogey the computer sends against him, those strange hands flying over controls as if they were designed to fit.

Irina hears a voice in her ear, the Captain's voice over her comm implant. "Gunner Lerenko, I want to see you right now."

"Da, sir." Irina smiles at the Ebettor. "Keep practicing. Here, I'll step it up a little to make it more of a challenge."

"Now, Lerenko."

With a sinking feeling Irina climbs the few steps to the command chair. Kassov touches a control; Irina felt a sonic curtain close about the chair. At least no one else can hear her being chewed out—whatever she's done.

"Lerenko, I am sure that the Presidium does not want us giving full details of Geledi Navy practices to the Ebettor. Do you understand what I am saying?"

"Not really." It is the wrong answer, but...there's no right one.

"You do not have to explain to them how our warriors are trained, nor any details about what our personnel did before they came aboard this ship. If the Ebettor want to believe that we are conditioned from birth as they appear to be, let them."

"I-I was just making conversation."

Kassov plumps a finger against her chest. "The Geledi Navy is not paying you to entertain aliens, merely to ensure that they do no damage while they are aboard. If you don't have enough to keep you busy..." The threat hangs unfinished, as it always does—Irina has no desire to test the consequences.

"I can keep busy, sir."

"See that you do. A word of advice, Lerenko: the Ebettor are more technologically advanced than we are. They found us, remember. They cruise deeper into the Galactic Core than our engines allow us. If it comes to war, Geled would have to put forth a full-scale defense to protect ourselves. I do not want to make their job one iota easier. So..." Kassov puts a finger to his lips. Irina nods, and the sonic curtain parts. She shuffles back to her station with her head low.

The Ebettor gunner has the computer set to a level fifteen times higher than Irina has ever been able to manage. And still he/she shows no signs of difficulty.

❁

7
Night Thoughts
[CIRCLE]
6484 CE

The stars rise silently over Alexandria as they have for almost seven millennia. From a peaceful balcony just off the Library building, Jedrek watches them with mixed feelings.

Stars that were familiar once. Now he has to learn them over again, tracing the constellations with the aid of star charts in the marble. Charts for each major inhabited world, at his fingertips. But...most of them are nearly four thousand years out of date, and in that time even the stars change a little. Nothing drastic; still, disturbing. He has a curious sense of being a visitor from some long-dead Imperial era inexplicably catapulted four millennia forward to the wreckage of the Capital Planet.

"Cilehe is right; you brood too much." He doesn't turn at Sukoji's voice behind him. In a few moments she comes to stand at the balustrade next to him.

"It's almost impossible not to brood." He waves at the sky. "Twelve thousand worlds—probably a good deal more by now—how many of them remember this speck of dust? How many remember what it was, or even that it *was* anything?"

"So this is what you think about when you can't sleep?" Sukoji smiles. "Earth is lucky that she has such a zealous advocate. Did you often say things like this on Borshall?"

"Borshall doesn't even know that Earth exists. Borshall remembers the Terran Empire but doesn't recall that there was ever a Terra."

"And why should they? Terra was a figurehead. After the Capital moved to Laxus, they might as well have called it the Laxan Empire for all the difference the change made. You know as well as I do that the Emperors and Empresses spent more time off Earth than on it." She sighs. "The Aetorian League remembers the Empire. They like to think that they're bringing back the Empire." She touches her marble. "They can't begin to comprehend the complexity of the entire Human Galaxy under one rule. Who am I to tell them that they're mistaken, that their League is but a fraction of a Province of the Empire? They're children at shadowplay— why spoil their fun?"

"I wonder what Drisana thinks of all this. If she ever does?"

"I've been meaning to talk with you about her." Sukoji pulls back from the railing and faces him with arms folded. "Why did you get us into this? Why did you encourage her?"

"I didn't get you into anything. You all agreed to come along. It was your own choice."

"Right." She turns away. "Like we all agreed to end the Library." She is silent for a moment, and Jedrek tries to frame an answer. Before he can speak, Sukoji turns and looks into his eyes. "Blast it, she has to learn that it's all over. It was all over eleven years ago, and for that long she's been living in an unreal world, trying to pretend. Now here comes the final straw, the last input that will allow her to break with her past, and you come along and tell her that it can be right again."

"I don't know what you mean."

"Jedrek, you don't understand Drisana. You never *did* understand her, and then you went racing off to the other side of the Galaxy. You didn't have to deal with her tantrums. Jedrek, she's a fanatic on the subject of the Library. It's her god, her sacred duty. She actually thinks the Circle can get together again. That we can be the same fun group we were before."

"I'm not interested in the group getting back together. I'm a professional, called back to a professional's work circle. Are you trying to tell me that I don't have an obligation to help?"

"I just wish you could see that for Drisana it's not all a professional matter."

"Isn't it? Maybe *you* don't understand her, Sukoji. Drisana is the last professional of her type in the Galaxy, the last

Curator of the Grand Library. If she's to stay in business she has to call us in; she has no choice but to get that Relay repaired. I know what I would feel like if some circumstance came along that made it impossible for me to design settlements—I would pull every string I could to change things."

Sukoji's eyes widen. "You don't honestly think we can repair Relay Alpha?"

"I don't know. I'd certainly like to try."

"Oh, would you?" She thrusts her marble into his right hand. "You think finding technical information about the Ultrawave Relays is going to be as easy as finding design specs? Give it a try, fellow Librarian."

He closes his eyes and feels the odd patterns of a strange data marble. It takes him a few seconds to attune himself to the flow.

Each one of them perceives the datasphere differently. They discussed the matter endlessly in earlier years, never tiring of the question.

For Jedrek, the experience is like following the complex threads of an immense tapestry—one fact leads to a dozen others by association, and thence he charts his way through the exabits of his marble.

Sukoji, he remembers, visualizes a vast library laid out in perfect subject order. By mentally trotting down the aisles she can isolate any fact she needs.

Sometimes Sukoji got her answers a bit more quickly—but she ran into fewer interesting detours along the way.

Jedrek closes his mind to all detours and concentrates only on finding information about the Relays. In less than a heartbeat he has it narrowed down to the right section of the marble—

"DATA ERASED BY ORDER OF TERRAD FOR SECURITY REASONS," a dull voice informs him.

He looks up sheepishly. "Wiped."

"Of course wiped. The Ultrawave Relays stitched together

the Galaxy and made the Empire possible. They also gave the Imperial government total control over long-distance communication. Naturally details of their construction were state secrets. I've already checked the large datasphere—all information about the Relays was wiped during the first Sack of Terra."

"Technology doesn't just disappear. There have to be other records we could trace to get a good idea of how the Relays are put together."

Again she shakes her head. "You're a tech. Try the problem on for size. When you get too many tachyon vesicles together in one place, conflicting gravitational strains evaporate them. Basse's Law. It applies to antigravs in the Galactic Core, with all the grav strains there, as much as to ultrawave sets in proximity. And a Relay is nothing *but* ultrawave sets in proximity." She plucks her marble from his palm. "The society that learns how to get around Basse's Law is going to rule the Galaxy. So far I haven't seen anyone do it. I know Aetor is nowhere near a solution."

She is right. "Borshall doesn't have it either."

"And if Borshall doesn't, chances are great that no one else does. So just how do you think you're going to fix that Relay when the technology doesn't exist any more?"

He shrugs. "It could be nothing more complicated than a burnt-out temp governor. We won't know until we look."

She snorts. "You're hopeless." She turns neatly and walks away.

Jedrek goes back to his railing and the stars. After a while he becomes conscious of a large dark shape in the sea—Cilehe's ship *Worldsaver*, her tanks filled with deuterium and tritium from seawater in preparation for tomorrow's departure. A few autoservants are barely visible by their running lights, making last-minute adjustments to the ship.

In the darkness of the balcony there is suddenly a presence next to him. Jedrek turns slowly and sees Sting. The boy's cap is missing and his hair is mussed more than usual.

"Hello," Jedrek says uneasily.

"Hi." Sting edges closer to him, looking out over the sea. "Nice ship."

"So I understand."

"She must've cost a pretty bit."

With a smile, Jedrek answers, "Why, are you thinking of stealing it?"

"I could do worse," the lad answers in an alarmingly serious tone. "She would be a nice ship to have, not just for what I could sell her for."

"You're a remarkable kid."

"Thanks. I guess."

There is silence for a while. Jedrek is very conscious of Sting's physical presence, the warmth of the boy's body less than a centimeter from his. He thinks of Denys.

He wonders what Sting is doing there. Here, at least, is an answer he can't look up in the marble.

"You're leaving tomorrow."

"That's right."

Sting turns his eyes on Jedrek, and the older man feels himself captivated. "Take me with you."

"You want to come along?"

"Sayyid Drisana said I could come if you agreed."

"Why should we take you?"

The boy shrugs. "If you don't I'll have to steal a ship and follow you."

"What makes you think you want to come out to the middle of nowhere with us?"

It is almost as if a film passes in front of Sting's eyes, ending what was a glimpse of his inner self. "I don't *think* it—I *know* I want to come."

"We're going into a dangerous area of the Galaxy. It's not the place for a young boy to go just to stay with his lover."

In no time at all, Sting's finger is resting lightly against Jedrek's neck. No weapon, just a finger...so why does Jedrek feel so close to death?

"I'm not sleeping with Sayyid Drisana. She's too fine a person for such suggestions, and if you make them again I'll let you find out why they call me Sting." Almost as quickly the boy is out of Jedrek's reach, and he settles calmly to the rail. "As for the danger—do you think the Solar System is any less dangerous? I was raised on Patroclus…after I killed my first two people I went to the Saturn settlements, and then I worked my way through just about every population center in this system. I know more about danger than you do, rest assured. And I know how to handle it." He bites a fingernail. "You ought to be begging me to come along."

Jedrek flips Sting his marble. The lad catches it and cradles it reverently in his right palm.

"Let me see what you can do, Sting. What was the gross production of wine on Euphrates during the year of the Elendan secession?"

There is a barely perceptible pause. "Calendar year or Euphratean Fiscal Period?"

Jedrek smiles. "Both." When Sting told him, he shoots a few more challenges at the lad. After ten minutes he is convinced that the boy has the skills of an excellent librarian.

"All right, Sting, you can come along. But remember that we were a Circle once, we have our own habits for doing things—you may not fit in very well. There's bound to be friction at first."

"Sayyid Cilehe."

"And others. We'll work together during the trip, and maybe by the time we get there we'll be used to one another."

For a while longer they are silent—the two stand side-by-side and look up at the stars. Jedrek wonders what thoughts are going through the kid's mind.

Finally he tousles Sting's short hair. "It's going to be a big day tomorrow. I want to get some sleep."

Sting touches his hand. "Need company?"

Jedrek thinks. Denys is half a Galaxy away…but a streetkid is hardly what he has in mind. He laughs, more at himself than at the offer. "How many of us are you sleeping with, if you don't mind my asking?"

"I'll tell you, but..."

"I know, it'll cost. Never mind." He slips an arm around Sting's shoulders. "Come on, let's get to bed."

With one last look at the stars, the sea, and the ship, Jedrek goes inside.

❀

Streaming moonlight paints cold shadows across blankets and floor as Jedrek lays awake, watching the boy at his side.

What is Sting about? Why should a Terran streetkid want to go to the stars? For that matter, why should he be so passionate about the Library?

Jedrek tries to recall his own childhood. Was he that way? No...in fact, he came to the Library for the same reasons that brought the others—because he always liked working by himself, because communion with the words and images of the past spared him from uncomfortable dealings with the people of the present.

Somehow, he doesn't think that motivation applies to Sting.

Is it Drisana, then? Jedrek knows that Dris could be overpowering—how much more so to a young lad craving attention? Has she infused him with her own vision?

Again, it doesn't fit. What little he knows of Sting tells him that the lad is his own man, serving his own goals and dreams.

But what are they?

Oblivious to his questions, the moon drifts slowly westward and its shadows lengthen. Eventually, Jedrek sleeps.

❀

The Few, the Proud...the Imperium Space Corps

The bond that holds Spacers together was forged nearly four millennia ago. Every Spacer inherits a legacy of those who have gone before and every Spacer is duty bound to uphold the traditions and legacy of our Corps and pass that on to future Spacers. From its beginning the long-ago days of the Terran Empire, the Corps has strived to produce not only the best warriors, but the best people. They are men and women who live by a code which form the bedrock of good character. These values guide the Corps, as well as its individual Spacers.

Honor: Spacers are held to a high standard of the utmost ethical and moral behavior. Honesty and honor are held in great regard. Respect for others is essential. Every Spacer is accountable for his or her actions and meeting the highest standard of the Corps.

Courage: Courage is not the absence of fear. It is the ability to face fear and overcome it. It is the mental, moral, and physical strength ingrained in Spacers. It steadies them in times of stress, carries them through every challenge, and aids them in facing new and unknown confrontations.

Commitment: Commitment is the spirit of determination and dedication found in Spacers. Every aspect of life in the Corps shows commitment, from the high standard of excellence to the vigilance the Spacers show for training.

There is only one explanation for people who accept a challenge this difficult. They're called to do it. They understand instinctively that the greatest things they will accomplish in life are the hardest things. Which path is calling you?

Touch here to contact a recruiter.

8
Arrival
[CREDIX]
Year 4331 of the Credixian Imperium

All things considered, Dalbert Ritter thinks he is pretty lucky. Not only is he on the most exciting ship in the whole Credixian Space Corps, but that ship is on the most thrilling mission in the Galaxy.

"Pay attention to worship," Gerda chides him in a whisper. Chagrined, he tries to force his thoughts back to the ceremony. He almost succeeds, but then comes the time for meditation.

Gerda places her Ancestral Ring before her; Dalbert takes his own ring from the chain around his neck (it is still a trifle big for his finger, and he doesn't want to lose it) and puts it next to hers. When laser light hits the ring, there stretches out a long line of holos, portraits of each and every couple of the Ritter Family, back to the very beginning of the Imperium. The line seems kilometers long.

By tilting his head a little he can see the equally long line from Gerda's Ring. They compared, one night long ago; the great number of similar and even identical faces testifies to the age-old friendship between Ritter and Lübchen. Too bad siblings don't show up in the line.

Dalbert smiles. In only a few days, Lars and Margrethe will be before ministers, pledging their love and their contract in the sight of Kaal, Brandix and Meletia. Dal hopes the Ancestors will bless their union with a healthy child—he is looking forward to being an uncle.

"Be solemn," Gerda whispers. Dal glances around the chapel; no one has noticed them. He starts to protest, then realizes in time that he should not be the occasion of the Captain talking through meditation period. He bends his head and lets his eyes run over the faces of his Ancestors.

Dal is not a very religious boy, but this time he manages to get in a short prayer—by all his Ancestors, he hopes their mission is a quick one, so he and Gerda can be home for his brother's Union.

It will be a difficult task. His Ancestors will have to work double duty if *Outbound* is to find the legendary Relay Alpha. Gerda has been over this with him before...although they know approximately where the Terran Empire placed Alpha, there is still an uncertainty measured in scores of parsecs. *Outbound* will need to painfully scour space one tenth-parsec volume at a time, hoping to find some trace of the Relay.

Dal sighs. If only those Ancestors displayed before him could talk. Some of them, from back in the days of the Empire, might know where the Relay is.

He fidgets. The ritual thousand seconds of Ancestor Meditation is too long; a hundred seconds is about all he can take. He sneaks a look at his datapad for the time, and tries to estimate—the period has to be about half done. Maybe more.

Dal concentrates on his duties. Has he left left anything undone for today's shift? The responsibilities of Captain's Cabin Boy are not great; they mostly relate to making sure that Gerda's autoservants are working well. He is also progressing with his studies to the satisfaction of the ship's puter. Small-arms practice is not going quite so well. Dal fingers his laser—he should be practicing his aim, rather than sitting in the chapel.

Maybe only five minutes to go. As he frames the thought, Dal knows with horrid certainty that disaster is near.

He has to sneeze.

"Be still, Dal," Gerda hisses.

But he can't be still. His nose insists on twitching, his lip starts quivering. He bends his head in the attitude of solemn prayer, hoping meditation period will end before—

With the effect of an Outsider spaceship caught by a fusion bomb, Dal sneezes. In the convulsive movement his Ring goes flying, and Dal almost fancies he can see a look of distress on the faces of his Ancestors. The Ring clatters to the metal floor and rolls under his seat.

Red-faced, he looks up. Not only has he breached military discipline and disturbed the silence of Ancestor meditation, but he has broken the the decorum demanded of a child of Ritter Family.

When lasers do not slice him into a dozen pieces, when his Ancestors do not rise up from the dead and strangle him, when Gerda does not even tell him once more to be quiet, Dal feels much relieved. He retrieves his Ring as quietly as possible, and spends the rest of the period silent as vacuum.

As soon as chapel is over for the morning, Dal runs right away to the ship's firing chamber, getting in a good hour of practice with his laser before Gerda requires him for duty. By that time, he reasons, the sneeze incident will be forgotten and the command crew will not give him a good ribbing.

As he enters the command deck, the pilot glances up, a twinkle in her eye, and makes the quick motion of a sneeze.

Dal hopes they find Relay Alpha soon.

❀

Are You One In A Billion?

Located in Alexandria, Egypt, the Grand Library is the central repository of all information known to the Human race. The Library's information is available from terminals all over the Galaxy. The Grand Library receives billions of inquiries every day. And each day, thousands of those inquiries require the personal assistance of a Human Librarian.

These Librarians are among the most talented and highly-trained professionals in the Galaxy. Ten times rarer than chess Grand Masters, Grand Librarians are gifted with a remarkable intuition, allowing them to sift through vast amounts of data to pinpoint exactly the information to answer any question.

The Grand Library is always in search of new Librarians. Only one in a million are neurologically able to undergo the delicate surgery that links the mind directly to the great databases. Only one in a billion have the combination of intuition nd imagination that make a Grand Librarian.

Are you one in a billion? If you think so, contact the Grand Library for recruitment information.

❀

9
The Crystal Ball
[CIRCLE]
6484 CE

When Sting sees *Worldsaver* perform, his opinion of Cilehe obviously goes up a few points. Watching the boy finger the copilot's couch, Jedrek feels compelled to caution him.

"Now don't go stealing this bird, Sting."

"She'd be nice to have."

"Drisana needs *Worldsaver* to get us to Relay Alpha...and back." Jedrek isn't at all sure of Sting—he doesn't know if the lad is joking or not, but the look of desire in those blue eyes is pretty convincing.

"Oh, I'll let it alone until we get the Relay fixed and the Library is back online."

"You'll let it alone longer than that." Suppose bringing Sting along is a mistake—no matter how quickly Drisana took to the idea? How can Jedrek possibly convince a punk like Sting to behave? "Listen, lad, if you like the ship so much we'll buy you one after we finish the mission."

If Jedrek expected astonishment at the wealth of the Library, he is disappointed. Sting turns shadowed eyes on him and puts on an expression half pout and half grin. "That takes all the fun out of it, don't you think?"

Kedar enters the control room, having stowed his belongings in his cabin. "I hope you're not going to hijack this ship, my boy," he says with a chuckle.

Sting throws up his arms. "I'd never get away with anything around here—you people all suspect me before I've even made my plans."

Kedar puts on his mentor look, and Jedrek suspects that he's decided to reform Sting. Silently, Jedrek wishes him luck.

Cilehe enters, grunts a greeting, and sits down in the pilot's couch to begin preflight checks. "Departure in fifteen minutes," she says to no one in particular.

Sukoji and Drisana come into the control chamber together, arm-in-arm and laughing. Sting bows to Drisana and gives Sukoji a quick good-morning kiss.

Drisana nods in Jedrek's direction; he returns the nod but carefully does not approach her. It's too soon to tell how things are between them…before they reach Alpha, he thinks, he will have to have a long talk with her. So far, she's said less than a dozen words to him—and he's returned the attention.

Hands in pockets, Jedrek stands behind the copilot's couch and wishes he could think of something to say. Sukoji breaks the spell by stepping to the control panel. "What departure vector do you have plotted, Cilehe?"

"One sixty-four, sixteen."

"Relative to the Core?"

"What else? Of course relative to the Core."

"Don't get upset. On Aetor we figure relative to Aetor's proper motion. Lets you know how provincial we've become." Sukoji frowns. "I hate to tell you, dear, but you're headed in almost exactly the wrong direction. Relay Alpha is precisely on a heading of zero, zero from Terra."

Cilehe smiles the smile of someone about to win an argument. "We have to make a little stop first, or have you forgotten?"

"Stop?" Sting echoes.

Wonder of wonders, Cilehe answers him civilly. "Drisana wants to leave the Library with its datasphere. So we have to pick up one of the offline data packages that the Empire scattered about. I decided to retrieve the one orbiting Iapetus."

"That's around Saturn."

"Yes, it is." Cilehe surveys the control board. "Whoops, it's almost time to lift. I'd like everyone to be both strapped in and very quiet."

Jedrek knows enough of piloting to know that he will never be a pilot. To be sure, he can fly a ship and eventually get to his destination intact. But the ability to instruct an autoservant does not make a good puter programmer, and piloting talent is as rare as any other.

Cilehe handles *Worldsaver* with the touch of practice and innate talent. She has a feeling for the everchanging fields of the ship's antigravs, a feeling like that one has for the moods of a lover. In addition, she has an asset very few pilots have: her palms.

She places her left hand palm down on a plate in the control panel, making direct neural contact with the ship's navigational puter. What Jedrek can be in relation to the Library, Cilehe is now in relation to *Worldsaver*.

The antigravs surge.

The complexity of the maneuver staggers Jedrek. Iapetus is swinging gaily around with both Saturn and Sol, a good deal further up Sol's gravity well than Terra; Earth herself is dashing in quite a different direction, and *Worldsaver* has all the potential energy of a multi-ton lump of metal and permaplastic sitting at sea level in Egypt.

The velocities, the energies that must be trimmed and matched. A lesser pilot—Jedrek, for example—would leave Earth in normal space, set up a velocity vector toward Iapetus, then briefly flick into tachyon phase for the trip out to Saturn. Then he would spend half an hour maneuvering near Saturn before all factors came together enough for him to approach the satellite. If he didn't become entangled in the Rings.

Cilehe runs her free hand over the controls as if playing a musical instrument, an entire bank of display lights flash from green to red and back again...and Iapetus is visible on the viewscreen.

"Don't bother telling me how sorry you are that you overshot by a tenth of a kilometer," Drisana says with a grin, "because you won't get my sympathy."

Cilehe smiles as well. "I still haven't found the data package. Let's hope it wasn't located and carried away."

"It was there last year when we checked." Drisana undoes her safety straps and leans forward. Cabin grav is a steady one gee. "It has a radar beacon."

"Well blast it, Drisana, someone's tampered with the package. I plotted from data in the Library—four thousand years isn't enough to alter a simple stable orbit, even in Saturn system." Cilehe bends over the controls, then chuckles. "There it is. Terra Salvage checked it out in one of their ambitious periods. I wish they'd put it back into the same orbit." She touches controls again; a point of diamond gleams in the ship's lights. It races toward them, then takes up a steady position about a hundred meters away. Already a few autoservants from *Worldsaver* are dashing about the package. "They'll have it aboard in a few minutes. I've already set up a contact to allow the ship's puter to read from the datasphere from here—Drisana, you won't object if the sphere is kept in the control room?"

"Not at all." Drisana roots in a pouch, produces a marble about half the size of Jedrek's. "I abstracted from the Library all data which has been added since this package was made. We'll have the complete Library to work from, at least."

The datasphere is packed in layer upon layer of meteor foam; as Jedrek helps the other peel back the insulation, he feels like a boy opening a Santamas present. At last the crystal datasphere is revealed, an identical twin of the one in the Grand Library on Terra.

Drisana holds the sphere up with her fingertips, inspecting it from all sides. "It seems to be okay."

"Only one way to find out for sure," Kedar says.

Six palms fit around the sphere, covering all faces. In the past, when Library Circles were larger, many leads had run from the central datasphere to palmpads like the one installed in *Worldsaver*. As many as several hundred could work with one datasphere at once.

Cilehe turns off cabin grav and they float in a mass about the sphere. There is embarrassment at first, Sting's presence is an added complication.

Jedrek closes his eyes and remembers. It's been eleven

years, yet still he recalls the exact position of his body, the outreaching hand, the cool feel of the sphere against his palm....

Fingers interlace with his. There is the warmth of human flesh, and the comforting feeling of being surrounded and protected, of belonging as a part of the Circle. Cosmos, it's been too long.

And then data flows. He is Jedrek nor Talin, Lord of the Universe. All knowledge is his, his to recover in the flash of a pulsar.

They move unconsciously into their accustomed positions. Jedrek feels Cilehe's body against his, is aware of Kedar on his left, and briefly touches toetips with Sukoji. Opening his eyes, he casts a quick wink at Sting, who holds himself back from the group. Jedrek reaches to the lad with his free hand, and meeting Sukoji's in Sting's short hair.

The datasphere is a magical doorway into another world. It is as if his hand reaches into a vast empty space, a huge room tangled with facts. And he is aware, in some mysterious way that they never quite managed to settle, aware that there are five other minds questing with his in this cavernous space.

Ridiculous. The datasphere is a vast space only in a mathematical sense, as a universe of discourse containing the Grand Library. But his mind can deal with the huge amalgamation of data only by treating it as a physical space. One thing is certain, substantiated by millennia of records—no acrophobe ever made a good Librarian.

Contact with the sphere is draining, draining of neural currents as well as of physical strength—and so much more so than the marble. Jedrek feels an old familiar flash of regret, then he takes his hand away and he is only in the control room of *Worldsaver*, only in the confines of his own skull and nerve network, and he feels crushing claustrophobia.

Around their crystal ball, the Circle has at last come together again.

❊

The Curious Voyage of the *Maria Theresa*

from *Mysteries of the Galaxy* by Raul Castoro,
Ibidem Publishing, 5892 CE

Perhaps the greatest galactic mystery is that of the *Maria Theresa*.

One of the legendary Imperial Starcruisers, the *Maria Theresa* was a passenger-and-cargo liner of unprecedented luxury. At an overall length of 8,000 meters and a width of nearly 500, the Starcruiser was a spaceborne city that could carry well over a million passengers. Each of the 25 Starcruisers endlessly plied the circumference of the Galaxy, making stops at each of the Provincial Capitals and completing a circuit in 11 days.

In TE 233, during a maintenance layover at the Tep Kecor shipyards, the presumed-empty *Maria Theresa* fired up her engines and, eluding pursuit, entered tachyon phase and was never seen or heard from again.

Lost along with the Starcruiser were her full complement of ancillary craft, including five fifty-meter liners, five twenty-meter cargo carriers, and one hundred ten-person escape boats. The liners and cargo carriers, respectable starships themselves, had FTL capability and limited weapons.

In TE 243, the *Maria Theresa* was replaced by a newly-constructed sister ship, the *Maj Thovold*.

Theories of the *Maria Theresa*'s fate include human or nonhuman pirates, other aliens, time-travelers, and unexplained behavior by the cruiser's onboard AI software.

❈

10
Maria Theresa
[MARIA THERESA]
Day 500 of the Reign of Her Magnificence
Olympia Marvelous VII

As tradition demands, the Queen departs Ship on her winged steed. The beast's wings beat strongly, and wind whips the Queen's red-dark hair into a flaming froth behind her. Below, *Maria Theresa* is alight with hundreds of colors; through ports she sees people going about their business, and the sight cheers her.

The steed gains enough momentum. She pulls its reins, directing it to the distant white bubble of Styriin. With one last thrust it pulls away from the Ship, they are beyond the atmosphere curtain, and the creature's wings cut nothing.

Olympia Marvelous VII feels her skin tighten, her nostrils and ears close up, transparent membranes seal over her eyes. She can almost sense the touch of what some ancient poet had called "the intangible wind of space."

Naked space is no place fit for people, but at least people can live to pass through it. Olympia clings to the warm neck of her mount and watches Styriin grow closer.

White is the color of Styriin...the white of cloud and snow and cold. A few large rocks jostle within Styriin's atmosphere curtain, and one volume features a grav field oriented southward; an area of several square kilometers of glaciers and ice and towering mountains looming over Styriin Town. Olympia hopes her beast can find its way there; it would be just too embarrassing to land far away and have to call for help like a lost child.

Through the curtain. At once Olympia wishes she'd brought a cloak, or at least a blanket. A Queen is a busy person, and she forgot how cold Styriin was. Oh, why couldn't this festival be in a *warm* place, like Needz or Veen?

With forlorn hope she claws at her saddle bags—to her

surprise, she finds a warm dark cloak and settles it around her shoulders to spite the wind. Her Special Assistant to the Queen, Dileene, takes her title rather seriously; Mother Superior might be a better name.

The winged beast has an instinct about the various habitats of Maria Theresa; it swerves just instants before a thirty-meter houserock comes dashing by. The rock is coated with ice, and looks rather forbidding in the muted starlight. Peering at it she sees windows; behind them, a family huddles around the comforting warmth of heating coils. A boy out the window—then they are all there, waving at her, noses pressed against plastic to witness the spectacle of their Queen careening by. She gives a regal wave of acknowledgment, then grabs at her reins as a gust nearly unseats her.

Near to the igloos and ice-castles of Styriin Town, she feels faint tugs of grav. Her beast flaps swiftly, bringing her down to a soft landing in one of the low-grav areas of the town; the creatures cannot fly in anything more than a trace of gravity. She dismounts and pats its flank affectionately. How much more useful are these beasts, than the dolphins they'd been gengineered from so many Monarchs ago.

Dileene is waiting with a car; together they ride almost high enough to see the pleasure domes beyond Styriin's curvature, then settle to the slopes of Mount Trivstock, where a glacier hangs in eternal menace of Styriin Town.

The amphitheater is all prepared, actors and singers ready, the audience waiting in dignified silence. Olympia takes the stage and tilts her head toward a hanging miniphone. Her voice rolls over the Town.

"Citizens...friends...First and above all must I thank everyone for this wonderful Jubilee celebration. The gifts I have received this past tenday marvelous have been, and sure I am you will enjoy the banquets tonight—everyone in the six Habitats and *Maria Theresa* invited is." She bows her head and dimples as best she can. "But that for later is—right now have we important business, and delay it further I will not.

Just want I, you all to know that today's winner designated will be, Queen's Minstrel for the rest of my reign. Now let the competition commence!" She claps her hands and retreats to her private box, where Dileene waits. The first contestant mounts the stage, his name flashing on her datascreen.

Olympia whispers to Dileene, "How did I do?"

"Good. Next time smile do not so much. Supposed you are to pay attention."

Olympia pays attention. As the Jubilee Competition wears on, she wishes she could avoid paying attention.

The singers and performers are not bad...but neither were they outstanding. And far too many of them have been at the history tapes in making their compositions. Midway through the tenth minstrel's performance, Olympia leans to Dileene and hisses, "If hear I one more song about how stole Dram Alvaad *Maria Theresa* from the evil Emper, or how managed some ancestor of mine I have never heard of to make an Imperial Starcruiser into a home, fully intend I to scream."

"Undignified is it, the Queen to scream."

"Queens sensibilities have too." Still, Olympia stays quiet during the next three repetitions of the earliest history of *Maria Theresa*.

The last contestant enters with a flourish: a young man wearing a flowing grey cape. He carries a simple stringed instrument. Olympia sighs, her eyes still smarting from the last-but-one performer, who dragged a chromatic harp onto the stage.

The grey-cloaked man bows to her, and when he straightens his eyes flash with light, almost as if green fire took root on a hillside against frozen snow.

He strums, then gives voice to an old song, older than *Maria Theresa*, older than anything Olympia knows...it is a song of the Galactic Riders, a hymn to Hesket, the alien goddess of snow and ice. As he sings, his voice lifts her and carries her over the white vistas of Styriin and beyond, out where comets fly without tails and chunks of primordial ices sparkle in the light of newcomer stars.

For days Olympia has been troubled, without knowing why. As if something dreadful is swooping toward them from the cool, eternal stars. Now for the first time, with this man's songs, she feels her burden of melancholy lift, blow away like powdery snow in a dry wind.

She taps Dileene on the shoulder. "He the winner is."

As if the singer hears her, he meets her eyes, and smiles.

❄

11
Relay
[CIRCLE]
6484 CE

The trip to Relay Alpha is slower and much more difficult than that to Iapetus. Tachyon-phase travel has an inherent speed limit—beyond that limit, conflicting gravitational strains from passing stars and dust clouds would rip apart the fragile tachyon vesicles at the heart of the ship's engines.

An additional factor complicating this particular trip was *Worldsaver's* trajectory. Their path led perpendicularly across the Galaxy's spiral arms and all the attendant gas, dust and planetesimals. Cilehe held her velocity down to a point where the trip would take just under three days.

Of course, in the upside-down mechanics of tachyon phase, to go slow takes more energy than to go fast. No matter ...*Worldsaver* has a more-than-ample fuel reserve. And if the ship should get low on fuel—then Cilehe explains that they would simply find a gas giant or skim a stellar atmosphere to pick up needed deuterium and tritium.

Jedrek is not exactly reassured.

The evening of the first day, he takes a stroll through *Worldsaver*. Cilehe's ideas of decor, he thinks, could stand a little improvement; most of the ship's volume is merely functional space used to store her incredible variety of terraforming equipment, as attractive as any warehouse. The few living areas are echoes of palaces and castles of long ago, beautiful but hardly comfortable.

Soon he finds himself in a buttressed engine room. Here, behind all-but-indestructible dellsite sheathing, is one of the antigravs that give *Worldsaver* its propulsion, interior grav, defense screens, and ultrawave communication ability. He rests his hand on the casing; it is smooth and cold to the touch but communicates nothing else to his senses. Odd that something so powerful, so alive, should give no indication of its presence.

"Jedrek, we have to talk."

He is oddly unwilling to turn at Drisana's voice. For all that he wants to clear the air with her, now that the time is come he wishes he were elsewhere.

"What?"

"Turn around, I won't harm you. That's better, now I can look you in the face at least."

"Drisana, I..." What? Good, Jedrek. Next time, have something to say before opening your mouth.

"I suppose I should thank you for coming along. The others might not have come if you hadn't. It was considerate of you." She sighs. "While we're at it, thank you for answering my rose to begin with. I didn't think you would."

He offers a feeble smile. "I couldn't ignore that. Anything else, but not that." Is it suddenly warm?

"We have to talk about Circle business. I don't mean to be personal..."

"If anyone has a right..."

"Don't. You'll make it harder." Her voice is emotionless, her eyes cold. "I want to know why you're not joining us."

"Huh?"

"We aren't a Circle, we're a group of specialists who just happen to be thrown together. You can feel it in our practice sessions."

"I thought we were doing well." Drisana has a way of pulling things in from intergalactic space.

"Think over. Remember what we used to have. That question about the reefbuilders?"

He knows the question she means. It was a dozen years ago and more, he hasn't thought of it for a long time. The Circle worked nonstop for sixteen hours on that question, all the knowledge of the Library spread out like a smorgasbord from which they chose the right morsels to create a gourmet dish. Then, they worked together for two days to get just the right phrasing in the final report to their patron.

"I remember the reefbuilders. I think we could handle that question now."

"You're wrong." Drisana leans forward, her hands braced on a locked control console. Still there is no feeling in her voice. She speaks as if reciting facts picked up from the datasphere. "It took all of us in concert to find leads for that question. I remember stumbling through xenopology and feeling you feeding me the engineering data that I needed to comprehend the inevitability of the reef structures. Answer truthfully; you've spent a day working with us, did you once feel anyone helping you on a question?"

"Cosmos, Drisana, it's been ten years. You can't expect us to pick up—"

"It's not the years that stand in our way. And it's been eleven. Kedar went away for two years, if you recall—when he came back he fit right into the Circle that afternoon. We've lost our common language, our common outlook on the world." She sighs. "It used to be that I could tell what you were thinking even as you thought it, and I could be there with the bit of data you'd need."

"If that's the problem, I don't see any way out of it. We'd have to practice together for a year before we got back to that intimacy."

Drisana shakes her head. "No. We could do it tomorrow afternoon, if all of you wouldn't keep running off every spare instant to be by yourselves. We used to spend a good deal of each day just existing in one another's company. Now Kedar is dictating an obscure monograph, Sukoji plays chess with the shipboard puter in her room, and Cilehe hates Sting so she stays in the control room. And I find you hiding among the engines. I don't understand you people any more."

You never did, Jedrek thinks. Not truly. "That's been going on for a long time. You just can't conceive of anyone having something better to do than play with the Library."

"At last you've said something right. No, I *can't* conceive of anything better to do. The sad fact of the matter is that we have a Library job to do now, and you'll all have to go back to being Librarians for just a little while longer."

And what's wrong with that, Jedrek asks himself?

The answer comes without words, in a foreboding dread: he might find that he likes being a Librarian again.

He closes his eyes and chops off the retort he was all ready to fire. "Drisana, I owe you a lot. I guess we all do. Hells, we're interdependent and I don't think anyone could say where one responsibility ends and another begins."

"I'm surprised you've realized that."

"This is your show, and I think we'll have to run it on your terms. Finding the necessary data to repair that Relay is going to be the biggest job we've ever undertaken, bigger even than deducing the history of Helettia and Cambolinee was. How do you want us to become Librarians again?"

"It's an old tradition, certainly not too much to ask…I want you all to Update."

Jedrek whistles. "Eleven years?" Updating the Library was a time-honored job of Librarians who traveled. All hard data, conjecture, and rumor was entered into the databank, where it could be sorted and cataloged by the Library's puters. "All the cultures and histories we've seen, all the subliminal data we've taken in? That's a job for years."

"If you'd thought of that to begin with, you might not have been so anxious to go tripping off across the Galaxy." Still she is not angry; eleven years has done something to Drisana that Jedrek can't understand. She always played at being firmly in control of herself, but it was an act, a mask that would vanish with a laugh, an angry shout, a few bars of music. Now it seems that she's lost the ability to turn off that façade.

"When I left I was scarcely considering ever coming back."

"And whose fault was that?" Abruptly she puts up a hand. "Let's not get into that again. It's all over and done. We have now to worry about." She drums her fingers a few times on the console. "Naturally everyone can't do a complete Update, there just isn't time. I had in mind a session or two of reading anecdotes into the databank; telling stories as it were. In the course of a night we should all become relatively familiar with one another again."

"I wish I had your optimism. You seem to think that the old rapport is waiting below the surface for some stimulus that will bring it miraculously into being again."

She shrugs. "Maybe I'm over-optimistic. Better than fatalism."

"You're probably right."

❈

Thirty-nine hours later *Worldsaver* drops back into normal space.

"I have to give the naviputer time to accurately determine our position before proceeding to the Relay," Cilehe explains. "Here it can get a good reading on some Cepheids and some of the major globulars."

Jedrek bows his head and joins the others around the datasphere.

It is hardly necessary to make this a group effort. Any one of them can easily abstract the position and vector of Relay Alpha from the last edition of the *Imperial Ephemeris*; any one can extrapolate the data over the intervening 3860 years and odd days. Galactic orbits, while not exceptionally stable, are very slow; Relay Alpha will not have moved much from its original position.

Still, Jedrek doesn't wonder that all six of them lay hands on the datasphere and search together for the information. They do everything as a team now...at least everything involving the datasphere. Drisana was optimistic, they are still nowhere near the level of co-operation of a true work Circle. But they're much further along than Jedrek expected. The Update sessions helped indeed.

"I have it," Cilehe says, and they all disengage. "Couches and crash straps, please."

Her hands move over the control console. The milky arch of stars on the viewscreen vanishes, instantly reappearing at a different angle.

The ship's puters are much quicker than the human eye. Even as Jedrek reaches to undo his straps, alarms sound and every display screen in the control room lights up with a different view.

"What in the cosmos...?"

"We have company," Cilehe announces. "Sukoji, I have tied in the defense puter but it wouldn't hurt for you to take gun controls. Just give puter the go-ahead or veto, please, and don't try to aim or you'll miss."

"I know how to gun, dear." Sukoji is in the copilot's couch; her left hand is already poised over the gun controls.

"Good. Now let's see what we have."

There is no light other than the distant stars; the forward viewscreen is useless. Cilehe points to a smaller screen, where the puter is busily drawing simulations in colored light.

"A multitude of shapes, asteroid-sized and smaller," she reports. "L-type pressure screens at moderate power, basically Terran atmosphere within six large bubbles. Something at the center...it's a ship, a whopping huge one, eight kilometers long. Numerous ancillary structures, all kinds of life activity reported. Nothing coming out on the standard ultrawave frequency. A few broadcasts in electromag, puter is analyzing them now."

Drisana leans forward despite her straps. "Where is the Relay?"

Cilehe taps the screen; a series of bulls-eyes pinpoint a tiny dot between several of the atmosphere bubbles. "In the middle of all that. Well, folks, this is a complication that I, for one, never expected: inhabitants."

❁

12
Tracking
[GELED]
GY 3216

Six days and no trace of the Relay.

Irina is heartily sick of scanners and puter simulations, sick of heel-and-toe watches, sick of the small half-parsec jumps that *Deathcry* takes in tachyon phase every hour. Her eyes burn as long as they're open, and threaten to stay closed every time she blinks. She hasn't had time to wash her hair in three days, and for the last hour a stiff muscle has made her hold her neck awkwardly tilted to the left.

As if all that is not enough, Captain Kassov is in the foulest mood Irina's ever seen.

Off watch, she sits in the crew lounge wedged between the galley and a gun housing. A viewscreen flickers to itself with some holodrama or other received before they left Geled space; Irina pays no attention.

Rur Chernoff, Power Officer Second Class, bursts into the lounge and throws a data module on the table; Irina rescues it from skidding into the disposal chute. "Rur, you don't look happy."

"The Old Man is on the rampage again. Do you know what he had the audacity to tell me?"

"What?"

"That the background noise from our antigravs is fouling up the detectors of his precious Ebettor friends, because I'm running the engines at ten percent overload. And he's the one who ordered the ten percent overrun before we left Geled, to leave enough leeway for quick maneuvering."

"Well, you don't think he's going to take the blame for an order like that, do you?"

Rur shakes his head. "I wish I could record every order he gives me. Then I'd have proof."

She leans back with a rueful smile. "It wouldn't help...that would just move you up on his crap list." It's time to change the subject. "How is the music coming?" Rur is painfully teaching himself to play the cyberharp; Irina heard some of his compositions and he's become quite good.

"I practice. This watch schedule is playing hell with my practice time, though. Funny, one of the Ebettor was watching me play a few rest periods ago and it couldn't seem to understand why I was doing it. The computer tried to translate a dozen times, but the idea didn't get across."

"Maybe they don't have music." She shrugs. "At least the Captain did his best to keep them off our ship…that decision was made for him by HQ."

"Yeah, but now he's playing along with them to the limit. And I don't like them. They make me feel, I don't know, like some kind of obsolete machine. At least, that's how I feel I'm being treated."

"At least they treat Cap'n the same way." They share a good chuckle over that. "Cheer up. This assignment will look good on our records when we return. I'm sure HQ will transfer us out of *Deathcry*."

"With my luck I'll be transferred to a Headquarters job under Kassov."

"No you won't. They don't want him. You'll be put on one of the Entertainment & Personal Services runs. I envy you in a way."

The intercom signals for attention. "Primary crew to stations immediately," Kassov's voice commands. The viewscreen flashes with "ALERT CONDITION URGENT."

The bridge is three minutes away from any point in the ship, and only forty seconds from the lounge—but Alert Condition Urgent leaves no time for movement. Irina dives for one of the five multipurpose terminals in the lounge, feels Rur settle at her left behind a second. In an instant, the puter laser-scans her retinal patterns and slaves the term to the bridge's gun controls. Display screens light up with data while her audio implant briefs her quickly. A strange ship has appeared at the extreme limit of *Deathcry's* sensory range, about half a parsec away. The entire crew is mobilized to track the ship and if possible learn its identity.

Rur flies into action, hands racing across the keyboard. By sneaking a glance at his display monitor, Irina sees that he is shutting down *Deathcry's* engines. Probably to stop interference from the ship's antigravs.

Irina does her best. Among *Deathcry's* armament are several drone missiles with tachyon phase capability; to keep track of them the gun station has its own tachyscope. Sure that every other faster-than-light instrument is already on the stranger, she brings her own tachyscope online and taps an order to track.

The other ship disappears.

The intercom is open; Kassov's voice echoes through the ship, from bunkrooms to empty cargo holds. "Get me the line of that ship."

"Vector measured and on your screens, Captain," A voice answers.

"That does no good," Rur counters. "They went into tachyon phase accelerating; it's a fair bet that they changed their velocity before translation."

"Navigation?"

"Wasn't able to track them, sir."

An Ebettor voice growls and the puter gives a belated translation: "Why are you worried about this one ship? We are searching for an ultrawave relay."

"Any ship in the area has to be going to the Relay; any other possibility is too remote to be worthwhile. Information Officer, what to you have on the make of that ship?"

"It was not constructed in Geled or any of our tributary states. Other than that I have no information."

"Who else tracked them? Gunner, I see your tachyscope was trained on them. What did you get?"

Irina takes a breath. "Nothing more than their original vector. As Power Officer Chernoff has pointed out, that is useless to us."

"Useless. Damn. Ebettor, didn't you get anything on your magic devices?"

"Captain Kassov, our sensors are tuned for detection of a mass of tachyon vesicles such as would be found in one of your Ultrawave Relays. We did not recalibrate the instruments to the strange ship."

"So no one was able to track them? So we have no idea where they went. Wonderful. Just marvelous." Irina hears Kassov's sharp intake of breath. "I want reaction drills for all off-duty personnel, two hours a day. The next time this happens, we will be ready for it. Alert condition is lifted; all stations return control to bridge."

❈

Rur comes to her bunkroom an hour later, holding his cyberharp. "Irina, I've been thinking about that ship."

"Da?"

"Suppose you were a very good pilot? Wouldn't you make all your course corrections with antigravs just before tachyon phase jump?"

"I'm not a good pilot. I suppose that's the way they do it."

"Let's assume the pilot of this strange ship was good, as good as the Ebettor claim to be."

"Then—?"

"If we knew what the ship's antigravs did just before tachyon phase shift…."

Irina pulls herself up on her elbows, wincing at pain in her neck. "It wouldn't help, Rur. Sure, that would probably give us the direction of the ship's flight. But we would have no idea of duration in tachyon phase, or total length of the flight. A flightpath like that could be kiloparsecs long."

"So assume Kassov is right and they're on their way to the Relay. We know it's within ten parsecs one way or another, if we knew the line it would make our search easier."

She pats him on the hand and settles back down into her bunk. "Well, we don't know what the pilot did with her antigravs, so the whole thing is academic."

"Not quite. You've seen the detectors I use to check the tuning of our antigravs? They're accurate to a ten-millionth of a directed gee."

"So you should have...oh."

"Gravitation propagates at lightspeed. There's a wavefront moving outward from where that ship vanished, and now it's about four thousand light-seconds out."

"I think maybe you should tell the Captain about this idea."

He strums. "I thought about that. Suppose I'm wrong? Suppose it was a lousy pilot who made corrections in tachyon phase? Suppose they weren't going to the Relay at all? It could be my career, Irina."

"You obviously don't want to keep quiet about it, or you wouldn't have come to me. What's your idea?"

"Could we mount a detector in one of your missiles? Then we could use the missile to check along their flightpath and see if I'm right."

"Now it's *my* career. Do you know what a talking-to I'll get if he catches me sending out an unauthorized missile?"

Rur keeps up his strumming. "You can do it. I checked; he's going to be dictating a report for HQ next watch in his quarters...you'll have an hour on the bridge uninterrupted."

She closes her eyes. Beating Kassov at the tracking game wouldn't endear her to the Captain—but isn't the mission the most important thing? And maybe HQ would hear of her ingenuity, and she and Rur could be promoted off Deathcry.

"All right, Rur. I'll give it a try. Get down to Armory and hook your detector up to Missile Number One. With any luck we can have it back in its berth before it's missed."

❋

It takes a few repetitions to accurately record the stranger ship's grav pulse. Then, after the puter drew a flightpath, Irina sends her missile skidding along the path toward the Galactic Core.

At three point six two four parsecs Rur's detector goes wild, clearly indicating a collection of grav anomalies.

Irina clenches her fists. She has to be sure. She calls over the Ebettor gunner.

"Why do you summon me?"

"I want you to use your vesicle detectors." She reels off the coordinates and gives direction. "See if that's the Relay."

"From where did you locate this information?"

She remembers her earlier talk with the Captain. "Military secret. Just check it, if you please."

Seconds later, she has her confirmation. Relay Alpha is found.

The bridge crew elects her to disturb Kassov with the news.

❖

13
Starcruiser
[CIRCLE]
6484 CE

Cilehe manages to raise someone on electromagnetic frequencies almost at once. The inhabitants are beaming a constant stream of voice-and-vision at *Worldsaver*...just as soon as the ship's puter digests enough data to be able to translate the alien tongue, they can begin a conversation.

"In the interests of security," Cilehe drawls, "I suggest we wait in the midst of their inhabited areas. They're less likely to shoot at us if we're surrounded by civilians."

"You're paranoid," Sukoji chides her.

"Nevertheless, I want a look at that central ship." Kedar fidgets with his inhaler. "For security, yes, but also to find out what these people are doing here."

Eyes go to Drisana. She becomes aware of them, looks up from the term where she is furiously punching out a description of the space around them. "Yes, take us in. Think of it, a whole new culture...I've already opened up seventeen data files." She frowns. "I could use some help with this, you know."

For a wonder, even Sting ignores her request. All eyes and minds are on the main viewscreen.

Cilehe takes them in on a slow course that threads between the bubbles of atmosphere.

"What are those figures darting between bubbles?" No one bothers to shrug at Sukoji's question, but even Drisana looks up to watch dark spots in motion against the stars.

Finally they near the gigantic ship that sits nestled between the six atmosphere volumes. Cilehe broadcasts messages of peace and friendship; apparently they work, as *Worldsaver* passes unmolested.

"Cosmos, that's a big ship." Jedrek checks the instruments; they are a full three kilometers from the ship and still it is immense. Ladar ranging gives its length as 8000 meters, width 1500. The thing is bigger than many settlements Jedrek had designed.

"I'm beginning to think that coming close to it might not be a good idea," Cilehe whispers. She slows their progress.

"Let's see what it's like in visible light," Kedar suggests. Cilehe nods, not taking her eyes from the viewscreen, and touches a series of studs on the control panel. The ladar image vanishes from the screen, replaced by....

Even in dimmest starlight the side of the massive ship gleams. Cilehe touches more controls, and cabin lights go out.

It is as if a silver wall is coming at them in a slow dignified dance. There are swellings here and there on the great ship, hillocks and protrusions whose nature might remain forever unknown. As they draw closer the eye picks up more details: lines grooved into the impeccable skin, occasionally a tiny pitted crater from some long-forgotten meteor impact, and the gaping maw of a fifty-meter access hatch leading into cosmos knew what.

Jedrek hears a long, slow whistle, and moves his eyes to meet Sting's face. The boy's eyes are wide, his lips pursed. "What a ship!"

Jedrek doesn't even have the heart for humor. Without any trace of levity he says, "Even *you* can't be thinking of stealing it."

"Doesn't look like it would be too hard." But Sting's reply is automatic, devoid of feeling and conviction.

"Bringing us around to the bow," Cilehe says. The silver wall seems to turn around them. *Worldsaver* pulls back, giving them an outstanding view of the large ship tapering off in the distance. He is suddenly able to grasp it as a ship, a unit with its own integrity. The ship's flowing lines make her appear almost a living thing. Her designer was a genius.

Drisana draws in breath sharply. Jedrek turns around and sees her with one hand on the datasphere, the other over her mouth. Her eyes are fixed on the viewscreen.

A majestic swelling at the very bow of the ship must to be the bridge. And below it, as *Worldsaver* continues in her orbit about the large ship, Jedrek can just barely make out markings that can only be identification.

Cilehe sees them too. "Bringing up the lights," she says. *Worldsaver's* working floodlights blaze forth, and dark against reflective surface Jedrek makes out a truly ancient symbol, the six globes of the Terran Empire; and below them, the words "MARIA THERESA."

From out of nowhere, six ships as large as *Worldsaver* swoop toward them.

❂

Someone has to explain to Sting, as they sit in the dark in a strange ship, surrounded by highly efficient and hostile autoservants, and Jedrek finds himself delegated.

"*Maria Theresa* was one of the Empire's Starcruisers...the largest and most luxurious class of ships ever built. There are full details in the Library, and if these servs had let us bring the datasphere you could read all about them yourself. Each Imperial Starcruiser had all the comforts of any planet in the Empire, without their disadvantages."

"Big ships. I get the point."

"*Maria Theresa* is a special case. She was stolen, taken right out from under the eyes of the Imperial Navy during a refueling stop. No one ever found out why or how an obscure tech from Patala managed to carry off the greatest heist in the history of Humanity. And the ship was never found in all the centuries afterward."

"And we've found it."

"Apparently."

Sting is, momentarily, as silent as the others. Then he smiles. "They sound like my kind of people."

"We don't even know if they *are* people," Kedar puts in. "It is not impossible to suppose that aliens found the *Maria*

Theresa and populated it."

"Who built all these environment bubbles?" Jedrek asks. "The aliens, or Humans who went with *Maria Theresa* when it vanished?"

"I have no ideas, Jedrek."

"It is useless to sit here in the dark and argue," Drisana says. "We could ask a million questions, starting with why we should find *Maria Theresa* nestled up to an Ultrawave Relay. One hopes these servs are taking us to someone who can give us answers. We'll just have to bide our time." She sighs. "I don't suppose anyone brought along their personal datasphere?"

There is a chorus of affirmatives.

"Good. Someone be sure to keep careful notes of what happens, so we can transfer them to the primary datasphere when we get the chance."

"*If,*" Sting says, "we get the chance."

❖

Jedrek feels the touch of metal waldoes on his arm, and under their urging he stands.

Suddenly the darkness is split, and the room becomes a montage of their own faces and uncannily distorted bodies in the strobe-light of laser flash. Sting is in motion, and with a flash of sparks one of the autoservants careens across a moderate-sized cabin and smashes into a bulkhead.

"Down, Sting," Drisana says. The boy sheathes his laser knife (Laser knife? Sheath? From whence...?) and clicks off the pale illumination.

"I'm sorry, Sayyid Drisana. I thought...."

"I know, and I appreciate it. We're not here, however, to make enemies."

Cilehe's sardonic reply comes out of darkness to Jedrek's left. "I'd say we've done a fairly good job so far."

The autoservants lead them out of the cabin and through

total darkness for quite a while. Jedrek is conscious of the faint smell of metal, and other odors less identifiable. Finally, they enter a huge chamber.

One entire twenty-meter wall is a viewscreen (or window?) looking out on the placid stars and the Milky Way like an artist's airbrush stroke across space. The pale light is barely enough to distinguish shapes: black-in-black forms that could be furniture, and two roughly-Human figures silhouetted against the stars.

One of them moves, folds in the middle; Jedrek feels Sting tense and puts his hand on the boy's shoulder.

"To *Maria Theresa*, be welcome. Sorry we are, forcibly to have brought you here. Necessary it was to prevent further harm to our people. Many blinded were by your lights."

Jedrek keeps his mouth shut; although he wants to ask a hundred questions, he knows that everyone else will speak and decides it's best to reduce confusion at first.

"How is it that you know our language—" Kedar begins, at the same time Sukoji starts with "Who are you—?" Drisana interrupts both and steps forward.

"We are at a disadvantage here; we cannot see in your dim light. We cannot continue conversation while blind." Her tone is not hostile, yet it allows no argument.

One of the voices says something in their language—Maria Theresan? Jedrek questions himself—and then drops back into Trader patois, "Sorry I am, to speak your language we ought. Now see I that you, us attacking were not, merely to see trying. If you patient will be, this regrettable state of affairs remedied can be. Our eyes tolerate cannot, the level of light you use, yet have we devices that amplify our light will, for you." An autoservant moves near Jedrek, handing him something; he fumbles and takes what feel like heavy work goggles. "Hope I they work will, for you."

He puts the goggles to his eyes, winces at the sudden onrush of light...then gasps.

He is in a room of brilliant color, with vistas of starscapes and fantasy beings all around the walls. The room's furnishings have the characteristic simple functional luxury of the Middle Empire: grav tables and chairs, datascreens and terms, here a shelf and there a door and on the far wall a series of lines that must be a map of the great ship. He surreptitiously touches his marble, seeks and finds the holos he wants—this is nothing more than a lounge of *Maria Theresa*, a place to rest for a moment and have conversation with a fellow traveler, or to watch the latest holodramas.

The two dim figures are Human women. No aliens Jedrek knows mimic the Human form so closely. Albeit their skins are tough and leathery, their fingers abnormally long, their feet like transplanted hands—they were Human.

One of them, with waist-length flaming red hair, repeats her earlier gesture, bending at the waist—obviously now not a threat but a ceremonial bow. "Again to *Maria Theresa*, welcome be. Queen Olympia Marvelous am I; this Dileene Shaarlin is, my Special Assistant." The other woman bows. He hair is dark and short, and she seems to be the older of the two.

Looking to Drisana for permission, Kedar performs introductions. "I must admit," he goes on, "that we are quite amazed to find life here at all. How did your people come to this place?"

The Special Assistant steps forward. "The story of our travels and our eventual arrival here in our archives is...it fascinating reading makes and allow you to peruse it I will, whenever you wish." She looks to the Queen. "Right now, and Olympia forgive me for being so rude, we must know why here you are."

"I can't blame you for being suspicious. This isn't one of the most peaceful areas of the Galaxy." Kedar continues speaking for the group; Drisana, after her aggressive outburst, stays quiet. "We came here to repair the Ultrawave Relay that floats about half a kilometer off the port side of this ship. We hope you will give us permission to carry out our mission; we will cause no harm to your people."

Olympia Marvelous smiles. "We no idea had, that piece of junk still operates."

"Olympia, please," her advisor says. "Kedar Yavam, give us can you, a guarantee of your peaceful nature?"

"Dileene, behaving you are, like a—"

Dileene Shaarlin whispers something to the Queen in their own language; Jedrek wishes he had a link to *Worldsaver's* puter.

"You may send people to accompany us and make sure we do no harm," Kedar says slowly. When there is no objection from either Drisana or Cilehe, he continues. "You obviously outclass us in might; surely it would be no risk to let us go back to our ship and continue as we planned."

Shaarlin nods. "Suppose I, no choice we have—short of you all locking up here. Return we will, to your ship, and then an escort will you have, to the Relay."

Jedrek takes a breath. He's spent the last few years listening to news reports of the relations between the various monarchs and government heads of the Sardinian League on Borshall...maybe that gives him the idea. "Your Majesty, Sayyid Shaarlin, would you consent to dinner aboard our ship so that we may show you how harmless we are?"

Dileene Shaarlin has no chance; Queen Olympia Marvelous accepts with such enthusiasm that Jedrek suddenly feels sorry for the older woman.

❋

Worldsaver's autoservants—more advanced but obviously the same design as *Maria Theresa's*—produce after-dinner drinks and drugs with an unobtrusive grace that only the machine could master. In deference to the visitors from *Maria Theresa* the cabin lights are turned down to only a trickle; wearing his amplifier goggles, Jedrek feels as if he is in a bright room. Colors take on new shades, but everything else is normal. What a world he's been missing in dim light and shadows!

Dileene is telling the story of how *Maria Theresa* had wound up next to Relay Alpha, and Drisana leans forward, wrapt. Jedrek hasn't paid much attention to the story. The Theresans do not have a modern approach to history...he is unable to date their arrival at the Relay and doesn't have the patience for long lists of Queens. Especially when filtered from the native language into Trader argot. Jedrek hopes the puter will soon have enough data to translate.

"Suppose I, a good deal of time passed has, since our language modified has, so much. This tongue you speak a very archaic language is, mostly used in religious ceremonies and official functions of the Queen—when heard we your broadcasts know we did not, what to make of them. Thus Olympia and I decided, to with you deal personally." Dileene sighs and sniffs her brandy. "Amazed am I, that Terra in existence is still, and that people the Emper remember. For us, nothing more than legends it is, tales mostly to children told, and in dramas enacted. And you keepers are, of knowledge. Understand I do not, why you must yourselves concern with the Ultrawave Relay."

Jedrek can see Kedar marshaling his forces to explain yet another time. Much good will it do him—Theresan astronomy is apparently content with a Universe only half a kiloparsec in diameter.

Dileene holds up a hand and cocks her head, touching her ear as if listening to an implant. Her eyes meet Olympia's, then both stand. "Afraid am I, that ask I must, you us allow to *Maria Theresa* to return. Accepted we you, in good faith, and now wrong have we been proven."

"What?"

Dileene turns on Kedar, her hands rolled into fists. "Peaceful mission—Suppose I, you know not that even now another ship into our space comes, from the same direction as yours?"

"What?!"

Cilehe touches her lapboard; a viewscreen blazes with nova-light and hands fly to cover eyes before she hastily tones down the screen.

It takes only a second for the puter to track with tachyscope. A ship, obviously a heavily-armed warship, is diving toward *Maria Theresa*.

"Oh, good," Sting says drily. "We *need* some further complications."

❁

Maria Theresa: Habitats & Populations

Maria Theresa: Main habitat and site of most manufacturing, official residence of Monarch, approximate population 0.5 million.

Kamtem: Recreational & residential habitat with many rivers and lakes, center of aquaculture, approximate population 0.7 million.

Needz: Forest & agricultural habitat, primarily recreational, approximate population 0.1 million.

Oberst: Residential & cultural habitat primarily known for musical & dramatic performances, approximate population 1 million.

Styriin: Recreational & residential habitat with many mountains, primarily devoted to snow & ice recreations, approximate population 0.7 million.

Teerell: Recreational & residential habitat primarily known for public festivals and markets. Approximate population 1 million.

Veen: Largest residential habitat, urban center, approximate population 2 million.

❈

14
Attack
[GELED]
GY 3216

From her first observations of Relay Alpha, Irina knew that it sat in the middle of an inhabited system. Now, as she dresses to take watch for the last leg of *Deathcry's* journey, she reads the orders on her datascreen and frowns.

"What's wrong?" Rur asks.

"Our orders. Look."

"So?"

"I guess I shouldn't be surprised that there's going to be fighting." She should have known. Gunner of a Geledi Navy Warship, she signed on for a five year duty tour of fighting, trained for fighting, spent every on-duty hour and many off in intimate contact with all the engines of fighting. What else was she to do, for gods' sakes?

And yet..."It's one thing to be battling away in our space, keeping down rebellions and skirmishing with the Escen Hegemony. I like that. But these people don't even know we're coming. They've never met us, we don't have any idea who they are. Ancestors, with the configuration of their habitats, they're probably not even Human. Yet we're going to come out of tachyon phase with all guns firing."

Rur puts a hand to her shoulder; she shrugs it off. He doesn't repeat the gesture. "Haven't you heard the Old Man's speech?"

"I've escaped thus far."

"This time he made sense. Look, Irina, as long as that Relay is inoperative we're out of touch with our outlying bases. That includes intelligence agents in Ebettor space. You've seen those creeps perform—do you want to face one of them in a battlevolume?"

"No...." She thinks of the Ebettor gunner, its fingers almost a blur as they stroked gun controls.

"Damn right. Apparently the feeling at Headquarters is that Geled wouldn't last a year if they decided to attack. So we need contact with those intelligence teams, and with the diplo offices for that matter." He cocks his head. "Do you want us to return home and find out that they're fighting for their lives against the Ebettor instead of against Escen?"

She switches off the screen with a chopping gesture. "Things aren't that crucial. The big ultrawave stations at Fleetcom can get through to our agents, I would think, and there are still telepaths and mail drones. The Ebettor Threat is a good excuse, but not good enough to go smashing up an innocent culture."

He shrugs. "Then try this one on: if you don't follow your orders, you're going to be court-martialed. When we get back home, they won't like the fact that you disobeyed, and they'll probably order psych-conditioning or even mindwipe. Either way, there goes Irina, never to be seen again."

"Damn it, I'm not thinking of disobeying orders." She looks uselessly around her bunkroom; she would never see a sound pickup if there were one. "You get carried away, Rur. All I was doing was making a philosophical point. You know as well as I do that when the order comes to shoot I'll be in there shooting." Having said it, she doesn't feel any better.

"Good decision."

"But at least," she stands, "I'll know that I'm doing something wrong." That has to count for something, doesn't it?

Doesn't it?

Please, gods?

❂

15
Summoning
[MARIA THERESA]
Day 503 of the reign of Her Magnificence,
Olympia Marvelous VII

Maria Theresa's Bridge is a sacred place, hardly ever used even for ceremony. The Starcruiser, after all, cannot move—her antigravs were long since torn out and used to construct the six habitat volumes. The Bridge is ten meters broad and fifteen deep; curving across the entire forward wall is a seven-meter-tall composite viewscreen that now looks out on star-strewn black and the distant fuzzy whiteness of Styriin. On the other three walls of the Bridge, control panels and datascreens line the sides of shallow alcoves. Halfway up the rear wall, a broad balcony holds even more duty stations.

Most of the Bridge instruments are dark now, as they have been for ages. Olympia wonders if anyone even knows how to turn them on any more, much less what they might be used for. Only a few of the duty stations are manned, and those by government techs who looked frankly silly in their skintight red uniforms marked with the Six Globes (can it be true, she wonders, that those globes represent the six original worlds of the Emper, and not the six habitats of *Maria Theresa*? So Kedar Yavam says, and she can't imagine why he'd lie.)

"Your Magnificence." Dileene bows; the rest of the Bridge crew stops their work and bows as well.

"Of that, none. No time for it. Respects pay me later, if you must...oh, know you all how important this is, your best do." Olympia is flustered, and that does not befit a Queen. Though what Queen would *not* be flustered under the circumstances?

"Dileene, how go things?"

Dileene's customary frown is deeper than usual; Olympia gets the feeling that she shouldn't have asked. "Tactical plot," Dileene orders, and the forward viewscreen fades into a multicolor holo display, a schematic of the volume under the rule of *Maria Theresa*. Various colored dots and stars have to indicate something, but Olympia doesn't try to figure out which are friendly.

"Things not well are going," Dileene says. "The aliens some drones launched and trouble enough we are having keeping up with them, without the mother ship about worrying." She glanced]s at the tactical display. "One thing good is. Our friends in *Worldsaver* fighting are, alongside the six—no, five now—destroyers we have. To hold off they managed, a concentrated attack on Oberst until two of our ships there arrived."

"Why these aliens are attacking us?"

Dileene spreads her hands. "I know not. The puter trying has been, to analyze their attack patterns—I it have, into *Marie Antoinette's* puters tied—but nothing of that has come. I no idea have, what their objective might be. Unless...."

"Unless?"

"One ship from far away comes, and interest expresses in the Ultrawave Relay. Too much of a coincidence would it be, that the second alien ship us to visit today would also want the Relay?"

"No communication from the aliens?"

"None. Nothing but hostility."

Olympia feels her stomach twist. This is nothing decent to be happening. People were dying, and she doesn't know why. "Offer them should we, the Relay?"

Dileene faces her with a pained expression. "If right I am, and that's their goal is—should we it give, to them? Ought not know we, what they with it want? Especially with such irrational behavior."

"You right are." They need more information.

Information. "What said have the newcomers from *Worldsaver*, about the aliens? What they want might, and why?"

"Kedar Yavam said, that they as ignorant are, as we. His people to work has he put, on the problem and will he notify us if anything they learn."

"Dileene, help need we."

"Afraid I am, that we do, your Magnificence."

"Call me that, do not." She feels like stamping her foot, know that is not a very Queenly thing to do either. "Magnificent have I been for only five hundred days, and I know I do not, what's the Magnificent thing to do right now. Just wish I, that I could go back home. Wish I, that Aunt Jesusita here was still." Olympia sniffs and reminds herself that crying is not dignified.

Dileene gives her a quick hug. "Queen you are. Know you, what that means."

"I know." Sniff. She hugs Dileene close. "Call will I, for help." Aunt Jesusita took her to the place...but she has never gone on her own. "Tell them will you, a steed to have ready for me?"

"Yes. Careful be, Olympia. No telling what those ships do will, or where the battle move next might."

"I will." She will need sturdy clothes. And..."The musician tell, that want I, him with me to come. Music will help."

"As say you, your Magnificence."

Leaving the Bridge, Olympia looks up to see one green dot vanish from the tactical plot. She doesn't wait to find out whose it was.

❊

Wind whips at her, and the musician holds tightly to her waist. She whistles to her mount, and it leaps off into space. All too soon the *Maria Theresa* atmosphere curtain closes behind them and Needz looms ahead.

At the center of Needz is a sphere of dirt that holds the great forest. Yellow and brown, green and red, these are the colors of Needz. Much work was done to gengineer varieties of plants that could live on infrared and other types of low-energy radiation; but there they are, and there Olympia heads.

The Hlutr, of course, are the main attractions of the forest. Six of them, set aside in their own domed and shielded preserve, with an artificial star shedding harsh and painful light over them, no traveler comes to Needz without looking at them.

How many of those travelers, she wonders, know that the Hlutr were intelligent beings? How many know that they are wiser and more intelligent than most people? And how many know that one can communicate with them?

As part of her Royal training, Olympia practiced singing with the Hlutr. Such communication became more difficult as she grew older (Aunt Jesusita said that was normal, even in someone with the Talent) and she came to hate the effort.

Now it is necessary.

Needz air closes about her with all its warmth and humidity. Her steed, perhaps harkening back to a forgotten aquatic heritage, shows no compunctions about diving through rain showers and emerging soaked; Olympia clings to its neck and does not complain.

As the steed sweeps to a landing in a low-grav area, fear suddenly grips her.

What is she to do?! One set of aliens attacking her people, and she is to call another? For what purpose?

The musician hops off the mount and gives her a hand down. "My Queen," he says. "Sung their songs I have, and told their tales all my life. The Galactic Riders help us will."

"Glad I am, that you confidence have." Let it serve for both of us.

Maria Theresa is nominally a member of the Free Peoples of the Scattered Worlds, the very loose association of intelligent races in the Galactic Halo—and so she is as entitled as anyone to call for the Galactic Riders when her people need help. And the Riders will answer, even though the Galaxy is large and their numbers few. But first she must contact them.

She thinks of trying to explain her misgivings to the troubadour at her side. Their culture is so ancient, she would say, and so wise, what will I say? I'll giggle, I'll stammer, I'll disgrace myself and my people.

He smiles, and she wonders if he somehow knows her thoughts. But he says nothing, merely follows her to the dome. She hands him blinder goggles, and settles another pair on her own eyes. Then Queen and troubadour enter the dome.

Bright, even with reduction turned to a maximum. Humid, and smelling of rich soil. Squinting, Olympia looks around.

Set amid lesser vegetation, the Hlutr are even more impressive than if they stood alone. They are arranged in a wide circle about the center of the dome, and their branches nearly touch the inner surface. Each is thirty meters tall; they are young, having been planted only a million days or so ago—virtually no time at all in their incredibly long lives.

Trees, she thinks, then No, drifting clouds low over hills. Twisted nebulae in far-off space. But they are none of these, they were Hlutr. Many-hued, their trunks and strong limbs radiate a comforting feeling of stability and security. She always wants to climb into the crown of one of them and settle down between those massive, protecting limbs, screened from the world by ever-changing colored leaves.

She takes a deep breath and tried to empty her mind. She is no telepath—but telepaths no better than normals in contacting Hlutr, so it doesn't matter. It is best, Aunt Jesusita taught her, to do nothing and let them come to you.

She becomes aware of a soft soughing, as leaves in the wind—but there was no wind in this dome, never.

The troubadour strums his instrument, and almost it seems to Olympia that the Hlutr sigh in tempo with the soft music.

Yes, Little One? The voice in her mind is everything that the forest could ever be: the lush greenery of air heavy with heat and dampness, the cool whispering dryness of the reds and browns and yellows of death-cycle, and under it all the strong brown support of friendly trunk and strong limbs.

I...I, she stutters. Then she looks to the troubadour, fixes her attention on his fingers plucking strings, and her thoughts firm. *Need I, with the Galactic Riders to talk.* She feels like a little buzzing insect, her thoughts so quick and shallow, and fluttering all about from image to image. What must the Hlutr think?

Be calm, Little One. Think with us, and we will carry your words to the Galactic Riders.

Olympia Marvelous closes her eyes and folds her arms. Across her inner eyelids swim blots of color, which firmed into the impression of vast forests of Hlutr all singing together—then she senses the perpetual gulfs of space, and feels them carrying her safely across the void on their music. The song of the Hlutr permeates and underlies all of space, she suddenly realizes, with a shock that almost jolts her out of their spell.

There is a bluewhite planet, and from tales and songs and legends she knows it to be Nephestal, the seat of the Council of the Free Peoples of the Scattered Worlds. Olympia quivers, and reaches forward convulsively, closing her hands over the warm roughness of Hlutr bark in an effort to hold on to the vision. *Do not be afraid, Little One, we will not let you go.*

Again a forest, this one faintly phosphorescent under starbright skies. Then she is before a towering edifice like unto the largest mountain in Styriin, and this she knows to be the Temple of All Worlds. Near you are to sacrilege, Olympia Marvelous, she tells herself...but at the same time she cannot believe the Hlutr would take her anywhere she does not truly belong.

An alien is there with her. In her vision she sees nothing of its physical form, she has only a dream-sense of age and wisdom. Can the alien see her? Not knowing, she makes a bow with her mind.

"How can we serve you, daughter?"

"Help need I. Being attacked are we, and...oh, doing this right am I not, who I am you know not." How to frame the thought that would give her identity and the location of *Maria Theresa*?

The Hlutr voices sound comfortingly in her mind. *Fear not, Olympia Marvelous of Maria Theresa, you are known to the Elder. Tell her what you want.*

"Aliens in a big ship came, and fighting with us are they. Killing people are they. Fighting them back are we, but know I do not, how long we hold them off can." She feels tears, feels her thoughts breaking apart in mental static. There is discord in the Hlutr-song. "Why doing this to us they are, do I not even know."

The Elder passes a hand (claw? tentacle?) over her in a gesture of benediction. "We will send a Rider to your place, daughter. All will be well."

"Thank you." She reaches for the Elder, but then the vision falls apart and she is back in the dome in Needz, watching swirls of color behind her eyelids.

Peace be with you, Little One, the Hlutr say, and then she senses their departure from her mind.

The troubadour stops his strumming.

She nods at him. "Thank you. Good for our people have you done. Now return let us, to *Maria Theresa.*"

Olympia takes her time returning. Her steed awaits them at the crown of a hill, as near as it dares to come to high-grav areas. She gives the troubadour a hand to help him up the gentle slope. About ten meters from the steed, she hears the singer gasp and follows his eyes skyward.

Moving quickly against the stars, one of the alien drones is diving. Lasers score vegetation on either side, then Olympia cries out in spite of herself.

The drone is flying directly toward the unprotected Hlutr dome.

❄

Meet a Galactic Rider
(from *Stars of the Galaxy*, May 6482 CE)

For millions of years, the Galactic Riders have served the causes of peace and freedom in the Galaxy. Yet Humans know little about this ancient alien order. Recently, on the planet Dovan, we interviewed T'to Yachim, a Dorascan Rider who was happy to answer some questions.

Stars: So tell us, what are the Galactic Riders all about?

T'to Yachim: The Galactic Riders provide help to those in need. In addition, we assist the cause of freedom over repression, maintain cultural continuity, act as mediators, and provide role models.

Stars: What sort of training do you need to be a Rider?

T'to Yachim: We are extensively trained in music, history, culture, and the accumulated wisdom of the Free Peoples.

Stars: Galactic Riders are empowered to act as judge, jury, and executioner. Who oversees them; who prevents them from abusing their power?

T'to Yachim: Galactic Riders act with the full authority of the Council of the Free Peoples of the Scattered Worlds. Riders are responsible only to their own consciences. A Rider's integrity is beyond question. On the few occasions that a Galactic Rider has misused power, other Riders have hastened to administer justice.

Stars: Where are the Galactic Riders based?

T'to Yachim: Our order is headquartered on Nephestal. Many individual Riders make regular circuits of various worlds and settlements, visiting each perhaps once a year or so. Some set up permanent homes, and operate out of them. Others consider their ships to be their homes.

Stars: Thank you for sharing this information with our readers.

❁

16
Resistance
[CIRCLE]
6484 CE

Aboard *Worldsaver* there is chaos.

Jedrek tries to concentrate on reading the datasphere. *Worldsaver* flashes between and around hostile battle drones, her defense screens winking on to radiate laser shots, then off again as Cilehe fires and, usually, misses.

He closes his eyes, telling himself not to look at the viewscreen. Back to the Library. Kedar's fingers move briefly against his.

No, no, no! Wrong section entirely. He doesn't need complete details of the placement of garbage receptacles in all Imperial complexes across the Galaxy. Start again.

Ships. The Terran Empire's Starship Registration Catalog opens around him in endless detail. Impatiently he flips through section after section until he comes to the silhouette identification routines.

A long shot. The ships they're fighting are surely not Imperial. But if they're Human—if!—they are almost certainly based on one of the innumerable Imperial designs. Jedrek's a tech, he should be able to determine which former Imperial shipyard might have built ships that could mutate into these. And with that knowledge, he might be able to guess where the ships are from.

"Cilehe," Drisana says, in a tone that demands immediate attention. Jedrek curses, his attention ripped from the Catalog. He opens his eyes to complain.

"There's a drone strafing Needz. Defenders aren't in the right position."

"Needz?"

"The forest habitat. Tracking data on your screen now."

Jedrek keeps quiet. Drisana's tracking and Cilehe's piloting are both more immediately important than his data search.

Cilehe tenses, then the view winks out and another replaces it; plants and trees and...an alien drone diving at an unprotected dome. Two figures are running up a hillside toward one of the strange winged animals.

Space careens about them and all at once *Worldsaver* is in the path of the attacking drone. The drone turns its lasers on them, and *Worldsaver's* defense screens come on full force, radiating into red. The drone makes a shallow, sweeping turn and flies away from Needz.

Cilehe whistles. "Sixty gees at that pullout. Well, my ship can follow any drone." Power indicators on the control board jump, and *Worldsaver* leaps after the drone. Cilehe fires a few laser shots, which go wildly off target.

"Blast, I thought I'd never say this." She glances into the cabin. "Sting, take the weapons controls. I'm busy keeping on this bogey."

Sting jumps forward and settles into the couch vacated just in time by Sukoji, slapping one hand on a contact plate, palm down. He fires a few laser shots and scores a hit on the drone; its screens flare yellow and then faded to invisibility once again.

"Try harder than that, Sting."

"Get us closer and I will." A broad grin is on his face. "What else do you have here?"

"Use anything you need." The drone goes through a complex course-change; Jedrek can't help noticing that the accelerometer hits one hundred twenty gees. If cabin grav overloads....

Best not to think of it.

"Hold on," Sting warns. The tip of his tongue shows between his lips, then a warning siren sounds and electric-red letters burn themselves across every available viewscreen: "GRAVITY WARP IN OPERATION."

Jedrek knows of the gravity warp. It was a Borshallan invention, back in the Late Empire—graity warps are still used occasionally for manufacturing in the Sardinian League.

Fearfully consumptive of energy, they are not used often.

A gravity warp projects a point-source of intense grav force up to a kilometer away. The small ones Jedrek is familiar with ranges from half a gee to twenty; he knows that military warps are sometimes more powerful…and there are always tall tales, although theoretically impossible, of a super-gravity-warp that could turn a planet into a mini-collapsar.

The drone disappears in a flash of bright light. *Worldsaver* swerved and, for less than a second, cabin grav fluctuates wildly.

Cilehe turns angry eyes on Sting. "How high did you have that set?"

"I thought you wanted me to get rid of the drone."

"What grav?"

"Two thousand."

"Two—!"

"Worked, didn't it?"

"Cost us a tenth of our reserve fuel. Nearly overloaded the reactor. Set up waves in our antigravs and nearly blew number six."

"But it worked."

Drisana interrupts. "Drone attacking Veen, Cilehe. That's a full-fledged city, seven million population if what Dileene told us is right."

Cilehe sighs. "Give me tracking data. Sukoji, take the copilot's couch. And someone please discipline this child."

For an instant Jedrek's eyes meet Drisana's; hers flash with amusement. It's the first honest emotion she's shown him. He looks to Sting; the boy shrugs and surrenders the couch.

Again Jedrek wonders why Sting is here at all. He acts as if everything—*Maria Theresa*, the gravity warp, the Library—is a toy for his own amusement.

And what happens when it all stops amusing him?

"We'd better get back to work," Kedar whispers to Jedrek. "If this battle lasts much longer they're going to kill one another."

❁

Too difficult. Too many ships, too many designs. In six centuries of Human-designed spaceships before the Empire fell, there were entirely too many radically different ways to build—and many thousands of them could have evolved into the alien ship they've holographed repeatedly through the tachyscope.

Jedrek keeps at it as *Worldsaver* chases and is chased all through the volume of space belonging to *Maria Theresa*. They fight a losing battle...already two of the Starcruiser's defense ships are destroyed, leaving only four—and *Worldsaver*.

"Cilehe, I need more information on the alien ship. If I could see doppler radar of their engine configuration, of the placement of primary screen generators, maybe I could narrow down the search."

"I can't get any closer to them. And they have full screens up, our ladar and radar are getting nowhere. Those exterior pictures are all you're going to get."

Only one alternative, much as he hates to admit it. "Drisana...I need your help. Can you spare some time to search with me?"

She hands the tracking station over to Kedar. "Of course. What do you have so far?"

"I've narrowed it down to five Imperial provinces: Credix, Neordan, Phuctra, Laxus and Geled."

"Say what you mean, Jedrek. You've eliminated three." She touches the datasphere. "You've probably been looking only in the Ship Registration Catalog."

"What else is there?"

"I'm not sure. Let me think." She purses her lips. "Is there any way we can get the exact frequency of their antigravs?"

"How exact? We can narrow it to the Ultrawave Scale note—to the thousandth of a vibration per second, maybe."

"They communicate on the same frequency as their tachyon vesicles, yes?"

"That's how Ultrawave works. But we can't get the necessary level of accuracy to pinpoint their exact ultrawave frequency."

"Do it to the best accuracy you can." As Jedrek fumbles with instruments, he sees Drisana close her eyes and touch the sphere. What is she after? He pushes *Worldsaver's* instruments to the closest measurement of frequency they can produce, aware that a difference of one part in ten million means an entirely different comm frequency.

He turns his attention back to the datasphere. Drisana takes his hand and places his palm in contact with the sphere. "This is a trick I picked up from Karl Loewenger's autobiography...he used it in battle with unknown Patalanian forces. Now look. Here's a list of the comm frequencies accepted by each of the Ultrawave Relays. You'll notice that they all overlap at some points, but this should cut your search down a bit." For the first time since the trip began, Drisana seems once again her old self. She only comes alive, Jedrek thinks, when she's working with the Library.

He skims the frequency list. "Most likely they used Relays Alpha and Beta. But that doesn't mean much. Tachyon vesicles come in all frequencies, and it's been millennia since the Empire distributed them along Provincial lines."

"It's in the best interest of a society to keep their Navy as attuned as possible, to prevent any interference during battle. And these people apparently think a lot of their Navy. So they will have continued using crystals of those frequencies even if they didn't quite remember why."

"You're telling me they're probably from the old Province of Geled. That leaves an awful lot of territory to cover. There were a total of sixty shipyards in Geled when the Empire fell." He sighs. "That still doesn't tell us if they're from around here, or elsewhere."

"You pay too much attention to tech matters. Now let me

see your work." She pokes her attention into Jedrek's workspace in the datasphere. "You've boiled it down to six hundred prototypes for that ship. Oh, Jedrek, you do make things complicated."

"I try."

"How many of these are from Geled?"

He counts and indicates them at the same time. "Seventy-three."

"Now pay attention. I'm bringing in the full power of the ship's puter. It would go quicker with the big machines at home, but this should suffice. Cilehe made a good choice." The images of the prototypes waver. "Now I'm going to key in what we know of the history of the Province of Geled after the Empire fell. Luckily we have tried to keep the Library up to date. Watch how these ships change and strike each one that doesn't lead to the attacker we're concerned with."

It takes almost an hour, many repeated trials, and complaints from Cilehe about filling puter memory. Jedrek finally convinces himself that only eight of his prototypes could have developed into the ship leading the attack on *Maria Theresa*. Four of those prototypes had been constructed in the shipyards of the planet Geled's largest moon; four more were from shipbuilding worlds and settlements within two kiloparsecs of Geled.

"We didn't need to take things this far, if you hadn't been so stubborn," Drisana says. "Fine. We know that they're not from around here. So this isn't some kind of local conflict we've stumbled into. They came nearly six kiloparsecs—why?"

"The Relay."

Kedar nods. "That makes good sense. Geled is a militaristic society; if I recall correctly, they're currently in an expansion cycle. The Relay has to be their primary target—there's nothing else in this system worth a major military effort."

Over her shoulder, Sukoji says, "And the Geledis are just the sort of people to enter a system with all guns blazing.

They border on the Transgeled, they're surrounded by enemies, so they don't know any other response."

Jedrek shakes his head slowly. "I'm sorry, I should have guessed that at the beginning."

"That's how you know that you've found the truth -- afterwards, it's so obvious that you know you should have guessed it." Drisana pats his hand, then turns to Cilehe. "Now that we know who they are and what they're after, we have a way to communicate with them. Contact Dileene and tell her we're going to take Relay Alpha under our protection—that should bring the Geledis to our airlock for a conference if nothing else will."

Jedrek frowns. She doesn't have to sound so self-righteous.

✸

Dorascans
(from *Cassaw's Field Guide to Nonhuman Species*)

Homeworld: Dorasc

Height: 140-160 cm

Physical: Bipedal, two arms, head with two eyes and beaked mouth. Extensible dorsal fin and bony ridges along back and head are primarily defensive. Stomach pouch for sheltering young. Dorsacans are long-limbed and very athletic.

Evolutionary: Dorascans are offshoots of the Avethellan race. The ancestors of current-day Dorascans returned to the ocean, where the dorsal fin developed; when they reemerged onto land, the fin became a primary defense against large predatory gliding animals. This fin, lined with sharp ridges, is a formidable weapon.

Special Features: With superb skills in vocal mimicry and empathy, Dorascans are highly-talented linguists and musicians.

Culture: The Dorascan Empire (c. 1.63-1.58 million BCE) extended roughly from present-day Elendan/Kellia/Frit to Vetret, with tributary states extending as far as Tethys and into Credixian areas. Today, Dorascans occupy a handful of worlds, and are part of the Free Peoples of the Scattered Worlds.

❀

17
Nephestal
[RIDER]
Galactic Revolution 561.19775508 following
the Migration of the Daamin

T'to Yachim kneels, a difficult enough posture for a Dorascan. He retracts his claws and feels his dorsal fin nestle against the small of his back. For a few moments at least, T'to Yachim is at peace.

Around him is the grandeur of the Temple of All Worlds; T'to has eyes only for the alcove before him. There, in a comfortable space only three meters square and looking much larger, floats a perfectly detailed holo of the planet Dorasc. T'to has not visited his homeworld since he was a cub, but still he knows homesickness and longing whenever he sees this image. After a lifetime of service to the Galactic Riders, when he feels that he his work is done and he deserves to rest, T'to Yachim will go to Dorasc and enjoy the last phase of his life surrounded by his kin and his people. The valley that has served as home for the Tribe of Yachim for over a million and a half years will be waiting for him.

T'to closes his eyes. Retirement is only a vague thought now, something he knows will happen, but doesn't actually believe. There is still too much to accomplish in the Galaxy before he retires.

"May I have speech with you, Galactic Rider?"

T'to's dorsal fin twitches in surprise, and he quiets the reflex. He turns to see one of the Daamin behind him. The creature stands about a meter tall, covered with fine white fur that cries out to be stroked. Her deep eyes are red as the giant stars near Dorasc.

"I give you greeting, Elder, this fine day."

The Daamin inclines her head. "I am Drac Trnas and I would give you counsel ere upon your mission you depart. Will you onto the Plaza follow me?"

"It is my pleasure to accompany you." T'to casts a farewell thought in the direction of Dorasc, then follows Drac Trnas past alcove after alcove, holo after holo of all the countless inhabited planets that make up the Scattered Worlds.

It is night, but the Great Plaza swims in light. In the sky above, T'to sees a jagged patch of almost sun-bright light: this is Rept Kretzlab, the Gap of Remembrance—a lane kept clear of interstellar gas and dust by Daamin watchships. This clear lane that lets in the dazzling light of the Galactic Core, only a score of parsecs away. The Daamin, it is said, originally came from the Core, the Gathered Worlds, and when they emigrated into the then-lifeless Scattered Worlds they kept this sign of their lost homes.

The light of Rept Kretzlab falls on the Singing Stones, oldest artifacts in the Scattered Worlds. T'to Yachim has spent many hours staring into the ever-changing facets of the Stones, listening in his mind to their melodies. Telepathic resonators, scientists call them, resonators which collect and focus the thought and emotion of an entire Galaxy, rebroadcasting them in the form of a music beyond any composer's art. Gifts of the Elder Gods, poets call them, given as a sign to the Daamin that all will be well. When the Stones break apart, when their song is stilled and they melt back into the primal essence from which they emerged, then the Universe will come to an end. So say the legends. T'to knows them by rote.

Drac Trnas brings him out of contemplation. "You go to aid *Maria Theresa*?" The Elder pronounces the name of the ship with the inimitable Human tone.

"Their call I answer. I am qualified. My student named Yevetha Krestin was born there and as an orphan sent to us."

"I hope that sentiment clouds not your mind."

"Elder Honored, I *am* Galactic Rider trained and true; you disappoint me to believe that I cannot objective be."

"T'to Yachim, I find within *myself* an unobjective fondness for this folk. Keep hold of your compassion but do not allow it to divert you from your duty."

"I do not think I understand, Elder."

Drac Trnas pulls herself up onto a stone bench. She does not invite T'to to sit next to her. "Among my people I am said to be the leading scholar of Humanity. Ten thousand years and more my clan has sought to understand the nature of this folk. Today stands Mankind at a crucial point; their history is shifting as we sit here."

"Honored Elder, could you more plainly speak?"

"Long ago we advised Galactic Riders to encourage the Theresans to abide beside the Alpha Relay. Then did we suspect this situation would occur. I have had reports from Riders on a hundred Human worlds, and what I hear disturbs me and puts fear into my heart."

"How so? The Elders rarely yield to fear."

The Elder's eyes go to the Gap, then back to T'to. "Other forces are at work here."

"You sense the hand of Kaylepeskrit?"

"Exactly. That great power that controls the Gathered Worlds is turning now its sight upon the Scattered Worlds, and I do fear. I hesitate to speak such matters here, yet they must needs be said before you go."

T'to glances again at Rept Kretzlab, and suddenly it is not quite a shining beacon. The Daamin had reason to leave the Core, for it fell under the domination of a power too tyrannical, too uncivilized, too repressive to be borne by any freedom-loving creature.

T'to Yachim knows well the power of the Gathered Worlds and of their ruler, the Gergathan. T'to's world, Dorasc, was once a tributary state of the grand Avethellan Empire. For seven hundred thousand years Avethell ruled the Galaxy, even conquered the Gergathan and took over the Gathered Worlds. Then, in a tragedy of betrayal and treason, the Gergathan rose once more and destroyed Avethell.

As for Dorasc, the evil ruler of the Gathered Worlds used its awful science and gengineering techniques to physically de-evolve the inhabitants. In the few generations it took for the Galactic Riders to halt the insidious attack, the people of Dorasc were reduced to little more than animals. Over three million years of natural evolution passed before the people of Dorasc rediscovered intelligence.

"It is against *this* that I caution you: do not allow desire for revenge to fill your heart and blur your reasoning. Galactic Rider, you've a job to do. Unless you wish another Rider to take on the burden of this heavy task."

"Honored Elder, there is not a one within the Scattered Worlds who has not felt the power and the wrath of the Gergathan. Your folk were driven cruelly from the Core. A thousand worlds Iaranor did rule, with life and joy and music on each one; now all lie ruined in the dust of time. Grand Avethell was torn apart by war, her people scattered 'cross the Galaxy. The Metrinaire were decimated when a Core-thrown comet struck their verdant world. The Human Empire's fall was largely due to machinations of the the Gergathan. Honored Elder, with respect I ask: where would you find a Rider who did not within her heart desire for revenge?"

"Well spoken, T'to Yachim. I was wrong to ever doubt your objectivity."

"Please tell me of this matter, what you know."

"Our knowledge is minute, yet I will share. This Geled, knowing not with whom she deals, sought out agreement with the Core worlds strong. Now that the Relay Alpha is burned out, a mission left from Geled for repair. Just recently we learned to our dismay, this mission carries with it agents from dominions under the Gergathan's control."

"And what, precisely, do the Elders fear?"

"We do not know. The futures are confused, and turmoil reigns within the Forever Dreams. I cannot divine the plans of the Gathered Worlds. I thought that when the Human Empire fell, they lost all interest for the Gergathan. Yet Geled hosts an envoy from the Core. A tragedy, if Humankind should fall under the power of the Gergathan."

"Drac Trnas, now I must confess uncertainty in having such a great responsibility thrown in my pouch. If I should fail, the stakes are very great."

"The thoughts and wishes of all the Scattered Worlds ride with you in this mission delicate. The cadre of the Riders give support. Yet all alone you go, for one may win, where millions fail. We cannot beat the Core with force of arms; they are too strong. Nor will we seek control of minds and wills. Convince you may, persuade but do not force. You are among our best, T'to Yachim. Master emotions and you will not fail." Drac Trnas pulls herself to her feet. "The blessings of the Elder Gods go with you." She bows and turns to leave.

"Most Honored Elder, I do thank you true." T'to looks again at the Gap of Remembrance, shivers. He calls after the departing Drac Trnas: "Elder. Do the Humans know the stakes?"

"Some do, some not. Your judgment will suffice. Tell them as much as you think they will believe." With that, the Daamin is gone.

The music of the Singing Stones behind him, T'to Yachim heads for his ship.

❄

The Daamin (aka Kien Khwei)
(from *Cassaw's Field Guide to Nonhuman Species*)

Homeworld: Nephestal (aka Kao Li)

Height: 120-130 cm

Physical: Bipedal, two arms, head with two large eyes and prominent ears. The Daamin have fine fur, usually in shades of white and grey.

Evolutionary: The Daamin originally evolved on the planet Verkorra in the Galactic Core. More than a billion years ago, a significant portion of the Daamin race migrated into the Scattered Worlds and settled on Nephestal.

Special Features: The Daamin spend a large part of their lives in an alternate mental state called the Forever Dreams. In this state of nonlinear causality, they experience a constantly-shifting kaleidoscope of possible futures.

Culture: The Daamin are part of the Free Peoples of the Scattered Worlds. Popularly called "Elders," they are considered to be among the most cultured and wisest races in the Scattered Worlds. Their homeworld, Nephestal, is the cultural center of the Scattered Worlds, and the meeting place for the Free Peoples of the Scattered Words.

❁

18
New Arrival
[CIRCLE]
6484 CE

Jedrek expected the Relay to be smaller. From everything he knows about the circuitry of the Relay, it could have been miniaturized into a housing as small as a two-man starboat. Instead, Relay Alpha is a sphere measuring a full hundred meters across, and doppler radar shows it honeycombed with tunnels and Human-scale living spaces, with comm rooms and lounges and all the paraphernalia necessary to support a crew.

"According to Imperial Chain-of-Command records, the Ultrawave Relays were manned at all times by a crew of from six to twenty," Kedar says from the datasphere. "Their purpose was to manually supervise the functioning of the Relay, as well as to be ready for repair of the equipment."

"We could use them now," Sukoji comments.

"We could use something." Cilehe points to the tracking instruments. "The Geledi ship is coming after us."

"All right," Drisana says, "Let's get ready. Send the message, Sukoji."

The puter had no difficulty translating from Terran Standard to the Geledi dialect; the message goes out on all electromagnetic bands.

"Attention the Geledi ship. We wish to arrange a peace conference with you. In case you have any doubts, please observe the planetoid we have just released."

Maria Theresa gave them an unused planetoid from one of the habitats; now Cilehe manipulates her ship's antigravs and guides it into position about a kilometer from *Worldsaver*. "Do it, Sting." She adds, "No higher than fifty gees this time, if you please."

The gravity warp triggers again, and the planetoid collapses upon itself until it is a glowing ball of white-hot slag.

"I can drive it to final collapse," Sting offers, but no one comments.

The Geledi ship halts in space, then starts to turn. "They're trying to run away," Cilehe says to no one in particular. "Watch."

Worldsaver's antigravs dragged a planetoid; a warship is no challenge. Cilehe applies power, and the other ship simply stay, her defense screens glowing faintly red. "They thought my range was shorter. They didn't know that I've been moving planetoids around at hundred-kilometer distances." Cilehe is obviously having fun. "Try to raise them, someone."

"Attention the Geledi ship." Kedar takes the tone of an apologetic parent. "We have you under our control. Our pilot frankly doesn't know whose antigravs would go first if you tried to pull away, but she advises you that our primary vesicles have a strain tolerance of twenty-two point six. You'll also notice that we can prevent you from going into tachyon phase by interfering with your grav field. Will you consider a peace conference now?"

There is no answer. Cilehe's face is taut; Jedrek sees strain gauges mounting as the other ship tries to break away.

"I don't know if I *do* want to try this," Cilehe whispers.

Jedrek thumbs his headset into the circuit. "Attention the Geledi ship…if you *are* from Geled. We are prepared to turn our gravity warp against the Relay unless you consent to a conference."

"No!" Drisana cries, and tries to boot Jedrek from the circuit.

He makes sure his headset is off. "I'm bluffing, Dris. If we're right and the Relay is indeed what they're after—"

"Attention the aliens," a thickly accented voice says from the speaker. "We are prepared to confer with you." Strain readings suddenly drops to zero and the Geledi ship jerks before Cilehe can adjust her tractors.

After a three-way battle of eyes, Kedar winds up in control of the mike. "We will meet you in this ship. Please send a gig over with someone who can speak for you. We will abide by all the rules of truce."

"Who are you? Where are you from?"

Kedar shrugs. "Can't hurt to impress them a little." Into the mike he says, "We're from Terra."

"Where is that?"

"Never mind." He rolls his eyes. "This is going to be a long conference."

❄

Gigabits of data about Geled, and none of it more current than five hundred years ago. For a second Jedrek almost understand why Drisana bitches about updating the Library.

Well, there is no help for it. They will have to get by on five-hundred-year-old reports by Independent Traders and hope for the best. Jedrek puts down the datasphere and goes to join the others in *Worldsaver's* dining room, which has been made over into a conference room. Cilehe remains behind at the ship's controls.

Entering the dining room, Jedrek dials the grav down to about one quarter of a standard gee. Geled's gravity is one and a fifth standard—that, at least, can hardly have changed in five centuries—but the crew of a warship might well be used to a lower grav, or even zero. He wants the guests as comfortable as possible.

"They're locking onto our docking port now," Cilehe reports over the intercom. Jedrek takes his seat beside Sting to Drisana's right; Kedar and Sukoji are on her other side. He doesn't comment that she wound up in the middle—it is, after all, her expedition.

The dining room door slides open and two figures enter.

The first is a Human man in military uniform. According to Jedrek's quick review of Geled's military hierarchy, the man's insigniae proclaim him to be a Captain, most likely the one in charge of the ship. He is slightly chubby, with black hair cut very short, a narrow mustache, and grey eyes. He nervously fingers a holster that is pointedly empty. Jedrek touches Sting's knee and inclines his head toward the holster. Sting nods.

Behind the Captain is an alien. Improbably tall and pale as the light of a lifeless moon, it has the same general bodily configuration as a Human. There is no mystery in that—Imperial biologists long ago verified that most lifeforms in the Galaxy sprung from spores loosed from seed vessels launched more than two billion years ago by some long-ago alien culture. The same patterns crops up again and again, both in the alien races known to the Empire and those entered in the Library after the Fall.

Drisana nods. The Geledi officer sits, the alien stands behind him with its head only centimeters from the ceiling.

"I want you to know," the Captain says, his words slightly more intelligible than over the comm, "that my ship is prepared to send a task force to avenge me if I am killed."

"You're not going to be killed." Drisana frowns. "So you *are* from Geled?"

"I am Captain Fedor Kassov of the Geled Navy Warship *Deathcry*. This is the Aydar of the Ebettor." He leans back and regards them. "I'm amazed that you're Human. I thought we were doing battle with some kind of advanced aliens. This world you come from must be very strong."

Drisana leaves the comment untouched. "You obviously know we're not from this region."

"It was not hard to guess." Captain Kassov's eyes narrow. "What do you want of us?"

"Why are you here?"

"The Ultrawave Relay you threatened to destroy is vital to the security of Geled. We came to repair it. We didn't expect to find a nest of strange creatures around it." He takes a breath—the man is obviously not used to lengthy speeches. The Captain produces a datapad. "I have here a legal brief prepared by the best lawyers in all our realm. It states that the

States and Territories of Geled have an unshakable claim to this Relay. Since *Deathcry* is the sole representative of the Presidium in this volume of space, I have the authority to take sole command of the Relay."

Drisana leans forward; Jedrek sees a data marble clutched in her left hand. She glances at the datapad. "I see that you base your claim on inheritance of authority from the Terran Empire."

"Da. Our lawyers found several documents giving the government of Geled complete control of all territories within the former Province of Geled, as well as any territories necessary to safeguard that control. This is such a region."

"And those documents were signed by Benjim Tattersall, Twelfth Duke of Geled, shortly after the Empire fell. *After,* mind you." She waves her hand in dismissal. "He had no right to make that claim, especially when the leaders of six other Provinces were quarreling with him about succession. I'm not going to touch the question of Imperial legitimacy, it's too complex a problem and too open to interpretation after this many millennia."

She fixes Kassov with a cold stare. "We come from Terra. Terra, do you hear? As in `Terran Empire.' Seat of the government. Home of the Human race. If anyone has a right to claim this Relay, it's us."

"Don't try to frighten me with legends. Terra never was, that's been conclusively proven. Mythmakers claim it was a planet, but history has proven that Terra was a family that first thought of going into space."

"Peers," Drisana says, addressing her remarks to her side of the table, "You've just heard one of the best arguments ever made for keeping a Library in good working order. Because if you don't, you may well sound as much an ass as this man." She turns back to Captain Kassov. "The fact remains that we have the most defensible claim to this Relay. Except for the people of *Maria Theresa,* who won it by right of conquest when your people were still fighting the first of your interminable wars with Escen and Dovan."

"We do not recognize their claim as legitimate. Nor yours."

"You make me tired. Kedar, make our offer. Please listen closely and remember that our gravity warp does not have a top setting."

Kedar leans forward on his elbows while Drisana closes her eyes and settles back in her chair. "Captain Kassov, we are as eager as you to see Relay Alpha repaired. We will allow you access to the Relay and are glad to offer you what records we have of Imperial science of the time. But before any such agreement can be made, you must withdraw all military force from *Maria Theresa* and its habitats. Only then can we be convinced that you are bargaining in good faith."

The alien suddenly makes a chopping gesture with one hand. It snarls and growls; from Kassov's datapad emerges a translation: "Geled and the Ebettor together will take what we desire. There is no bargaining."

Drisana's eyes pop open.

"I see that you have reconsidered," Kassov begins.

"Quiet," Drisana says. She glances at her lap; Jedrek sees a tiny holo of Cilehe whispering to Drisana.

"Well, my good people—and whatever you are, Aydar— negotiations have just entered a new phase. Another ship, has just appeared in this volume. The design is radically different from yours, ours, or *Maria Theresa's*. They are on a course that rather obviously leads here to the Relay. I suggest that you return to your ship and let us know what happens. We'll be waiting here."

❖

19
Showdown
[CREDIX/GELED]
CI 4331/GY 3216

As Captain's Cabin Boy, Dal is privileged to accompany Gerda to all the hurried meetings awaiting the Captain of *Outbound*. He is a bright boy; he pays attention, asks Gerda questions, and soon he is able to piece together what's happening.

Three different alien cultures in one space. First, the strange people of the *Maria Theresa*, who spoke a weird language only slightly related to Dal's own. Then, the single ship of Librarians—Librarians?—from out of legend and long-ago. And last the Geledi ship, with not one but *two* species aboard. And as far as Dal can tell all these people—except for the *Maria Theresa* folk, who after all live here—all these people are here on the same mission as *Outbound*.

"If we're all here for the same reason, why can't we just repair the Relay and go home?" he asks.

Gerda gives him a tolerant smile. Dal knows that smile, it means she's thinking of him as only a kid again. She should know better. "It is very, very complicated, Dal. We did not expect anyone else to be here. Ja, it would be nice if we could all get together and repair Alpha, but a few things stand in our way."

"Right. I guess we have to do something about the Geled folks attacking *Maria Theresa*."

Gerda tousles his hair. "That is part of it. As long as they have a military cordon around that mother ship, then we must consider this a war zone. The librarians have asked us to join them in demanding cessation of hostilities; right now I am waiting on a decision from home."

"Why is it taking so long?"

"Do you remember when I took you to that meeting of the Reichstaag? That was only a simple inheritance question, but you know how long it took them."

"Oh, ja. First the Imperator had to speak, then all the heads of the Noble Families, then the High Priests and Priestess, then that lady from the Kala Phenkae...by the time it got back to the Imperator everyone was ready to go out for lunch."

"Yes, well, it is not going to be quite that complicated this time. The Privy Council will decide what we are to do. They will have to look through all sorts of information, try to determine what we know of these people, if anything, and whether they present a threat to us."

"Ancestors, I'd hate to make a decision like that. I'm glad I don't sit on the Reichstaag."

"No, you only sit on my bunk. Is there not something you should be doing right now—other than talking?"

"Oh, Gerda, I want to know what's going on. You might need me to...to...." Dal isn't quite sure what the Captain might need him for—sometimes he wonders why she needs a Cabin Boy at all. "To run errands," he finishes. That's vague enough to cover all manner of sins.

She smiles again. "All right. There *is* something you can do. I have a crick in my neck, and if I am any judge it is going to get worse." Gerda stretches out on her bunk. "Would you mind?"

"Not at all." Dal starts kneading her back, moving his way up to the sore spot. He's glad Gerda hasn't sent him away to school or something stupid like that; he'd die of frustration if he couldn't know what's happening, after having met all those strange people face-to-face.

"Captain?" The first mate's voice comes over the intercom.

"Ja?"

"Telepath is ready to report."

She pulls herself up on her elbows. "Put it on display, please."

The face of the ship's Telepath appears three meters before Gerda's eyes. Dal has never felt comfortable with the Telepath. She is an ancient woman, kept alive more by virtue of her numerous implants and cyborg supports than natural ability. Telepaths are rare, and so the Navy has to take what they can get. *Outbound* is fortunate, Dal supposes, if you could call it that—only one ship in a hundred had a Telepath at all.

Dal remembers his first few weeks on the ship, over a year ago. Telepath met him in the hall as she floated by on her antigrav implant; he bowed and greeted her, as he did to everyone in those early days of uncertainty about ranks.

She stopped and stared at him with watery-blue eyes. Then there was a whirr of servs and her one living hand approached him, settling on his shoulder. "Nice little boy," she said, and cackled. And into Dal's mind she projected a scene involving himself and what he assumed to be the Telepath before her body failed, a scene whose intensity rivaled the fantasies of a pubescent boy. He blushes even now, thinking of it.

From that day to this, Dal has kept mental blocks firmly in place whenever he's near the Telepath.

"Message for you, Captain Lübchen, from Fleet Headquarters on Credix. Message follows in code."

Gerda fumbles with her datapad. "Go ahead."

Telepath drones out a series of nonsense syllables. Dal has to admire the woman. He doesn't see how she can remember those phrases for a second, much less repeat them verbatim.

The puter digests what she says and, when she is finished, issues a decoded version.

"By order of the Imperator and the Reichstaag, there is to be no hostility repeat no hostility in connection with repair of Relay Alpha. The Credixian Imperium stands now and has always stood for interstellar peace, and will enforce such peace whenever necessary. You, Captain Lübchen, are the personal representative of the Imperator and you are expected to set an example of the Imperator's love of peace. No reply necessary."

Gerda shakes her head. "Another ambiguous directive

from Headquarters. I did not ask if we were supposed to attack; I asked if we were supposed to keep the *Geledis* from attacking."

"Isn't that what they meant?"

"They are covering their tracks. In case I screw up, I guess. When a Captain gets a message like that, she knows that they are saying one thing only: 'If you succeed, we will swear it was our idea. If you fail, you acted contrary to orders.'" She sighs heavily. Dal keeps working on her neck. Finally she sits up.

"Well, I guess I have an obligation…if not to my superiors, since they aren't giving any guidance, then to my conscience. I cannot let them go on killing people out there. Now if only I can figure a way to make them stop without using force." Gerda thumbs the intercom, dials the dispensary. "Doctor, how is Telepath? Can she transmit a few more messages for me?"

"Where to?"

"Home. Fleet Headquarters. Obron. Central Intelligence."

"I don't like this. She's never been worked this hard before. I don't know what the drugs are going to do to her system. Let me ask the puter." There is a pause, then the doctor returns. "All right, but nothing too lengthy. I'll tell you when to stop."

"Good. I will be there in minutes." She clicks off the intercom and stands. Dal watches her, trying to keep his face impassive.

"All right, little pup, I can tell you are just dying to come along. You have seen this much of it, you might as well see it through to the end." She rolls her eyes. "This is the price I pay for having promised your mother to take care of you—Mother Meletia rest her soul and our Ancestors receive her."

"Aw, you don't mind that much, do you?"

"I will never tell."

❖

As *Outbound's* Captain, Gerda has two great advantages over any other military commander in the Galaxy. The first is her Telepath. Dal only now appreciates what wisdom Fleet Headquarters showed in sending a ship that did not have to rely on Relay Alpha for instant communications with home.

The other advantage is that Obron, a small world only one and a third parsecs from Credix, is the Galactic Seat of the Kala Phenkae.

Not *every* world in the Galaxy is touched by the Kala Phenkae. They supervise only two hundred six bloodlines—even with literally tens of thousands of collateral lines added in, they actually control breeding for only a vanishingly small percentage of the Galaxy's people. And with each failure of an Ultrawave Relay, the area in direct contact with the Kala Phenkae dwindles a bit.

No matter. Until Alpha died, the Kala Phenkae ran several lines on Geled and in the Geledi sphere of influence. A few of them are persons and families of importance. So the Kala Phenkae Headquarters has some fairly complete information sets on Geled.

It takes Gerda very little time to convince Obron to release their information. Every child knows that the Kala Phenkae is completely independent of the government of Credix, that they have the power and loyalty and votes to enforce their independence—but the matter of Relay Alpha impacts directly on their control of bloodlines, and those in charge of the Two Hundred Six are no fools. They were among the groups pressuring the Imperator to send *Outbound* on a repair mission in the first place.

So when Gerda sits down before her comm screen and calls the Geledi ship, she is fully prepared with all the information she needs. Too many lucky breaks.

An unidentified face appears on the screen.

"Hello. This is Captain Lübchen of *Outbound*; I would like to speak with your Captain." There is virtually no pause at all before Captain Kassov is visible on the holoscreen. "Good morning, Captain," Gerda says.

"It's evening here."

"So sorry. I have had something of a sleepless night, and the people at home did not appreciate me waking them with my calls." Dal noticed that Gerda doesn't specify *how* she called home; Gerda told him that she's reasonably sure the Geledis don't even know how far away Credix is, and she hopes she can bluff him into thinking their home is nearer than it actually is.

"What do you want?"

"My government has instructed me to take a stand. We must demand that you end hostilities this instant. We cannot allow you within fifteen hundred meters of the Relay unless you comply."

"Ha."

"Do not force me to be crass, Captain."

"Don't let me stop you, *Captain*."

"Very well. I understand that you are in line to receive a large inheritance from your maternal grandmother now that your mother has passed away. Sorry to hear about that, by the by. Now I am sure that your courts do accept the records of your local chapter of the Kala Phenkae. Well, by a strange coincidence that is simply too improbable to go into here, the Kala Phenkae has discovered that your line of descent is actually illegitimate. You follow me, I hope? By the cosmos, my dear Captain, you look pale."

"Go on."

"Now Captain Kassov, I am sure that the Kala Phenkae— who have a great interest in this mission we seem to share—would be very interested in getting the job done as quickly as possible. They would probably find it in their records to legitimatize the person who made progress possible. Since I am compelled by my government to continue acting like a stubborn mech until you give in, perhaps you can see your way clear to calling a truce?" Gerda gives a smile that almost turns Dal's stomach.

"How do I know you're not bluffing?"

"Are you all set for datafeed? Good, then, I will send along a complete genealogy of your family for the last—oh, let us make it two hundred years just to be interesting. No one on your ship would have given us such information, would they? No, I did not think so." Telepath was up for almost an hour copying that family tree; Dal hopes Kassov enjoys it.

Gerda gives that smile again. "We certainly want to give you some time to decide, Captain. Shall we say ten trillion vibrations of Cesium 133? I will expect to hear from you then."

In far less than the roughly one thousand seconds Gerda gave him, Captain Kassov calls back with a declaration of truce. *Deathcry* recalls all of her drones, and peace settles over in the volume controlled by *Maria Theresa*.

At least for the moment, Dal thinks. He doesn't like Captain Kassov at all.

❄

The Kala Phenkae
(*Encyclopedia of the Interregnum,* edited by Oskar Bartlett, Terra-Prime Publishing, 20,832 H.E.)

Little is known of the origins of this secretive breeding program. During the First Terran Empire, various Idara conducted programs of genetic enhancement, most notably Idara Kuchta under Sten Kuchta (TE 123-237) and the Hoister Family. By TE 250, many of the veterans of these programs had joined an ongoing effort under the sponsorship of the Idara Kristeller. The combined program settled in permanent headquarters on the planet Obron.

By TE 320 the program coordinated two hundred six distinct bloodlines, on about four hundred planets; thus, it was popularly referred to as "the Two Hundred Six." During the Interregnum, the program became known as The Kala Phenkae, supposedly from "Cealla Faenke" ("Two Hundred Six" in the Heloxan language). The Kala Phenkae included Idaras Adelhardt, Carroll, Loewenger, and others, as well as many non-Idara bloodlines.

Over the millennia of the Interregnum, the bloodlines were kept reasonably pure. During this time, the Kala Phenkae were one of the few institutions that remained Galactic in scope, although communications difficulties and political circumstances often limited the program's effectiveness.

In many parts of the Galaxy, and particularly in the Credixian Imperium, the Kala Phenkae wielded great political influence, even though it was practically unknown to the population at large.

Due to the security surrounding the program, the mission and ultimate goals of the Kala Phenkae remained a secret until the time of the Second Terran Empire....

❁

20
Possibilities
[GELED]
GY 3216

Kassov is furious. Irina does her best to stay out of his way, but he hovers around the bridge even when it isn't his shift, squinting this way and that and making everyone miserable. She and Rur speculated on what the Credixian Captain might have said to Kassov on a sealed circuit behind the privacy screen...they couldn't come up with anything bad enough to account for his mood.

"Gunner, keep your eyes on your screen."

"Yes, sir." Irina sighs—a rather silent and timid sigh, but a sigh nevertheless. She prefers not killing the aliens of this area—but things were certainly much more peaceful on *Deathcry* when they were fighting.

"You are not concentrating on your duty," the Ebettor tells her.

"No, I don't suppose I am." For a moment she has a desire to take the Ebettor to her cabin, to sit the alien down and try to explain to it why she isn't happy, why the Captain's mood affects the entire crew.

Why bother? It's no use...the Ebettor follow orders from their superiors without ever seeming to think or hesitate. Maybe that's how they're constructed, like ants or bees or cybs. Maybe they never feel resentment against a commander, or irritation at a man who can't seem to delegate even the tiniest responsibility.

"Navigator, I said I wanted tracking on all traffic in a hundred-kilometer radius."

"I'm trying, sir. Some of the smaller forms are hard to track. The puter's tied up in knots as it is."

"If you're incapable of performing your duties, maybe I'd better bring in your replacement."

"I'll try harder, sir."

Irina sneaks a glance at the six Ebettor. They might be cloned copies of one another. Wouldn't Kassov like that—clones of himself to do all the ship's jobs for him?

"Your leader does not seem clearheaded," the Ebettor gunner observes.

"The Credixians beat him somehow...some underhanded trick or other." Which he probably deserved, she adds silently. "He's not sure what to do. We sent message drones home for orders, but they're not going to return for a while yet."

"Captain off the bridge," an autoservant announced. There is a brief break while protocol is satisfied, then a feeling of relief sweeps the bridge. Irina leans back in her chair and tries to keep her attention on her screen.

"Your Captain resents the ship from Credix."

"Da, he does." I don't want to talk about it, Irina thinks. Yet this is the longest continuous conversation she's had with her Ebettor station-mate; she wants to continue it.

"But they are the same race as you."

"That's not been conclusively proven. Sure, they have the same physical characteristics...but so do you and I, if you look on a gross enough level. Some of our scientists think that Human life sprang up on several different worlds, maybe from spores carried around in space. The Credixians probably have a totally different biochemistry."

"You are the same race. Both of your societies claim descent from the same Empire."

"Yes, well, the Empire was a long time ago. There were hundreds of different worlds in it, each with its own species of Humanity."

"Credix is strong."

"They have something going for them, to be able to make Captain Kassov give up so easily."

"And Geled is strong."

There seems no answer to that. Geled *is* strong...but she doesn't particularly want to get into a discussion of the relative strengths and weaknesses of the Geledi State.

Treading dangerous ground.

"Geled is strong. Credix is strong. The Ebettor are strong. The inhabitants of this volume of space are weak." The puter translation gives the Ebettor the tone of completing a mathematical equation. "Tell us, have your people never thought of restoring the Empire?"

"Captain on the bridge!"

Kassov barges across the bridge like a cargo airship under full power. He halts before Irina; she shrinks back, expecting a lecture as strong as a whipping.

Instead, Kassov faces the Ebettor. "What was it you just said about restoring the Empire?"

"You are strong. Credix is strong. The Ebettor...."

Two other Ebettor come over and stand behind Irina. They speak in their curious unanimous way. "Do you not think that Geled and Credix together could conquer the rest of the Galaxy?"

"You mentioned the Ebettor. What is your part in this?"

"We are not empowered to speak for our leaders. Your leaders may speak with them. Long have we been interested in the Scattered Worlds—in the rest of the Galaxy. We might give you aid."

Kassov is silent. For the first time since Irina set foot on deck, he is speechless. Then he turns to the comm officer. "Comm, I want a message drone to Geled. Top priority, to supersede all previous messages." He eyes the Ebettor. "I think my leaders might be interested."

❋

Medical First Aid Diagnostic Leech
Emergency Instructions

You will need:
- Series A-1 First Aid (red) or B-1 Diagnostic (white) leech
- Datapad(s) or dataspex
- Phone or other communications device

1. Peel back the leech's transparent covering. Attach leech to patient's exposed skin. (If the patient is wounded, attach the leech as near as possible to any wounds.)

2. It is normal for the leech to deflate as nanos enter the patient's bloodstream. Leech casing will drop off or disintegrate when no longer needed.

3. Nanos will perform diagnosis and begin any necessary treatment. Consult your datapad and follow any instructions.

4. Provide a means for nanos to communicate with medical resources or authorities.

5. Further, specialized leeches may be required. Be sure to match color and number before attaching leeches to patient.

6. If medical professionals are available or needed, they will be summoned by nanos. Please be prepared to assist in locating patient for authorities.

❁

21
Meeting
[MARIA THERESA/RIDER]
Day 507 of the reign of Her Magnificence,
Olympia Marvelous VII
Galactic Revolution 561.19775508

T'to Yachim has never visited *Maria Theresa*. That fact in itself does not hinder him—he has the guidance of records made by every other Galactic Rider who flew to the settlement. Pausing at the very edge of the system, well out of range of Human detection equipment, he scouts.

His ship's puter picks out at least three ships radically different in design from *Maria Theresa* and her attendant vessels. Three sets of invaders at once? He better be careful.

The ships of the Galactic Riders are the best in the Scattered Worlds. They must be—a Rider depends on his ship not only for survival, but mobility, aid, and even company. The Daamin supervise construction of these ships on a world not far from Nephestal. The chief advantage of a Galactic Rider's ship is the tunable antigrav—a Daamin invention that allows a pilot to tune his engines to different frequencies, thus avoiding much interference from surrounding gravitational fields and other sets of tachyon vesicles. Wars would have been fought to learn the secret of the tunable antigrav, if not for the fact that the Daamin are eminently able to defend their worlds.

Keying up his antigravs and adjusting his field to match the background grav radiation of the area, T'to Yachim slips his ship indetectably into the heart of the *Maria Theresa* settlement. Before too long he docks with the great Starcruiser itself. Long ago, *Maria Theresa* set aside one docking bay for the exclusive use of the Galactic Riders; T'to is pleased to see that it is still clear. Sometimes a long while went by between visits by Riders , and he's worlds that distrust or even actively resist the Riders.

Before leaving his ship, T'to Yachim remembers to drop his music-synth in his pouch. Music is the trademark of the Galactic Riders, transcending cultural and species bounds, and the old songs and legends are a good way to teach lessons about present situations. Thus, T'to is always embarrassed that he cannot play an instrument or sing his way out of monomolecular film. The music-synth helps.

Brushing one last time the unruly bit of fur between his horns, he leaves his ship and goes forward to greet the people.

❀

Docking bay is like a drawer that receives T'to Yachim's ship and then retracts into *Maria Theresa*. By the time he leaves the ship, atmosphere-retaining side walls have slid down and a crowd awaits him.

T'to takes great care to greet the youngest ones first. The affinity of all young creatures in the Galaxy transcends physical form or cultural background. Only after he's patted and stroked and crooned to the cubs does he turn his attention to the adults.

"Thank you, Rider. To save us, you have come."

T'to sighs. Always the same misconception. Always the idea that visitors from the sky are here to bring salvation. Why is this attitude so prevalent, in direct contradiction to the facts? T'to thinks with sadness on the archives of the Galactic Riders, on the thousands upon thousands of civilizations which were not saved, which were allowed to follow their own paths to thermonuclear self-annihilation or economic strangulation or physical regression, without any effort by the Galactic Riders to "save" their cultures. At least four races in the Galaxy are right now in various stages of self-destruction, and the Riders are honor-bound not to interfere. Cultures and races, like individuals, must choose their own destinies.

"Friend, I have come only to persuade you to save yourselves." Doesn't *that* sound pious and trite? T'to tries to remember what Drac Trnas told him on Nephestal...he must not get too emotionally involved with these people.

One of the Humans steps forward. "The Queen you awaits, in her chambers."

"Indeed? And will you take me there?"

"When ready you are, Rider."

"Good." T'to folds into a crouch on the floor of the docking bay. He takes one of the very young cubs into his lap and produces a little plastic toy from his pouch. The youngster delights in it. T'to doesn't think his own cub, now coming into maturity and far more busy with her own training than with toys, will mind; he gives the gewgaw to the Human child. "Tell me what's been going on since a Rider last visited you. You have a new Queen, of course, I read all about that. And the people from Outside. But what else?"

"A great festival there was in Teerell when crowned the Queen was," one of the younger adults says with enthusiasm. "To have seen it, you ought. Singing and dancing and drinking like there never before has been."

Another young adult pushes forward and bows politely. "Rider, of Ras'prekkeh tell us." An Avethellan was the last Rider to visit *Maria Theresa*; according to her chronicle she had stayed for hundreds of their days and had made many friends. T'to whips out a datapad and calls up information from his ship's puter.

"Ras'prekkeh is doing well," he says. "She is currently serving a Mietharan scientific team elsewhere in the Scattered Worlds." T'to feels happiness at the next news. "She left a message to be delivered here. Can anyone tell me where I might find a Human by the name of Mitia Krahn?"

There is silence in the group surrounding him. T'to has the terrible feeling that he's committed some kind of awful *faux pas*. But the message contains no warnings that it should be delivered in private, no cautions at all. "What's wrong?"

"Us forgive, Rider. Mitia Krahn killed was, in an attack by the aliens not two days ago. Close he was, to Ras'prekkeh."

T'to feels his back fin twitch. "Perhaps you'd better show me to the Queen now," he says.

❋

It doesn't take long for Queen Olympia Marvelous to explain the situation to T'to. T'to picked up enough of the background on his trip here, that he knew what to expect. The words of the Queen and Dileene Shaarlin only confirm fears...and those of Elder Drac Trnas.

The Core is at work here. He especially smells the hands of the Ebettor in this new idea of Galactic Union starting here and now with Credix and Geled.

The Queen's chambers command a view of surrounding space. T'to was warned in advance to come with light-amplifying goggles, and so he is able to see the not-too-distant forms of the three alien ships against the stars. He muses over them. "This may very well be one of the most important diplomatic incidents in Human history for the past million of your days." T'to isn't particularly good at arithmetic and still tends to think in terms of Dorasc's years...but his ship's puter is very good at translation, and he keeps half his eye on his datapad. "And yet, since hostilities have ceased there has been no movement on the part of the aliens?"

Dileene Shaarlin moves her upper torso convulsively. "Each ship a party has sent, the Relay to investigate. Think I, they all it find, too difficult to repair. Nothing else have they done."

T'to knows what to do. The answer is in every textbook, on the lips of every instructor, burned into the biochemistry of every Galactic Rider's brain. In a disagreement between several different viewpoints, hold a conference. "Would you be willing to host a negotiation conference here on *Maria Theresa*?"

"Any number have we, of rooms for such a purpose."

But something's missing. "They're trying to go ahead and

fix the Relay. How do *you* feel about that?"

Dileene spreads her hands. "Think I do not, that matters it, what we feel. Shown us have they, that they the power have, to force our compliance with whatever decision they make. Suppose I, we grateful ought to be, that our people killed are not being, and our territories destroyed."

Olympia Marvelous leans forward, looks into T'to Yachim's eyes. T'to senses a quiet urgency in her posture. "The Hlutr happy are not, about this. Went I, back to their dome, sure to make, that they harmed were not. Fine they were, but filled was the air, with discord. Tell me, Rider, what we in the middle of are, and why they so unhappy are?"

T'to reaches for his music-synth, then halts the gesture. He must tell it his own way, without the old songs. "What you're in the middle of, is a conflict that's been going on since before your race or mine were sprung from the seed vessels of the Pylistroph (blessed be!) It is a struggle that's been pursued across the coils of the Galactic Spiral, and has involved more peoples and more individuals than you or I could hope to imagine. This is just one phase of one side-track of the entire Grand Scheme. I don't know what any part of us will have to play in its ultimate conclusion, if indeed our actions play any part at all. The Daamin may know; they live part of their lives in unseen worlds where the futures are real." He finds himself absently tugging at the end of his right horn; he forces his hand away. "There is...a presence...that seems to want Credix and Geled to join together and form a new Human Empire. Another...group...would not like to see this happen."

"And we on which side are?"

This is the hard part. Gods of all peoples, this is the part where every Galactic Rider must strain his integrity to the breaking point...and then must wonder forever if he succeeded. Many have resigned the cadre rather than face another such cusp.

T'to gathers his courage and finds that he can stand fast by his convictions one more time. "You must decide for yourselves what side is the right one. We may guide, and teach, and even lead—but we can never force. I can answer your questions, but I can't tell you which side is best."

Olympia's mouth stretches. "Rider, heard have I, the ballads of the Galactic Riders since I a child was. And listened have I. Know I all the old stories, the Tale of Ocnert and the Legend of Mooredann and all the other inspiring tales of heroism and goodness. Think you, I in doubt could be, about which side to choose? Dileene, the council call, which T'to Yachim recommended. Want I, the aliens to tell, that they allowed will not be, the Relay to repair."

Instead of exhilaration, T'to felt uneasiness. She made the right decision—but out of blind faith rather than reason. And her people will need more than faith to keep them true to their course in the hard times that will follow. Can one tone-deaf Galactic Rider inspire them to hold fast, in the face of attacks worse than the ones they have already suffered?

He feels for his music-synth. He will need it before long.

●

22
Explanation
[CIRCLE/RIDER]
6484 CE; Galactic Revolution 561.19775508

Jedrek can't help liking the Credixians. First, there's Credix itself. The Independent Traders carry tales, across half the Galaxy, of a huge, powerful Imperium that retains memory of the Terran Empire in word and deed. The very existence of Credix is legend; there, it is said, time stood still and the High Days never left. Credix is like a whiff of the same forgotten fragrance that still lingers on Terra—the evening meal aboard *Outbound* is conducted with a quiet dignity and solemnity that Jedrek sometimes sees in meetings of the Terran Council.

The spell of Credix touches each and every one of the Circle. Drisana even pulls herself away from cataloging the wonders of *Maria Theresa* in order to supervise the dumping of *Outbound's* databanks into the Grand Library datasphere...wherein all the information disappears like a glassful into an ocean.

Second is the Credixian crew, and particularly Captain Gerda Lübchen. Jedrek dislikes serving under officers; he's known that since an abortive childhood stint in the Terran Home Guard. But if he had to serve under any Captain at all, he imagines he would want it to be Gerda. Her entire speech to her crew before allowing them to visit *Maria Theresa* consisted of a wistful expression and the words, "I will be disappointed if I hear any reports of misconduct or infringement on the natives' rights." And so far there were no such reports. Jedrek has to admire the Captain for the loyalty of her crew, let alone her sense of humor and evident joy in the face of what has to be a tough assignment.

And the Captain's little shadow, Dalbert, is so cute in his diminutive uniform. Sting sniffed at the child and has stayed away from him, but the rest of the Circle instantly adopts him as mascot.

A salon of *Maria Theresa* adjoining the conference room has been set aside for the use of the various "aliens"—here light levels are set to a comfortable intensity for eyes that grew up under suns. There is access to the Starcruiser's food and drink stores, and autoservants to fill every need. Jedrek watches a viewscreen that looks out on the stars, and now and again sips a fruity drink provided by the food-synth.

Captain Gerda enters, Dalbert tagging along behind her. Jedrek lifts his cup in salute. "Evening, Captain."

She yawns. "We are going to have to do something about compromising on time schedules. Why in hell do the Theresans count by a thirty-hour day?"

"Who knows?" Drisana probably knows, he thinks. But it isn't a good idea to bother her now. "Have you spoken with Credix?"

"I sent a message home. There has been no response yet, nor do I expect one for a time." She sighs and settles into a chair. Dalbert stands at the keyboard of the food console, scratches his head, then shrugs and punches. He takes a cup of faintly orange liquid to Gerda and sits on the floor next to her. "After all," she continues, "the Theresans did drop something of a fusion bomb at today's meeting."

"Agreed. Drisana's taken refuge in our control room everyone is off trying to get her to talk. Good luck to them, I say." Jedrek raises his cup and drains it. Whatever the food-synth put in his drink, it is making him nicely happy, without any ill effects. He punches for another.

"Why do the Theresans not want the Relay fixed? By my Ancestors, Herr nor Talin—"

"Jedrek."

"Jedrek, then. They will not be bothered once it is repaired. They did not even know the verdammt thing was working, much less that it had stopped. What great disruption will it cause to their society?"

"I don't know, Gerda. They haven't seen fit to inform me of their reasons." The cold of his cup feels strange against his palm. It is porcelain, and feels a little like the texture of the datasphere. "I can't say I'm displeased." He forces a chuckle. "I couldn't figure out how to repair the thing anyway, and I hate admitting failure."

"Our technicians are baffled. The Geledis seem to think that they know how to fix it, though."

"Queen Olympia won't allow any Geledis within a hundred meters of the Relay." If I'm so happy, Jedrek asks himself, then why am I sitting in the lounge getting high? Is it only reaction after spending so much time researching the problem?

"Kassov has invited me to his ship for what he terms 'discussions of our plight.' I do not think I like the tone of that."

Jedrek shrugs. "The Theresans don't want us to repair Alpha. That's our plight, and I see no way around it."

"That is what I am afraid of. Kassov sounds desperate, and desperate men are capable of desperate actions. He has already attacked once."

"He can't get anywhere with us here to stop him."

"As long as we stay united." She closes her eyes and rubs her temples. "Relay Alpha is of great strategic importance to Credix as well as Geled. How do I know, the Imperator might order me to attack with Kassov. And you said yourself that Frau Hardel is not happy about the Queen's decision. She is the leader of your expedition, nein?"

"Not really." Jedrek thinks quickly around the Circle—if it comes to that, who would support Drisana? Kedar, probably, Kedar is like that. And Sting...could anyone wrest control of a ship from Sting? "The question is academic. *Maria Theresa* has a defense fleet—"

"Such as it is."

"And there's always the Galactic Rider. Surely even Credix doesn't want to move against the Galactic Riders?"

"Jedrek, Credix is a long way from here and the people who make my decisions are not on the bridge of *Outbound*. I do not know what Credix might see fit to do. Friend, it would pain me to strike against such a peaceful and defenseless people—but my personal feelings matter little, weighed against an order from the Imperator. I simply want you to appreciate the forces in motion here."

"Gerda, I'm a tech. I deal with physical forces, with gravity and electromagnetism and the nuclear forces. I don't have the knowledge or patience to deal with historical forces. That's for people like you. My job is to repair what I'm told to repair." As he says it, Jedrek knows that he's wrong, that the drug is helping him to delude himself. His job is the interdependency of knowledge, and he knows well that his physical forces do not exist in isolation. If only they did.

For the first time since he left Borshall, Jedrek finds himself missing Denys. For a moment he wonders at that—why hasn't he thought of Denys?

Because he might as well face it: Denys is as much—or more—a business partner as he is a lover. And who misses a business partner?

"I have to leave for my appointment," Gerda says. "I hope I will be able to see you later."

Jedrek waves a hand. "Sure. Stop by whenever you wish." The Captain leaves.

Dalbert, the cabin boy, sticks his head back into the lounge. "Herr nor Talin...Cap'n can't say so, but she really wants you to do something to save these people. The Queen might listen to you—can't you talk to her?"

Jedrek hates to lie to children. He smiles weakly and drunkenly. "I'll try, Dal."

What to do? If he really thought about it, Jedrek considers, he might come up with a way to change Olympia's mind. The Theresans like him, like the Circle, like the information they bring.

A portal opens and the Galactic Rider strides in, hung about with a variety of strange equipment including what is rather obviously a laser weapon. "Good morning, Jedrek nor

Talin of Terra."

Jedrek yawns. Terra, said the proverb, is where all times meet—but Terra's prestige is next to nothing, and for him this is the middle of the night. "T'to Yachim, isn't it? Sorry I wasn't able to welcome you properly before the conference."

"It matters not." The Rider peers into Jedrek's viewscreen for a few moments. "I need to speak with you and your people," he finally says.

Jedrek pulls himself to his feet. "Everyone is commiserating in *Worldsaver*. If we're in luck we can catch Drisana in the middle of a tantrum." With T'to Yachim following him, Jedrek leads the way to the docking port where *Worldsaver* is temporarily linked to *Maria Theresa*.

"Your people are not happy about Queen Olympia's decision?"

"You're perceptive, T'to Yachim. No, they aren't. Drisana is like to have a fit." He looks over his shoulder at the Rider, sleek and graceful despite apparent clumsiness. "Of course, we all know it wasn't completely Olympia's decision. A Galactic Rider arrives, charms the populace with songs and stories, and then they all decide not to let us repair—I know the kind of tricks you play."

"You need not be hostile, Jedrek nor Talin. We are both, after all, on the same side."

Are they? Probably, Jedrek has to admit. Wasn't he just a few seconds ago arguing with Gerda that the Theresans had a right to their own decision? He frowns. The Circle has a stronger hold over him than he expected, if he is willing to change his tune this quickly in the presence of Drisana's adversary.

"I'd apologize, T'to Yachim, if you could convince me that you had nothing to do with today's conference." The Rider doesn't answer.

Worldsaver is a scene of chaos. Cabin grav is at zero. Drisana's body, twisted snakelike, floats in the center of the control room with the datasphere clasped between her palms like a fragile egg. Her eyes are closed and her lips set tight. Behind her floats Sting, arched but not tense, his face showing readiness to do quick battle with anyone who disturbs his mistress. Someone, Jedrek thinks, should give that boy a spanking…if anyone could.

The rest of the Circle are in various positions about the room. Cilehe sits at the control panel and, as Jedrek enters, is producing a staccato flash of display lights in time to her drumming fingers on control surfaces. Kedar floats before a display screen, reading fine-printed matter. And Sukoji merely hovers cross-legged in the middle of the room, a rather pointless-looking knitted trail emerging from her lap like a fuzzy umbilical.

"Look alive, Drisana," Jedrek says. He approaches her; Sting moves. "Don't bother me, Sting. How long has she been at the sphere?"

"Since we returned from the conference. Two hours?"

"Well, lad, she has things to deal with here in the real world, and retreating into in masses of dry data isn't going to help her." It must be the drinks, Jedrek thinks, making him speak so boldly. Or maybe the reawakening of his own awareness of the real world he left behind?

Drisana opens her eyes and fixes Jedrek with a sullen stare. Once, Jedrek saw Borshall's sun blue and frozen through the half-kilometer thickness of a tumbling ice asteroid; Drisana's eyes are just as cold.

"Real world, is it? Look, Jedrek." She holds out the datasphere. "In here is a world that was real to you once. Projects we worked on together, the five of us busting our skulls to track down data. In here are five lives that were one. Do you remember?" She lowers her eyes, and something of the stiffness goes out of her posture. "Why can't we bring those years back, Jedrek? Why can't we be what we were to one another?" She turns unseeing eyes around the cabin. All attention is on her now. "Why are you all here, making mockery of the single most precious thing we ever had? Do you care, any of you? Do you care?" She returns to Jedrek. "Real worlds. I was part of your real world once, and then it was the Traders who were real, then some group of techs on Borshall of all places. And now your blind little friends in their big ship are the real world. Blast it, how can you expect me to deal with reality if you keep changing yours?"

So that's it. He takes a breath, organizing his thoughts, and then she points to T'to Yachim. "What is he doing here?"

The Galactic Rider executes a fair imitation of a zero-grav bow; in the creature's fluid motion Jedrek glimpses a hint of what makes the dorsal fin such a deadly weapon for a Dorascan. "My lady Drisana Hardel..."

"Rider," she interrupts, "You have no obligation to be polite to me. First of all we are obviously on opposing sides of this present conflict; and second, if you poll my companions I think you might get a range of opinions as to whether I am a lady."

"Well spoken," the Dorascan says. "I came to address you and your group; to justify myself and the Theresans, if I may. I know that you have traveled far and made sacrifices to repair the Relay, and I think you should know why they have decided not to permit you to do so."

"Go ahead."

"If the Relay is repaired, it will facilitate communication between the Geledi and Credixian spheres of influence. Based on their chance meeting here, the two cultures might come to some kind of...alliance. I fear—and the people of *Maria Theresa* fear—that such an alliance would be dominated by the creatures that the Geledis know as Ebettor. Geled itself is even now in danger of domination by those creatures. And the Ebettor themselves are under the control of a far worse society, one that would love to get a stranglehold on the diversity and fullness of Human culture in the Galaxy. If the Relay is not repaired, we are certain that a Credix-Geled union will never come to be."

Drisana hands the datasphere to Sting, and drifts closer to

T'to Yachim. "Let me tell you why I want the Relay fixed. That globe contains a good percentage of all the knowledge of the Human race. It is my trust, and I have taken care of it as I was charged to do." Jedrek can't miss the barbed comment obviously meant for his ears. "As far as I know, that globe before you and an identical one on Terra are the only two in the universe that are functioning. The Empire dumped a few more in other locations, but none of them are on-line and it's likely that a few have been destroyed. To the best of my knowledge, if the Grand Library on Terra fails, then all that incredible store of knowledge will be lost. It is the birthright of every Human being, and it is in imminent danger of being blown away on stellar wind."

"Oh, Drisana…" Jedrek begins.

"Listen to me. If the Library is not used, the data will perish. Oh, it will last my lifetime, because I will move worlds rather than have one bit lost. It may even last beyond my time." She turns to Sting with the attitude of a psych tech showing off his trained cybs. "Sting, when I die will you care for the Library's data?"

"Yes, Sayyid Drisana."

"Be truthful."

The boy chews his lip. "I would. I don't think I'd stay on Terra but yes, I would take care of the data." He closes his hands about the sphere.

Why? Jedrek wonders. Terra obviously means nothing to him. Why does the Library mean any more? Yet Sting certainly seems to be telling the truth.

Or perhaps the truth as he sees it?

"And will you train a successor to do the same?"

Sting looks pained and turns his face away.

Drisana looks self-satisfied. "You see? Unless that information is used and there's a reason to keep it, it will eventually be discarded. Now do you understand why the Relay must be repaired?"

T'to Yachim holds out a hand. "I will personally deliver

your datasphere to the Temple of All Worlds on Nephestal, and there it will endure as long as the Scattered Worlds."

"Did you honestly believe that offer would tempt me? Do you think I intend for this data to languish in some alien attic until its existence is forgotten by all but a million generations of file clerks?"

"When you put it that way, Sayyid Drisana...I should never have made such an offer. I respect you for refusing."

Sukoji very pointedly looks from Drisana to T'to Yachim. "All right, now we all understand each other. We respect each other. The fact remains that you're on opposite sides, and only one of you can win. Who?"

T'to Yachim's teardrop-shaped eyes don't leave Drisana. "I wish I knew."

❄

The Right Datapad Makes All the Difference

When you're looking for a datapad, you want high resolution, quick response, durability, and compatibility. And above all, you want value.

All *Ipuwer* brand datapads feature near-molecular scale resolution, with nano-addressing to achieve results that exceed the limit of unenhanced human eyesight. With a refresh rate less than 0.01 seconds, *Ipuwer* datapads can display even the highest-speed video with no trace of breakups or artifacting.

Constructed from permaplast polymers that will last for decades of normal use, *Ipuwer* datapads are crumple-resistant and fully-rollable. And *Ipuwer* pads feature Snap-Smooth technology to eliminate folds and creases at the touch of a corner.

Ipuwer datapads are the most compatible on the market, fully compliant with all major data and networking standards, including FLBLA, Terran Empire Standard, and GalactiNet. Each *Ipuwer* pad comes with a minimum 2 TB of onboard memory, with access to local and wide-area network storage. Input methods include stylus, virtual keyboard, and auto-congifure data transfer from any system or network.

Ipuwer pads are available in all standard sizes, from wallet (5 x 7.5 cm) all the way up to Display (60 x 80 cm). Pads can be linked, physically and virtually, to make larger displays as needed. Available in multi-packs of 10, 25, and 50, *Ipuwer* datapads provide superior performance and value.

❖

23
Suggestions
[CIRCLE /CREDIX]
6484 CE; CI 4331

Dal can't help noticing that the Geledi ship is much smaller on the inside than *Outbound*. At first he thinks it odd, since the ships are very nearly the same overall length; then he realizes that it was only the living spaces of *Deathcry* that are cramped, as so much of the ship's hull is filled with weaponry and spare reactor fuel.

Cramped it is. Whereas even Dal has his own cabin in *Outbound*, fully half the Geledi crew share living space on a watchstanding basis. While Gerda goes off to her appointment with Captain Kassov, Dal is set down on a bunk in a room barely two meters by three and told to wait. A drab blue autoservant floats beside him and makes no comment.

After a few minutes Dal is delivered from terminal boredom when a couple in Geledi uniforms wander into the space. The woman is short, shorter than Gerda, and younger too. The man is taller, dark-haired, and carries a cyberharp almost like the ones Dal's seen at home. Margrethe is learning to play the cyberharp, at least that's what she said in her latest holo. Dal is sure he's seen this couple before, on his last trip to the Geledi ship. Isn't she a gunner? Or something?

She smiles at him. "Dalbert, isn't it?"

"Yes, Ma'am."

"I'm Irina, this is Rur. I hope you don't mind if we sit with you. There's so little space on this ship to enjoy off-duty time."

"I'd be pleased to have you. Otherwise it's lonely."

Irina nods. "That's right, of course they wouldn't give you anyone to speak with. I'm sorry we haven't been able to see more of your people. I guess the diplomatic status of all this is still up in the skies."

"I think you're right, Ma'am."

"No need for that. We ought to be friendly with one

another. I understand you've just come from a conference with the Terrans."

"That's right." How does she know? Dal wonders.

"How is everyone there? Did you see their crew?"

"They're okay, I guess. I think they're upset. Frau Drisana is not very happy, I gather." He has a sudden attack of truthfulness. "We didn't actually see them, only Herr Jedrek."

"We don't get much news here other than the official announcements." When she says that, the man looks at her with a strange expression, and Dal senses it might be time to change the subject.

"Do you play the cyberharp?" he asks the man.

"I try."

"My brother's Spouse-to-be plays it...not very well, she's just starting out." In a strange ship without even Gerda near, Dalbert realizes that he honestly misses home, misses Lars and Margrethe. "Would you—I mean, if you wouldn't mind...?"

The man (Rur? Odd name) gives Dal the sort of grin that adults are always giving him, and he knows he's been cute again. Then Rur strums the cyberharp and adjusts a few outputs, and Dal sits back to listen. He can't help thinking that Margrethe might be playing at this instant back on Credix, and Lars listening as he, Dal, is listening to Rur. It's an exciting thought.

Another creature enters the area, and Dal shivers at the sight of it. Too tall, too thin, too pale—limbs that don't look or bend right—this has to be one of the Ebettor. He glimpsed one across the bridge of *Deathcry* earlier, but this is the first time he's seen one so close. Its skin is covered with coarse translucent hairs, stippled with a network of furrows that look about as inviting to the touch as the rind of an overripe cantaloupe.

The Ebettor's eyes are wide and mostly white—but Dal catches sight of dark flecks like a negative-image of a globular cluster. The way those eyes gaze upon him, he feels almost the way he did when *Outbound's* Telepath caught sight of him in a corridor....

The Ebettor puts a hand on Rur's cyberharp. Rur stiffens but keeps playing. The alien grunts and gags; from nowhere the ship's puter produces a translation: "Why do you make this sound?"

"It's music," Rur answers. "It may not be very good, but surely you can recognize it as music."

The puter takes a long time with this one, jabbering in the Ebettor language. Finally the alien lets go of the harp and responds.

"What you do is not music. Music is for the temple only. Music is order and structure, and it calls for us to give our most to our master. What you have made with this box, that is noise. You do not know what music is."

Rur shrugs. He holds out the harp. "Would you like to show us how your music sounds?"

The beast takes the harp in its strange hands. For a moment it does not move, then its fingers explore the keyboard. One or two exploratory notes sound.

"I am not of the temple and I do not make music as it should be. Nevertheless I will give you a sample of what we make." The Ebettor moves its fingers deliberately over the keyboard. From the cyberharp emerges a pattern in minor chords, a pattern that repeats and repeats, begins to grow upon itself, becoming something that seems a composite of dirge and march and the worst bits of all the intolerable hymns that Dal has sat through in Ancestor Worship. It lasts only a minute or two, and when it ends Dal is glad—yet at the same time his fingers long to beat that selfsame beat.

"*That* is music," the Ebettor says. "I will have one of those aboard play you more sometime, I am sure you will be inspired by it." The creature turns, and in turning its eyes meet Dal's. All that terrible music seems compressed into one instant, racing like a lightning flash from the Ebettor eyes into his brain. The creature's mouth twists, it licks its awful lips with a grey tongue, and Dal shivers.

"Perhaps the young Credixian would like to learn our music?"

"Nein," Dal says without thinking. Irina moves between him and the Ebettor, and he feels infinitely better.

The alien walks out without another word.

They say nothing. Rur goes back to his playing and keeps it up until Gerda comes to take Dal away—but every once in a while, the Ebettor's tune creeps into Rur's song, and something in Dal is always glad to hear it resurface.

❂

As they ride back to *Outbound* in one of the ship's gigs, Dal doesn't even ask what Captain Kassov said. Gerda always tells Dal everything, told him since they were both children, and it never occurs to him to doubt she will. She told him first when she passed her Naval Academy exams, told him first when she became a Captain, told him first when she was given *Outbound* to command. Out on the borders of the Imperium and beyond, Dal and Gerda are the only family each one has, and they are close enough to keep secrets for, not from, one another.

"Captain Kassov has heard from his government," she tells him. "And they have come up with a proposal that sounds very big."

"What is it?"

"They want us to sign treaties between Geled and Credix. Treaties for co-operation in the repair of Relay Alpha, to begin with—then other treaties, and more co-operation, and then talks designed to lead to the formation of an official union between Credix, Geled and the Ebettor states."

Dal tries to imagine chubby Captain Kassov saying such words, wonders if the Geledi even knew what he mouthed. "That *is* big."

"I will have to tell home about it right away. There will be a meeting of the full Reichstaag over this for sure. It might take them tendays to make their decision."

"Do you think they'll go along with it?"

"That is a good question, Dal. I wish I knew. I have no idea what the Imperium might decide." She must notice his wrinkled face, for she says, "You do not like the idea?"

"I'm not sure. I just wish they could pick nicer people than Captain Kassov and those Ebettor to get along with." Still, Irina and Rur were nice to him, and one of the things his teaching program is forever trying to get across to him is that he should be objective in his judgments.

The ship looms closer out the gig's starboard ports.

❖

Dal stays out of the way while Gerda consults with the Telepath. Actually he doesn't have fun at all, since Gerda told him to keep absolutely quiet about the notion of Credix-Geled Union until there was some kind of preliminary reaction from home. Rather than take his chances with the crew, who are a curious bunch, Dal stays in Gerda's cabin and tries to read.

Union with Geled? If what the Terrans say is right, then Geled is one of the major remnants of the Old Empire—the third most important one being someplace called Borshall, too distant to worry about. A union between Geled and Credix could mean the foundation of the New Empire that everyone's always talking about and no one ever believes would happen.

Dal crosses the room and sits down before Gerda's term. He keys into his teaching program, and calls up what he studied years ago of myth structures. He spends the next few hours happily reading about the promises of the New Empire and the Priest-General who would bring it about, and all the wonders of the Old Empire it would resurrect.

Finally Gerda returns. Her eyes are tight and Dal can tell she has a headache. He springs to her side as she slides onto her bunk. "What's wrong?"

"Rough session with home. They needed a replay of the interview with Kassov, so Telepath pulled it from my memory and transmitted. Medical," she says to an autoservant; it drifts over and attaches a diagnostic leech to her arm. While the leech deflates, the autoservant vanishes into a maintenance tunnel. Within a minute it—or another just like it—returns with another leech, which it presses to Gerda's thigh. She sighs.

"That feels better. What a time for a headache." She is still for a moment, and Dal wonders if she wants to sleep. Then she sits up.

"Where are you going?"

"To the Terran ship. We have to know where they stand on all this."

"I'll come with you."

"Maybe you had better not."

He has only to make the shadow of a pout and she relents. "All right, come on."

⦿

The Terrans are getting ready for sleep, and Frau Drisana made no pretense that Gerda has not dragged her from a comfortable bunk. But when Gerda tells them what Kassov proposed, they all stop complaining and Dal feels like the Telepath—he can almost see them starting to think.

"This whole matter very obviously turns on Relay Alpha," Gerda says. "Kassov did not try to hide the fact that his technicians cannot fix it. Even those wonder-creatures he brought along, they say they can't understand certain things about the technology. If we pool our forces, he says, we stand a good chance of either being able to repair it or building something that will serve us just as well."

Herr Jedrek, whom Dal has liked since he first heard him speak, yawns. "Captain Lübchen, I hate to burst your bubble, but there isn't anything that can serve us as well. With the technology that you and the Geledis have shown, neither of you know how to put thousands of high-powered ultrawave transceivers together in such a small space without blowing out your transceivers and every ultrawave set in this side of the Galaxy."

"If we work together, we can construct large-scale projects. Thousands of little booster stations separated by parsecs, rather than one big station to do it all."

"I doubt it. Thousands of stations? Each with its own in-tune tachyon vesicle? That would cost the ransom of several dozen planets, if you could get them at all. And then who's going to protect all those little stations from the hostile Galaxy around them? Would the military might of even Credix and Geled be good enough for the job? When you can't even extend your boundaries to the point where they were a thousand years ago?"

Sayyid Drisana strokes the crystal ball she holds between her palms. "Kassov is right. There's no other way but to repair Alpha. Of course we give our support to that effort."

"Now wait a minute, Drisana...."

Gerda holds up a hand. "I do not want to cause a quarrel. You have given me something to think about; at least I can present your arguments to the logisticians at home. You don't have to give me a decision right away. Talk it out among yourselves. You know how to reach my ship." Gerda gives Dal a signal, and they both prepare to leave.

"Haven't you forgotten to consult one party in this matter, Captain Lübchen?" Herr Jedrek's tone sounds awfully insolent—close as he is to Gerda, Dal knows that *he* could never get away with using such a voice to her. He somewhat admires Jedrek for not withering away to nothing instantly. "Have you asked the Theresans what they think of your Union?"

Gerda turns back to him with a sad face. "Jedrek, I have received no instructions from my superiors to consult the Theresans about anything. And that frightens me."

She leads Dal out, and they make their way back to *Outbound* in silence.

◆

24
Data
[CIRCLE]
6484 CE

Sting turns out to be as conscious of Jedrek's moods as Denys—and before him the Circle—ever were. For once the lad stays in for a night and does not practice his tomcattish sleep-period wanderings. From the darkness of their shared cabin Sting says, "You're not happy."

"Perceptive."

"You're easy to read. Look, Jedrek, I know you don't trust me, but I can listen if you want to talk."

Listen, Jedrek thinks. Then run to Drisana and tell her everything. Why does he like this boy? Oh, he's long since gotten over the fear of ending up with a laser burn along his side or something even worse...Sting is not a murderer. At least not an unprovoked one. In Sting Jedrek senses some of the same control that T'to Yachim displays when he clasped his hand to his sidearm and said: "The weapons of a Galactic Rider are never used in anger."

Still...T'to carefully explained that his control came from the gun as much as from himself—the weapon had detectors that would not allow it to trigger when his body produces the hormones of anger. Jedrek has no such guarantee that Sting will show restraint with whatever his weapons are.

Besides, there's the whole nagging question of what Sting is up to on this voyage. Jedrek suddenly realizes that the lad has expressed no opinions of his own about their situation. In the back of his mind, he has all the others categorized as being on "his side" or "Drisana's side"—what side is Sting on?

He sighs. Sensible or no, brat or not, he trusts Sting. "We're in an awkward situation here. I happen to want to befriend the Theresans and the Galactic Rider, but every force in the Galaxy seems to be against them. I take solace in the fact that my decision is already made for me—no matter what political machinations take place around the Relay, there still remains the fact that no one *can* fix it."

"Drisana thinks you can do it. She's angry that you won't."

"Knowing how much it means to Drisana, I'm just as glad I don't know how, because I'd be in a very touchy moral position." Jedrek shakes his head. Years past are years past, frozen like data in the Library, no matter how memory seems to bring them back to the present. And he hasn't seen Drisana for eleven years, there's no reason she should mean any more to him than the other people he left behind on Terra.

Even so, he wishes he could believe in something as intensely as Drisana believes in the Grand Library.

"You're sidestepping my question, Jedrek. I know you can't fix Relay Alpha, no one can. But apparently you're the best bet any of them have, or else they wouldn't be going to such lengths to convince you. They'd just elbow you out of the way."

Sting is right. They all believe that he has the expertise. "But I don't."

"Could you learn?"

Ah, the question that's been on his mind for days. *Could* he learn to repair the Ultrawave Relay? With access to almost all the science of the Empire, able to tap at will into the technology of Geled and Credix...he reaches out blindly and his fingers close over his data marble. If he really tries, can he do it?

I'm a tech, Jedrek thinks, not a librarian or a politician or anything else. I see a mechanism that doesn't work, and I itch to repair it. Nothing as strong as the all-consuming fire that burns behind Drisana's eyes, but still the itch is there.

And so he can never satisfy it, never allow himself to know that it could be satisfied.

"I don't think I could."

"Nonsense. You're not the kind of person who says 'I can't.'" Sting knows him too well. "What stands in your way?"

"Ignorance. I've been through all the technical data of Credix and through the files that the Geledis have released to us. I've reviewed everything I learned about ultrawave on Borshall, and I've spent hours with the big datasphere trying to track down every bit the Empire ever knew about ultrawave relays. Nobody knows the secret of how they kept the Relay from shorting out, and those who did know wiped it very effectively four thousand years ago."

"*Someone* must have the knowledge you need. All right, not the Empire, not those ships out there, not *Maria Theresa*. Who, then? The Galactic Rider?"

"If he knows, he would never tell us. No, I don't think T'to Yachim has any idea of how Ultrawave works. Maybe their scientists on Nephestal know, but we'll never get anything from them." He lets Sting feel him shrug in the dark. "The Ebettor seem to think they have the technology to effect the repair. But they don't tell anyone, they want to do it themselves. And Olympia won't let them near Alpha."

"Suppose they gave you what they know. Could you repair the Relay then?"

"I don't know. I'd have to see what data they have." Safe enough. The Ebettor are paranoids even more security-conscious than Geled, they will never give up the slightest bit.

"Suppose it's the right information. *Would* you repair it?"

"Blast it, Sting...I'm trying to avoid that choice. Let's not talk about it. If it comes up, fine, I'll deal with it then. But they're not going to give me data." He pulls the boy close. "Forget it, okay?"

Sting doesn't answer.

❖

The word "Teerell," ship's puter guesses, is from an old Anglich or Kerman word meaning "festival." The guess is very astute, considering the puter has never seen the habitat of Teerell.

"Festival" is a good first approximation of the real Teerell. Thousands of people in fantastic costumes mill about joyfully greeting one another, eating and playing and in general having a good time. Teerell is something of a marketplace, Olympia explains; here one can purchase just about anything that the *Maria Theresa* system produces, and by examining the wares of the many vendors Jedrek believes her.

With his light-amplifying goggles off, Teerell is nothing but a confused crowd shifting and muddling through darkness. With the goggles in place and starlight bright in the sky, it becomes a fair that dwarfs even Cairo's annual Vernal Equinox celebrations.

Peoples and customs and environments change, but the Galaxy over, liquor is liquor and happy-drugs are happy-drugs—and although Olympia does not indulge, both Jedrek and Sukoji are soon in hilarious spirits. While the Queen hangs back in pained dignity, the Terrans allow the Theresans to convince them to sample some of the Carnival's rides. Soon they're swinging all about the tiny planetoid, bodies whirling about every possible axis.

Jedrek throws back his head and feels wind whipping up his hair; then his amplified vision catches sight of *Maria Theresa* and behind it the compact stylus-shaped bulk of *Deathcry*, and the laughter vanishes from his lips.

Soon after, Olympia and Sukoji sit with him at a streetside table, chatting against a background of ten thousand happy voices.

Olympia is the first to turn the conversation to business.

"To me tell, what out there is going on." She nods toward *Maria Theresa* and the three visitor ships. "Informed we are not, only rumors have we, and what you to give us have been willing."

Sukoji spreads her hands. "Nothing has changed. Credix and Geled are still going through talks aimed at Union. If they can agree, they'll most likely use force to repair the Relay."

"And where stand will you, in that eventuality?" The

Queen's eyes are tight, her voice anxious.

Sukoji shifts her weight. "Why must you be so intransigent? You're only making it easier for Credix and Geled to unite in defiance of you as the common enemy."

"Think not, do you, that I know that? Were there any other way, think not do you, that I take it would?"

"Then why?"

"Because convinced am I, that the alternative much worse is. Give not, must we, the Ebettor and their master an easy route into the Scattered Worlds."

"Nonsense."

Jedrek looks up from his drink, and there stands Drisana. She wears coveralls and her hair glints in reflected star-highlights. She props her foot on a stool. Around her neck hangs a clear pendant that can only be another form of data marble.

Drisana bows her head. "With all due respect, Queen Olympia, no one fights for the good of the Galaxy. I have the entire Grand Library at my disposal, and I can't even *conceive* of the Galaxy—I don't expect you to be able to, whose astronomy is only now *discovering* the Galaxy as a structure. You may have your reasons for not allowing that Relay to be fixed, but saving the Galaxy can't be one of them."

Olympia stiffens. "Sorry I am, for you, Sayyid Drisana. Respond let me, on your level. If Union make Geled and Credix, then trampled will be my people, a servant race will become. Removed will we be, to one of your planets us to prevent, from with the Relay interfering. Say you, that I comprehend cannot, the whole of the Scattered Worlds, and possibly you right are—but comprehend I can most certainly, my duty to my people." She stands. "If you excuse me will, I things have to do." She turns, and is lost in the crowds of Teerell.

Jedrek shakes his head. "Drisana, sometimes you amaze me."

"Oh, and now *you're* my moral superior also? Well I have

a few things to tell you, Jedrek, things I ought to have said quite a while ago—"

"Stop it, both of you." Sukoji removes her goggles, rubs her eyes, replaces them. "I had enough of your bickering eleven years ago, and absence hasn't made me grow fonder."

Jedrek opens his mouth, Sukoji puts a finger over it. "No, Jedrek, don't escalate it another step. Cosmos, I wish one of you would learn how to let things lie."

"I'm learning," he snarls, and leaves the table. As he pushes through the crowd he rather hopes someone will come after him...but of course they don't.

❀

On any world or settlement, a carousel is a carousel. Teerell's carousel is fifty meters in diameter, and its track makes a delightful möbius twist as the animals march around on their poles. And oh, what animals!—beasts from every mythology Jedrek is familiar with, and a good many he can't place at all.

The spinning of the track makes his head spin faster. He settles onto the back of a six-headed rearing reptile, and lets the music and the animal carry him about through darkness while innocents cry out in joy on every side.

"Here, Jedrek."

He puts on his goggles. "Sting!"

The boy climbs atop one of the beast's necks and holds out a hand. "This is yours." Sting's face bears a smile, part of which Jedrek reads as self-satisfaction and part that seems sheer pleasure in existence; the kind of smile Jedrek himself wears after a good morning stretch.

A tiny bit of plastic drops into Jedrek's palm. A data chip—

The silvery lines engraved in his palm come alive, and Jedrek feels the carousel's motion spinning him into the world of the chip....

A physics he suspected, but never saw evidence for. Better,

a whole raft of engineering principles based on that physics, engineering that makes possible the containment of hundreds, thousands of fragile tachyon vesicles. And with such arrangements, frozen in space and anchored to gravity like beautiful equations and matrices frozen and anchored to a terminal screen—why, with such lattices of vesicles one could build vast world-moving space fleets, defense screens that could protect planetary systems, gigantic Ultrawave Relays....

Cosmos!

"Sting, where did you get this?"

"Is it what you need to repair the Relay?"

"I can't be sure but...yes, it could very well be. Where did you get it?"

"From the Ebettor. You said they knew it."

"How?"

"How does anyone get anything? I traded for it. I nosed about, and found out what one of the Ebettor wanted, and I gave it to him." Sting smiles, this time a smile of simple triumph. "I've bedded worse, for less noble purposes. I'll tell you one thing, Jedrek—those Ebettor, I don't care what everyone says, they're Human. Or they *were*."

"T'to says that they're descended from Human stock. Maybe from the Cambolinee settlements of Imperial times, but they can't be considered completely Human...."

"T'to's wrong. I don't care how they fit into the evolutionary scheme or what they're descended from, there are times when Humans behave one way and others don't, and these Ebettor are closer to Humans than they are to other."

"You liked it?"

"It was odd. They don't use sex for reproduction or entertainment, the way we do. For them, it seems to be entirely about status and power." Sting's eyes sparkle. "Why, are you jealous?"

"Don't be sick." All this is automatic banter on the top of Jedrek's mind; under, he swims through the no-longer-murky waters of the data chip and Ultrawave physics. Had the Empire known all this? It seems almost unbelievable.

"I'm tired." Sting settles down onto the back of the reptile, his back braced against Jedrek's right leg. Jedrek clings to the beast's pole and struggles to make sense of the data in the chip. Teerell swims past them.

Finally, with eyes that look at a world changed in the way that only new knowledge can change it, Jedrek notices Teerell and the stars and his gaze goes to Sting.

The lad is asleep, and in sleep he loses something of his assurance, becomes the child hidden inside every Human. Jedrek knows from experience that Sting will awaken at a touch, ready to defend himself—but for now he is an innocent little boy.

And now that innocent boy set Jedrek on a tightrope across a wind-whipped canyon. Gifted with the very data he wanted most not to have, Jedrek knows that he now has an important decision to make.

Leaving the carousel to spin and Sting to sleep, he goes off to walk among the crowd.

❖

25
Painbird
[GELED]
GY 3216

Irina knows what she must do. As soon as the orders come
in, as soon as she knows what they mean, there is no more
choice in her mind. The only question is how. Kassov will
certainly never allow her to leave the ship, especially
now...and using any of the comm equipment is out of the
question.

"How" answers itself rather quickly. Whatever else,
Kassov is a loyal Geledi from Geled—which means he follows
the god Kaal. Irina, raised in the outlying worlds, is not very
religious, and she's never made a practice of attending
worship services. Now, on the eve of such an important
military encounter, Kassov will be cloistered in the chapel
interceding on the crew's behalf to everyone's father figure
Kaal, giving Irina at least two hours out of the Captain's sight.

Feeling very much like a foreign agent or traitor of some
kind, Irina lets herself into the main airlock and cycled it.
There is no need for a pressure suit; *Deathcry* has taken up
station only a few meters from the atmosphere curtain of
Maria Theresa, and she can survive a short jump in
shirtsleeves.

Vacuum tugs at her skin, then it is over and she drifts
through gentle breeze with the hull of *Maria Theresa* scarcely
two hundred meters before her. Irina tucks her body into a
ball and rotates slowly until she faces back at *Deathcry*; there
is no sign that anyone witnessed her jump.

It takes an inconsequential time to reach *Maria Theresa*,
and only slightly longer to crawl along the ship's hull until
she reaches a hatchway. It is open—these people don't seem
to know know what hatch locks are for. She pulls herself in
and squints through darkness trying to get a feel for the room
she occupies. The hatch's tiny patch of starlight does nothing

to relieve the gloom.

A form moves before her, light flares, and Irina finds herself looking into the face of the Galactic Rider.

The Ebettor, Irina thinks suddenly, are *in*human—this alien facing her is *non*human. And the difference is immense. She can't help seeing the Ebettor as travesties of her own form—but T'to Yachim's horned countenance, his great small-pupilled eyes below the curling depressions of ears, the nasal slits lining his stocky neck—these could no more inspire repugnance than could the scales of a fish or the bark of a soaring oak.

"I observed your dive here, Irina Lerenko. I came to greet you in the light that you are accustomed to." He speaks Geledi with no trace of an accent, as if he learned it on the plains of Geled herself. Irina is astonished to think that *she* has more of an accent than him.

"I came in search of you, Galactic Rider. When I was a girl, a Rider came to my settlement—I remember that he was fair and told us nice stories. Some people were having an argument about the use of some volume, it was a family quarrel and had a lot to do with inheritance. They asked the Rider to decide. I don't remember what he said, but after that there was no more fighting." She shrugs. "I don't know if I should be doing this."

"What have you to say, Irina Lerenko? I will listen, and I swear by the Golden Throne of Avethell that I will be fair about whatever you tell me."

Irina takes a deep breath. There is always the split second after you launch a missile, or just before you tell the puter to fire laser, when you wonder whether you're doing it right—but it is a point-of-no-return, and you can only act on momentum and hope. This is one of those moments.

Her words come out like atmosphere escaping a breached hull. "A new ship is coming from home. Once *Painbird* arrives, we're going to attack the Theresans to force repair of Relay Alpha. The Credixian ship is going to help." The more she says, the easier it becomes. "Captain is under orders to hold down casualties as much as possible, but he's arranged a crew exchange that will put Ebettor gunners in charge of the offensive weapons of all three ships. I don't know what I want you to do, but I wish you'd do something."

The Rider is silent for a time. Irina wishes she knew how to read the emotions of his unfamiliar face. When the dangerous-looking backfin tenses and moves slightly downward, does that mean he's happy or angry? Or is it nothing but a neutral motion, like the way the tip of Irina's tongue emerges from between her lips when she concentrates heavily?

"I am disturbed by what you have told me, Irina Lerenko. I thank you very much for giving me the information. You may very well have given us the time we need to save many lives and prevent much misery."

"I wish you could just blow up the Relay. I wish it had never existed."

"Ah, we cannot do that. If we destroy it, then your governments would only build another. We must somehow convince them that they ought not to have any. For the nonce, it is good that this Relay remain to focus their attention on *it* and prevent them from ideas of building a new one." He expels air from his nasal slits. "Irina Lerenko, you have done right." He holds out his hands to her. "I have some idea of what your Captain is like. If you wish it, I offer you asylum from his wrath and from your government."

Irina shivers. "I couldn't. Nyet. I have friends, family at home. And—and all of this aside, I don't think Geled is wrong. There are bad ones like Kassov, but we're basically a decent people. If the members of the Presidium were here, I'm sure they wouldn't vote to hurt these people. No, I don't want to give up Geled. I can get back to the ship before I'm missed."

"You have earned my respect, Irina Lerenko."

"Thank you." She isn't quite sure what to say.

"The Galactic Rider who visited your settlement when you were young—I think he would be proud of you."

Unbidden, a smile creeps onto her lips. "Thank you. Thank you very much."

Somehow it is all worthwhile now.

❖

He has little time. Geled is efficient, it will not be too much longer before *Painbird* arrives, and shortly after that the attack will begin.

T'to finds Queen Olympia and Dileene Shaarlin with no difficulty, explains the situation to them, and then leaves at the dead run that four million years escaping predators on the grassy plains of Dorasc bred into his race. His ship, warned in advance, is ready for flight by the time he jumps through the airlock.

Stars wheel. *Deathcry* was alone—good. There is time yet.

The sphere of Relay Alpha grows before him, while T'to takes inventory of his weapons.

Weapons—ha! The weapons of a Galactic Rider are his voice, his ingenuity, his reason. Persuasion, never force. But when force is called for, options are available. Defense screens that make Human screens look like soap bubbles. Generators that drew power from starlight and gravity to produce streams of particles so energetic they tear the fabric of space when they pass. An energy-absorption field that is actually within the scope of Human technology, would they but look in the back pocket of the right set of equations....

Voice, ingenuity and reason. Defense screens. And hope.

If only, T'to thinks, the myths were true. If only Hesket and Jaseni and Den and all the other Elder Gods really existed and could be called up through song to fight on the side of right.

If only the entire cadre of Galactic Riders could be assembled into the most effective army the Scattered Worlds had ever seen, to descend on the Geledi ships and prevent them from destroying *Maria Theresa*.

T'to chides himself. Muddy thinking. What would his

teachers say, if they could hear him?

He docks his ship with the Relay, and starts at once moving equipment. Physical exertion helps put his mind at rest. As he works, he set his music-synth to play some of his favorite ballads; music always makes things go faster.

What if *Maria Theresa* and all her people are destroyed, he thinks. The Galactic Riders stood by and watched the Terran Empire fall, and did not raise a digit to save many deserving worlds. For that matter, Dorasc itself was left free to fall, and none interfered. A few art relics and cultural items saved for prosperity, that was it. Death and decay are part of the natural processes of an entropic Universe.

He sighs. Looking at it practically, if the Theresans cannot save themselves from Credix and Geled, then he will be doing them no favor by stepping in and saving them.

No, his place is here with the Relay. This is not the property of the Theresans, not their construction, they are at best its unwitting guardians. And as it is one of the most crucial pieces of equipment in the Galaxy, T'to feels obliged to help protect it.

Yes, Irina Lerenko, it *would* be easier to destroy the Relay. What Galactic Rider ever allowed himself to choose the easy way?

For a moment T'to feels a childish regret, regret that a Galactic Rider is bound to follow only his conscience and no other force in the Universe. He would like nothing better at the moment than to have someone give him a direct order and follow it to the best of his ability, without any responsibility should he be doing the wrong thing.

Ridiculous.

Music playing, T'to Yachim settles down for his vigil.

❋

Aladdin Systems:
Not Your Greatmother's Autoservants

Who could imagine life without autoservants? They cook and clean for us, tend our homes and businesses, keep everything in good repair, and take care of our every need. Servs and mechs and cybs are indispensable to modern life.

Yet how often do you think about your autoservants? If you're like most people, seldom. You inherited them, or they came with your home, your business, your ship. They work perfectly—and when they don't, mechs fix them.

Would it surprise you to know that your autoservants may have been in service for thousands of years? It seems incredible, yet it's true: the average autoservant in today's galaxy dates back to the days of the Terran Empire.

What must fill your poor serv's circuits. Think of the inevitable bloat and clutter of that long a lifetime. Your grandfather's drink preferences. Great-Aunt Matilda's favorite breakfasts. The social schedules of a hundred generations. Millennia of trivia.

At Aladdin Systems, we specialize in making old autoservants new again. We'll clean out your servs' memories, peel away generations of clutter, and update their software with state-of-the-art routines. You'll find that your autoservants are more responsive, more efficient, better able to serve.

Touch **here** to contact a representative for a consultation.

❁

26
Plan
[CIRCLE]
6484 CE

Stars should not be as bright in the sky as a sun. That's only one of the things Sukoji finds wrong with the environments of *Maria Theresa*. She doesn't know why she ever left Aetor anyway. This place has nothing to offer her, Terra has nothing to offer her, even the reformed Library Circle has nothing to offer her.

Nothing but a dream.

Drisana holds court for the people of Teerell, her hand clasped about the crystal data dewdrop she wears around her neck, her other hand on a stack of datapads. Like an oracle she holds forth on the questions and problems of the populace, dispensing answers in the best tradition of the Librarian.

"My child from strange allergies suffers. What do I, should?"—two hundred pages on allergic reactions and their treatment. "My business failing is, how to increase can I, production and yet high quality maintain?"—four of the Grand Library's thousands of volumes on management make their way onto another datapad.

Drisana is in her element, happier than Sukoji's known her in all the years since the Circle broke up. Surely she was born to do this work, to manipulate data and present it clearly. Watching her, Sukoji feels that she knows what drives Drisana, that she understands what went out of the other woman's life when the Relay failed and the Grand Library's last link to the Galaxy died.

Is it any wonder that Drisana would do anything to get that link back? Is Jedrek blind, that he can't see how overwhelmingly *herself* Drisana is? All the rest of us went off to search for things we wanted, things we thought Terra and the Library couldn't give us—why shouldn't Drisana have the same option?

Comms buzz. Sukoji narrows her eyes and touches her headset, exchanging a wondering look with Drisana. A tiny holoimage of Kedar forms in the air before them.

"Ladies," he says in typical Kedar fashion, "you are standing in the center of a war zone."

"What?"

"Look in the right place, and you will see that *Deathcry* has been joined by a sister ship. The three of them, two Geledi ships and *Outbound*, have filed a declaration of war against *Maria Theresa*. I've managed to persuade them to hold off hostilities until all of us are back safely."

"You can't be serious." Drisana's eyes do not show through her goggles, but from her tone, Sukoji imagines them narrowing.

"I don't think they mean to attack," Kedar says. "I think this is a ploy. They're hoping that the Queen will give up and let them try repairing Alpha. Just the same I'd like you to come back to the ship in case the Theresans are more stubborn than we think."

"They won't give up. The idiots." Drisana gathers her datapads and tucks them into her shoulder bag. "Kedar, we're on our way. I want you to put a special watch on the Relay to make sure these people don't try something stupid. They're fanatics, they'll do anything to prove their point."

Cilehe's dry voice sounds over the circuit. "The same might be said of you, Drisana dear."

Drisana actually smiles. "There's a big difference," she says with laughter in her voice. "I'm *right*." Not giving Cilehe time to reply, she continues in a more serious tone, "Jedrek is also on this hunk of rock. Is he all right?"

"He's fine. Sting is there too, and hasn't answered yet. I'm still trying to raise him."

"Never mind, I'll take care of him." Drisana takes a data slab from her bag, touches it to her headset. Then she cradles the slab in her palm and punches instructions.

"He'll answer you. Come on, Sukoji."

"What is that?"

"Nothing sinister. Just an ultrawave link with Sting. It's a high-priority channel that feeds into a slab he can palm-read, just in case he doesn't want to answer publicly or go through a long conversation."

"And what made you think you'd ever need something like that?"

"It was Sting's idea."

"Drisana, I sometimes wonder about you."

Drisana says nothing, she merely tugs at Sukoji's hand.

❋

Jedrek is trying to tag along with a native on one of the winged steeds when Sting emerges from the crowd. "Jedrek, I've found you."

"That you have, little Librarian."

"I-I wanted to make sure you were getting off this rock. You heard what happened?"

"I've heard." He turns back to the Theresan, who stands by patiently petting the flank of his mount. "Can you take my friend and me to *Maria Theresa*?"

"Going I am, that way; the beast will three bear. Your hand give me, help you up I will."

The creature's skin is warm and firm beneath him. Jedrek turns to offer Sting help, sees that the lad is already astride the beast.

Jedrek sighs. "Listen, Sting—" the creature kicks off and its wings bite air; Jedrek feels gravity ever-lessening as the creature climbs away from Teerell. Starlit, the whole settlement is laid out below him now, the carousel and midway and the moving throngs, the too-sudden curve of horizon that cuts off sight of the rest....

"What?" Sting demands.

"Sorry. I'm not going back to *Worldsaver* right away. Kedar wants me to run messenger to *Outbound*. Do you want to come along?"

"I'd better. You've forgotten to wear your knife again; in a fight you'd be——" The rest of Sting's remark is cut off as they breach the atmosphere. Jedrek keeps his mouth open, feels air whistle from his lungs, feels the tingle of vacuum on skin. He is of unmodified Terran stock—he doesn't even have the slight advantage of Sting who was born in a space settlement where a jump through hundred-meter stretches of vacuum is considered easier than donning a vacuum suit. At most, Jedrek can count on two minutes or so of consciousness.

Long before his time is up *Maria Theresa's* atmosphere curtain closes about them. He gasps, his lungs burning from the sudden inrush of air.

"I hope Captain Lübchen finds your speech more convincing than your breathing, big fellow, or we may all be in trouble."

Jedrek says nothing.

❁

Gerda makes time to listen to Jedrek. Even her little shadow is not there—when he asks after Dalbert, Gerda says the cabin boy is busy tending to the many jobs necessary to put a ship on combat footing.

"That's what I came to talk to you about, Captain Lübchen."

"Captain, is it? So we are being formal? Should I record for my log?"

"That's not a bad idea." Jedrek takes a breath. Here goes, he thinks. "I bring a message from Drisana Hardel, Terran Councilor." As Head Librarian, Drisana holds an automatic seat on the Terran Council. Gerda doesn't need to know that Drisana hasn't sat in Council in her life. "We do not wish to see war in this volume, as we are a peace-loving people. Therefore, on behalf of the Terran Council I am empowered to make this offer for compromise: come to Terra and let the

Terran Council hear all arguments in the case, and then decide as impartial witnesses whose rights are being violated and which point of view should be upheld." It is not bad, for a hastily-composed speech of Kedar's—even if he *did* borrow from several documents of the pre-Imperial Colonial Wars.

"I am going to stop recording now, Jedrek." Gerda touches a button on a control panel. Then she smiles. "What is behind this?"

"Drisana thinks the Relay's going to be destroyed in the fighting. I went along with it because I don't want to see the Theresans suffer any more. I'd just as soon see the bloody thing blown up."

"Off the record, I think I would too. But there is not much chance of that with our Dorascan friend sitting on top of it."

"T'to Yachim is guarding the Relay?"

"He flew his ship there before *Painbird* ever arrived. He has issued no statements—he does not need to." She clasps her hands, looks over knuckles at Jedrek. "Do you expect me to say yes to this compromise?"

"We seemed to think there was a possibility. There's precedent. Remember how the Independent Traders held the Council of Escen to end the Geled-Natal War a thousand years ago?"

"I come from the wrong side of the Galaxy to remember that. I will take your word for it."

"And if you stretch a legal point all out of shape, Terra has the best property claim to this Relay."

"That is something that must be decided by the courts of the future, my friend. Probably a good many millennia into the future. So far you have given me no good reason to accept."

"I'm not here to give you reasons. I'm here to offer a justifiable excuse. It's got to be your choice to stop the fighting."

Gerda frowns. She touches her term, and on the screen there appears a holo of an old woman in Credixian uniform.

"Jedrek, that woman is our ship's Telepath. Right now she is in rapport with Fleet Headquarters on Credix. Behind the Commander-in-Chief stands the Imperator. I am not free, you see, to make my own decisions. What I think does not matter—any more than what Dal thinks. But I will make your offer. You will excuse me?"

"Certainly."

Gerda leaves the room, and Sting stands. He holds a durasteel knife, the blade sharp and gleaming; he picks at the dirt under his fingernails. "They aren't going to accept."

"I knew that to begin with. It was a stupid idea. But we had to make the offer."

"Well," Sting makes a flourish and the knife is gone, "Now it's made and we can get down to serious business. I love a good fight."

"Yes, but on whose side?"

The door opens and Gerda steps back in. "I am sorry, Jedrek. The Commander-in-Chief sees no reason to accept your offer. He apparently does not think we will have any trouble getting what we want."

"Do *you* think you will?"

Gerda spreads her hands. "Three battleships—and you ought to see what those Ebettor can do with a firing puter. I do not see that *Maria Theresa* has any chance at all."

"I'll work on it. Thanks for the try." Jedrek turns to go, Sting behind him. At the door, he looks back.

Gerda gives a wan smile. "I wish you luck."

The door closes behind him.

❖

27
Retreat
[CIRCLE]
6484 CE

By this time, *Worldsaver's* control cabin is as familiar to Jedrek as the workrooms of the Grand Library, or his office on Borshall. The space is just about the same size as his office—which means when everyone is milling about or talking at once, it is bedlam.

One of the datascreens, he notices, shows a puter-enhanced image of the three warships, each wheeling in perfect formation with the other two. Hard to believe they are real, deadly ships, ships that could any moment explode with attacking fury....

He slams his hand flat against a bulkhead; everyone falls momentarily quiet.

"Thank you. I've just returned from taking our peace offer to Captain Lübchen."

"And?"

"What did you expect? Another Yavam plan meets with disaster." He narrows his eyes at the older man. "Don't you ever get tired of the pattern, Kedar?"

"That's cruel, Jedrek," Sukoji protests.

"No more than necessary. I've *been* kind, and now three warships are poised to wipe out these innocent people. I think the time for kindness is over."

In response to nothing, seemingly connected with nothing, Cilehe observes, "Puter says that they're running wargame sims. It theorizes that the Ebettor are training in the two new ships—when they're done, the attack will start."

"And what are we going to do when it does?" Jedrek feels a note of rage in his voice. Good. All the better if they know he's not going to put up with any foolishness. "Are we going to sit by and watch *Maria Theresa* get blown to ions?"

Drisana gives him a look that he remembers all too well.

"What would you have us do? Charge in there and act as first target? We've made the best offer we could—that's all that's in our power."

"You mean that's all you *want* to be in your power. Blast it, Cilehe, this is your ship. Does she have the firepower to stand off the others?"

"We fought back *Deathcry* pretty effectively. We could probably hold them off for a while. But even *Worldsaver* doesn't have infinite fuel reserves and I know we don't have infinite vigilance."

Kedar puts a hand on Jedrek's arm. "*We* have made an effort at compromise, Jedrek. Now it's your turn."

"What?"

"Tell your friends in *Maria Theresa* to surrender. Let the Geledis and Credixians repair the Relay."

"Don't talk nonsense. They can't, even if we let them try. That's what makes this whole struggle so useless." What he says was true…he has all the data in his marble, and he knows that not one of the pieces will do without the rest. Terran, Credixian, Geledi, a dash of Borshallan technology, and the vital Ebettor contribution—together, the secret of the Relays; separately—nothing. And he, Jedrek, is the only one with all the parts.

"Then help them," Sukoji says. Jedrek turns pained eyes on her.

"How can you say that? You were always devoted to life, Sukoji—how can you let them win? Do you want to see the whole Galaxy run by the Ebettor?"

She laughs. "Is that what you're worried about? This Union of theirs? Jedrek, stand back for a moment and look at this from a historical perspective. You can't seriously expect that they're going to found a new Empire?"

"What about me?" Sting asks. He is ignored.

Jedrek shakes his head. "Say what you like, justify it any way you wish, I…just…don't…care. I know what's right, and that's not attacking a neutral system when they stand in the way of something you want."

"This neutral little system," Drisana says, "stands in the way of the future. Stands in the way of our last link to the past. I'm not saying that Credix and Geled are going to bring about a new Empire—but *someone* has to do it *sometime*. You must believe that, Jedrek, or you wouldn't have spent so many years tending the Library with us. No Terran can help but believe it, long for it. Cosmos, I've heard you moan often enough about how Terra has gone downhill, how beautiful it was during the Empire, how wonderful if worlds could be like that again. Well, if anyone's going to remember and dream and eventually bring it to reality, they're going to do that through the data in the Library, just the way *you* know of the past and can dream of the future." She closes her eyes and rolls her head. Drisana's icy calm has broken at last, and now she is on the edge of hysteria. "Or do you want all of Humanity to be like your Theresans, little self-sufficient pockets of not-quite-Humans who don't even know the rest of the race exists?"

After all the years and all the emotion, she still has the power to make his head spin. "I know what's right, Drisana, and I know what I have to do."

"At least you could respect what *I* know is right. That's all I ask. Tell the Theresans to surrender."

He grits his teeth. "They wouldn't, even if I told them to."

Cilehe gestures at the viewscreen, the image of the three ships. "I have a feeling that surrender, or lack thereof, will be academic before too long."

Kedar bends his head, avoiding Jedrek's eyes. "Cilehe, you'd better take us out to a safe distance from *Maria Theresa*. We don't want to be in the way of stray fire."

Jedrek goes to his cabin, and doesn't even let Sting in when the lad knocks at the beginning of sleep-period.

❉

The Only Headset You'll Ever Need

Introducing the KL-1000, the most powerful and durable headset on the market. Combining superior connectivity with sophisticated intelligence, the KL-1000 may very well be the last headset you'll ever need.

Comm functions? The KL-1000 is a multi-spec communications device, seamlessly interfacing with all known comm standards for unparalleled voice/vision clarity. And translation to/from over 250 languages and dialects is built in. Whether it's across the room or across the Galaxy, the KL-1000 gets the job done.

What about data? With tons of onboard memory, state-of-the-art processors, and no-worry networking, the KL-1000 makes data management effortless. Personal contacts, schedules, holos, music, documents—the KL-1000 manages any and all data in your life…and provides quick & easy access to local, wide, planetary, and Galactic internets.

Powerful as it is, the KL-1000 is small enough to fit behind an ear. The unit interfaces with standard datapads, screens, and spex for hassle-free input and output. It also responds to voice commands, with outstanding natural-language processing. The optional neural-induction interface* outputs directly to optic and aural nerve centers, and can be configured to read and interpret eye movements and subvocal commands.

To top it off, the KL-1000 is sturdy and durable; this is a unit that you could easily pass along to your great-grandchild.

* Neural-induction interface carries a small risk of brain damage.

❀

28
Cabin Boy
[CREDIX]
CI 4331

Dal doesn't know what to do. Go to Gerda? But no, for the first time in his life Dal knows he can't talk to Gerda. Nothing in his adolescent puppydog relationship set the stage for what he needs now. Gerda is a friend when things are well, a confidant for all the gossip of a young life—but in this crisis, he can't go to her.

Dal sits in the corner of his bunk and hugs himself tightly. The ship's solid bulkhead is strong and secure against his back. His cabin is dark; he doesn't want to move, doesn't want to expose himself to the terrors that every Human being sees in the dark. A tear trickles down his cheek; he tightens his arms and wipes his face on a shoulder.

For Dal Ritter, the night's terrors are all too real.

Outside his door he hears movement. The very possibility of returning horror sparks him into action—he grabs his commpad and stuffs it into a flight bag containing a uniform change, toilet articles, his Ring, and his lucky rock. Then, moving quickly and praying to his Ancestors he won't be seen, he ducks into the autoservants' access tunnel and makes his way through the confusing network of low passages toward the hangar deck.

It is never difficult for a crewmember to sign out a gig—in this case Dal simply taps in Gerda's authorization codes and decides to worry about the consequences later. Puter will not question the Captain's use of a gig; the report won't land on Gerda's desktop for another ten hours at least, and by that time—

Dal doesn't know what will happen by that time. All he knows is that he has to get away from *Outbound*.

Quieting his sobs, he punches orders into the gig's control panel; then *Outbound* is tumbling away on the main viewscreen and Dal is alone with the stars. He relaxes and finally gives himself over to the anguished cry he has not been able to sound before.

Where to go, what to do? The gig's autopilot stops its tumbling, orienting it straight against the snowy band of the Galaxy. The gig is a planetary craft, with antigravs but no tachyon drive...else Dal would cast off and try to lose himself among the distant, cool stars. There has to be a way to forget, to erase the images still burning in his mind.

The curve of the Milky Way reminds him of the turn of pale arms, and shattering memory comes back to him...visitation from out of the night, inhuman caresses, the unbreakable grip, the pain...and worse than pain the terror, the horror like every dream he's ever had of not being able to move, to cry out for help....

No, no! Dal pounds his fist against the gig's viewscreen. Through dull thudding he can barely feel pain. Will he be like this forever, unable to feel anything?

Like a flash of ship's docking lights in planetary eclipse, out of the darkness there comes to him the image of the Galactic Rider. There are few Riders in the Imperium, but Dal knows the stories that everyone knows—the Riders love children. Despite the shattering experience that took away his innocence, Dal is still a child—the Rider would take him in.

Involuntarily, he shivers. The Rider is an alien, and he can't face another alien right now. It is asking too much. If the Galactic Rider offers him all the solace in the universe and the comfort of a mother's lap, he still would not be able to go to him.

Inspiration hits. Of all the people in the Galaxy, there is one Dal can go to, one who will understand and will not dismiss him as a little boy with a little boy's problems.

He taps orders to the autopilot, and the gig turns toward *Worldsaver*.

❈

"Ship coming up on us," Cilehe says. Jedrek jerks himself out of a doze. How can she remain vigilant all the time, without sleep? Since this journey started, he hasn't seen Cilehe sleep for more than a few minutes at a time. She is certainly a wonder.

"What is it?" Kedar leans over the control panel; Cilehe pointedly turns her back on him.

"It looks like a Credixian gig. Maybe Captain Lübchen has changed her mind."

"Not bloody likely." Kedar thumbs his headset. "Attention the Credixian gig. Your approach has been noted."

A tiny voice comes from the speaker. "If you please, sir, this is Dalbert Ritter of C.I.S. *Outbound*. May I have permission to dock and come aboard?"

Kedar looks around the room; no one says anything. "Come ahead."

"Sir... I-I don't know how."

Kedar rolls his eyes. Cilehe thumbs into the circuit and gives him a look of dismissal. "This is Cilehe, lad. Slave your autopilot to our puter and I'll bring you in. You'll be entering our docking bay number two; I'll have someone there to meet you."

"Please, Ma'am, I'd like to talk with Herr Jedrek if I might."

Cilehe's eyes questions Jedrek; he nods. "He'll be there." She closes the circuit and turns to the difficult task of bringing the gig aboard.

"Now what do you suppose is going on?" Sukoji asks.

Jedrek shrugs. "I'll find out soon enough, I wager."

❋

The boy is nervous, Jedrek can see that at first glance. He takes Dal to his cabin—not the most comfortable meeting place, but better than trying to deal with the rest of the crew. He sits the boy on Sting's bunk, then settles onto his own.

"What's wrong, Dal? I don't mind telling you that you look terrible."

The Credixian lad clenches his fists and sniffs. "I don't know how to tell you. It was horrible." Bravely, the boy sniffs again. From a meter and a half Jedrek feels the tension in the young body.

He reaches across his bunk and fumbles in a drawer. "Here," he takes a pill from his box, "Take this. It's nothing but a trank, it'll help you relax."

The lad takes the pill and swallows it with an effort. "Thanks." He closes his eyes. "If I tell you something, promise you won't think I'm awful."

What...? "I promise."

"It's about...about the Ebettor gunner. He-he came to my cabin when I was asleep...."

Realization hits Jedrek. He kneels next to Dal, puts an arm about the boy's shoulders. "What did it do to you?"

"He...fought with me, and knocked me down, and—and...." The boy flushes and turns his eyes away from Jedrek.

Jedrek feels angry. And *these* were the kind of animals Drisana wants to turn the Galaxy over to.

Painful as it is for the child, Jedrek has to know for sure. "Dal...was it rape?"

"I'm not sure what that means, but I think so."

"Tell me."

Before the boy is finished, Jedrek tells him to stop. He knows enough...knows too much. "Have you told Gerda about this?"

"I couldn't."

"I understand." He rests Dal's head on his own shoulder, holds the boy as reassuringly as he could manage. He reaches past him into the drawer and pulls out a bright red first-aid leech. "I want to check you over, just to make sure you're okay."

"Al-alright."

Jedrek attaches the leech to Dal's arm and watches it deflate. After a few minutes, he checks a datapad; the medical nanos report that Dal is physically unhurt. The damage is emotional.

Nothing could justify this treatment of a boy...and yet, Jedrek knows that this incident could be the key to saving *Maria Theresa* and millions of future Dalberts. "Listen, Dal, you've done nothing wrong. You have nothing to be ashamed of. A bully picked on you, that's all. Do you understand that?"

The boy sniffs. "If you say so."

"I do say so. And you were very brave to come tell me. You did the right thing. Now about Gerda...she's got to know."

"She'll be mad at me. I-I stole a gig."

"Nonsense, she'll be proud of you for doing the right thing. She isn't going to think any less of you, believe me. We have to get those vermin off your ship and out of this system as soon as we can—in order to do that Gerda has to know."

Wet eyes look up at him. "Will you tell her?"

"If you want me to."

"Please." The trank is taking effect; Dal is turning to soft mush in Jedrek's arms. He eases the boy down on Sting's bunk and, keeping one hand on Dal's cheek, he punches the intercom with the other. "Cilehe, I want to use one of our boats."

"Number two is ready for launch."

"Thanks. And send Sting down to our cabin, will you? I'll need him to pilot for me."

This time Jedrek remembers to take his laser knife.

❀

Sting pilots the boat, while Dal sleeps in a rear crash couch. Jedrek frowns. "The Ebettor are scum. I can't believe one of them would do this."

Sting shrugs. "From what I know of them, it makes a

perverse kind of sense."

"How so?"

"I told you, they use sex for status and power. In their society, sex goes downhill from higher-status individuals to lower-status ones. Dal is the lowest-status person on *Outbound*."

"But he's just a child."

"I agree it's heinous. But that doesn't mean the same thing to us as to them. Their children are brought to maturity pretty quickly."

"Sting, you can't be defending those monsters."

"No, of course not. You're right, they're scum. Their whole society is based on this kind of status-based domination. It's awful."

Jedrek nods. "Well, with any luck, we can prevent them from spreading that society."

❀

"Boat, identify yourself."

"This is Jedrek nor Talin and I have important words for your Captain."

"This is Captain Lübchen," Gerda's voice says.

"Gerda, this is a highly personal matter of greatest concern to all of us. Will you please cut that defense screen and let me in?"

The defense screen fades. "Come ahead. Dock at airlock six on our starboard side."

Sting plays with the controls, tracks for a green-outlined rectangle on *Outbound's* side, and in minutes the boat is docked. Motioning Sting to move ahead of him, Jedrek lifts Dal's sleeping form and carries him through the airlock. Two security personnel wait for them. Sting looks them both over very obviously and cooly. "Our business is with your Captain," he says, in a tone far more serious than any Jedrek's ever heard him use, "And you're well advised to take us to her without any delay."

"What have you done to the boy?"

"That's for us—"

"Quiet, Sting. Dalbert is asleep. If you want to find out more you'll have to ask Captain Lübchen after we've spoken with her."

Gerda steps out of a dropshaft. "I'm here, Jedrek. You've upset our sched—what's wrong with Dal?"

"Sleeping. Gerda, it's not that I don't trust your crew, but I don't trust *anyone* at this point. Could you come into our boat?"

"Surely."

"But Captain—"one of the security men starts.

Gerda touches a stud on the wall. "Commander Messer, you have the conn." She follows Jedrek into the boat. As the airlock closes behind her, she puts her hands on her hips. "What is this about?"

Jedrek sets Dal down in an acceleration couch. The cabin boy twists in sleep and cries out, then grasps Jedrek's hand and settles down.

"One of the Ebettor gunners you've given free run of this ship broke into Dal's cabin and raped the boy."

"Mein Gott! No!"

"If you want to wake him, he can tell you himself."

"No, I believe you." She kneels next to the boy, puts her hand on his neck. "Damn. I promised his parents I would take care of him, and now…."

"Gerda, you know what you have to do."

"Bloody right I know. I don't even have to consult Fleet Headquarters for this—there's precedent enough. He's a citizen of the Imperium…." She stands; Jedrek watches the color drain from her face. "If they think they can get away with this—" She forces a breath. "Jedrek, thank you. You are a true friend."

"I try."

She picks up Dal; he turns and puts his arms around her

neck. She smoothes his hair. "I'll be back in touch—right now I have a lot of work to do." The boat's airlock opens before her; as soon as her foot touches Credixian deckplates she is shouting orders. "We are now in alert condition crimson. Security, round up those aliens and send them back where they came from. If they co-operate, give them their pressure suits. First Officer, draft a provisional declaration of war against the Ebettor. And get me Telepath."

The hatches slide shut and Jedrek turns to Sting. "Let's get back home. We have our work as well."

"What makes you think I'm on your side, Jedrek?"

"For one thing, the murder in your eye when someone says the word 'Ebettor.'"

"I just don't like to see children hurt."

"Maybe that's what it's all about, Sting. Take us home."

❋

29
The Circle Broken
[CIRCLE]
6484 CE

When Jedrek and Sting return to *Worldsaver*, everyone is clustered about the central datasphere in the control room. There are two spots left.

This time, Jedrek doesn't even try to frame objections in his mind. If they are to meet, if they are to salvage anything from the Circle and the Library, it must be on the common ground that they inhabited for so many years. He pats Sting's bottom and the lad scoots into position. Then Jedrek moves forward...and pauses, his hand centimeters from the sphere.

Olympia, Dal, Gerda, Denys....

He moves his hand, cupping his palm against cool plastic.

There is a tangible shock, and almost he is tempted to pull his hand back...but he knows if he doesn't maintain contact now, he can never go back to it.

Swimming through endless data, pages and volumes and kilometers of holos streaming past him, Jedrek senses five other minds: minds torn apart with battling. Then he is caught up in the storm of emotion and intellect, of pain and anger and stubbornness, and the control room of *Worldsaver* wavers and is gone.

The largest Library in the Galaxy, hundreds of kilometers of shelves loaded with volume upon volume. And in this Library, a great whirlwind personified, a discordant clash of wills that tears books from the impeccable shelves and throws them at random, trying to break itself apart on the shoals of long-ago knowledge. Someone else's mental image pervades the sphere, and for the first time in his life Jedrek is not fully in charge of the data in the Library.

"Stop it!" he screams. At the same time, echoing his words, he hears a shout in Drisana's strained voice: "You're tearing the Library apart!"

How have they come to this?

A packet of data in this sphere, a minuscule corner between opposing shelves, contains all the records of *Worldsaver*, all the data Gerda gave them about Credix, all of Drisana's observations about *Maria Theresa*. Jedrek finds himself thrown by the swirling wind, dropped into this packet, surrounded by swimming chaotic images. The crowds of Teerell, the spires of the Imperator's Palace on Credix, their first sight of *Maria Theresa* framed by *Worldsaver's* control panel and six wondering faces....

Throw it all away, Jedrek.

He shakes his head, draws himself slightly back from the datasphere. He almost feels sparks of electricity between his palm and the sphere. This isn't right. The Library is no place to vent their feelings. It is far worse, now, than the worst days years ago, when the Circle broke up. Think what he will about Drisana and her obsessions, it is a blasphemy to run rampant through the stacks of the Grand Library. If they never agree on another thing as long as they live, at least he and Drisana have to agree on this.

With his free hand he reaches through crowded bodies until his fingers close about Drisana's shoulders. Then he feels her answering grip on his own, and the turmoil within the sphere begins to quiet.

Heaving a sigh of relief, he pulls back.

He hears a sound like a cosmic thunderclap, and as one the members of the Circle withdraw their hands from what is suddenly only a tiny clear ball floating in the center of the control room.

Drisana releases her hold upon him. She faces the group. "We have a decision to make. Jedrek, we heard what Captain Lübchen has done. She's asked us to declare ourselves for one side or another, for Credix or Geled."

Kedar's face is strained—he looks much older than he ever did. Jedrek thinks, with a shock, that Kedar is a dozen years older than himself. He remembers how incomprehensible

Kedar's life had been when he first joined the Circle as a youngster...years brought them closer in age. "I don't see that we should get involved. We are having enough trouble deciding where we stand in relation to *Maria Theresa*—Jedrek, I must say that you've complicated the issue immensely."

"I don't see any question of where we stand," Jedrek says. Calm, he tells himself, shouting will help nothing. "We can't condone what the Ebettor did. And if Geled is going to stand by them, then we've got to stand against Geled."

Drisana's lips are white. "I think you are all losing sight of why we are here. We are not a court of judgement, we are not a great military power looking for spoils, we are not the avenging angels trying to make sure that Right prevails. We are a Library Circle, trying to repair the Relay and get away so we can carry on our business."

Calm. "Your trouble, Drisana, is that you see everything from one perspective...repairing the Relay. I don't think you even realize that there are larger issues at stake here." Jedrek throws up his hands. "You can't mean to tell me that any of you think we should side with *Geled*?" There is no answer. "Well, then, we side with Credix."

Sukoji frowns. "I hate to remind you, but *I'm* not going to side with anyone except the Aetorian League. We each have a home world and a home system now, and if this is going to escalate into a Galactic war I think we all ought to stand with the places we call home. If it doesn't touch Aetor, well, then, I will stand neutral."

"Cilehe?"

"Jedrek, I don't want to side with anyone. I don't want to fight. Who are these people, and what do their concerns mean to me?" She shrugs. "If you remember, I was against this expedition. If attacked, I will defend my ship—that's as far as I'll go."

"Sting?"

The boy narrows his eyes. He looks to Drisana, then back

to Jedrek. Finally, wordlessly, he moves to Drisana's side and floats defiantly.

"Why?"

Sting touches the datasphere. "Do you know what this is? Have you ever thought about it, or did you just take it for granted? This is the greatest culmination of knowledge we've ever had. With this information we can build a new Empire, or renovate the old one, or all go off in a hundred different directions and find out what we can see. But for the few of us and Sayyid Drisana's single-mindedness, this might very well be forgotten and ultimately lost. Do you want to take the responsibility for *that*?"

"I see." Five faces, five voices, five opinions. And Jedrek remembers eleven years ago, near an identical datasphere, facing four opinions and saying the hardest words of his life. This time, at least, it will be easier—if nothing else, there's precedent.

"I'm leaving."

"For cosmos' sakes, Jedrek—"

"No, Drisana, I have had it. I should have known you wouldn't be any better, should have known that nothing ever changes. Well, I allowed myself to get caught up in your destructive games and the passions of the rest of you...but now I'm saying goodbye, and that's it."

Drisana pulls herself to her full height and crosses her arms over her chest. "Go ahead." He voice is close to panic. "Go, leave, get out again and leave us all stranded. You did this to me once before, Jedrek nor Talin, and I lived through it. You broke the Circle and took away the only people I ever cared for, and you left me alone on Terra to cry myself to sleep for a solid year. But I lived, and I kept the Library going. *I don't need you*, do you hear me? I got along without you before, and I can do it again. Because I'm strong, and I can live through anything you throw at me. So go away, and help your blind people in the big ship, or fight your battles, or sail away and join the Galactic Riders. I don't care what you do, because I'll get along without you!" Her eyes are red, her hair straggled, and tears puddle in the air around her face.

He would have liked to have the last word, but he could think of nothing...and if he stays any longer, the lump in his throat will blossom and he might change his mind. Blindly Jedrek turns and moves as quickly as he dares to the hangar deck.

❁

Olympia Marvelous seems actually happy to see him. "I glad am, that you for us stood up, Jedrek nor Talin of Terra."

"Borshall," he corrects. No, try not to think of that. He doesn't know if he will ever see Borshall again. What will Denys think? Will he be able to finish the project without Jedrek?

Why doesn't he care?

"Borshall, then. We glad will be, you with us to stay. Give you will I, a suite in the *Maria Theresa* itself."

"Queen Olympia, there's going to be war. Geled and Credix will fight one another, and Geled will try even harder now to get the Relay, to summon reinforcements. I guess the same goes for *Outbound*. I'm afraid that I'm nothing more than a bad-luck charm to your people."

"Nonsense."

He stirs, reaches for his data marble. "I have information here that may help you. I can teach you how to beef up your defense screens, and possibly we can get the parts to build a gravity warp. That would at least help even the odds."

"Jedrek—Know you how, the Relay to fix, no?"

"I do."

"So much easier would it be, for you if you it fixed. Credix and Geled at war are now...the Relay fixing, no longer their Union would bring about."

"I don't suppose you've ever heard of the god Brandix, but you're playing his advocate. All right, I'll play." He forces a smile. "First point, we can't be sure that Credix and Geled are going to stay angry at one another. Putting their governments in contact through the Relay makes it much more likely that they will patch up their differences. Second point, Geled and the Ebettor are just as much a threat to the Galaxy without Credixian help. Third and most important, to fix that Relay I would have to face T'to Yachim and tell him what I'm doing and why...and I'm sure I couldn't come up with a compelling reason."

"But you your home are giving up, a chance taking, of killed getting in a war that your own is not, when so much easier it would be...."

"Don't try to pretend to me that you think that way, Olympia. If you do, then all my work on your behalf is useless."

She smiles. "If of us survive any, your name sung will be, eternally in legend."

"I'd be satisfied just to be an excuse for lifting glasses and making merry on Teerell."

"So shall it be."

"If," he says with a wry grin, "We survive."

❖

30
Wartime
[MARIA THERESA/RIDER]
Day 513 of the reign of Her Magnificence,
Olympia Marvelous VII;
Galactic Revolution 561.19775508

Not enough time.

Jedrek paces *Maria Theresa's* bridge and worries. On all sides, viewscreens show the progress of his various defense projects...though perhaps, he thinks, "lack of progress" is a better term.

The Geledis have already made two abortive Geledi attacks on *Maria Theresa*, one foiled only through the intervention of T'to Yachim's ship. It won't be too much longer before the real war starts, and Jedrek can't get things ready by then. Everything takes time: time to train Theresan techs, time to gather materials, time to wrench effective weapons out of chaos. And meanwhile a population of seven hundred million is in danger.

Maybe he should concentrate on defense screens, rather than offensive weapons. But no, that's not effective military strategy. The Imperial Formation Wars demonstrated that lesson. Any defense screen can radiate only so much energy, and then it gave up. Ships outside the screen access unlimited energy—starlight, fusion, galactic magnetic flux—while the generators inside rely entirely on their reactors. None could survive a siege under a defense screen; at worst, the best screens he can build will only prolong the agony.

Still, unless he comes up with something, the weakly-held screens around most Theresan areas will collapse at the first hit.

Jedrek sits in an acceleration couch and rests his head in his hands. No way around it, no way at all. He rolls his data marble between his palms, desperately searching for some way out. All the technology of the Empire is here, plus refinements introduced by the Credixian Imperium and Borshall, plus the morsels Sting was able to steal from the Ebettor. Surely somewhere in that morass are plans for some new superweapon that will send Geled's ships back where they came from, that will guarantee the freedom of *Maria Theresa* forever. It works that way in all the holodramas.

There is no superweapon. Glimmers of hope, perhaps. The Ebettor have taken Imperial tachyon vesicle technology far beyond what the Empire knew...a competent physicist might be able to deduce all manner of new principles. Some of the equations have singularities that seem to hint at teleportation, for example, or maybe duplication of matter across interstellar distances. But Jedrek is not and never will be a competent physicist, and so the hints and promises must remain merely that.

And meanwhile two warships are ready to pound at *Maria Theresa* with everything they have, and Jedrek can do nothing.

He pulls himself out of the couch, triumphant over lethargy one more time. Maybe T'to has some ideas.

❖

The minute after her shift starts, Irina knows there's going to be trouble. When she reads the orders on her screen, she clenches her fists and frowns. There is to be a full-scale attack against one of the *Maria Theresa* settlements today, an attack coordinated with *Painbird* and ending up with a two-pronged assault on the Credixian ship. How soon, she thinks, allies became enemies.

Kassov wears the insigniae of a Commodore now; *Painbird* arrived with a field promotion for him and he is now provisional director of the Maria Theresa Territory, as well as commander of all Geled forces within fifty parsecs. Which means *Deathcry* and *Painbird*. Irina steals a glance at him as he converses with the Captain of the sister ship...she searches his face, not sure what she's looking for but not finding it. It was not that he was a bad man, or inhuman . . . that would be easier to understand. No, in the final analysis he's nothing more than another person doing the job assigned him. His face shows neither sympathy nor anger nor hate—it echoes only boredom. When all is said and done, she supposes that Kassov does what he does for the same reasons she herself carries out *her* orders...because it's too much trouble to change.

Their best demographic information says there were over six million people in the target area. She knows now that they are not aliens, but Humans like herself—Humans like every other, doing *their* jobs and living their lives in near-total disregard for the universe around them. And now that universe is going to swoop down in fusion flame and laser fire, and they will be forcibly and fatally reminded that there are others.

How did I become *other*?

No. It has to end somewhere. Some time. This is the time.

"Commodore Kassov?"

Kassov looks up in surprise. His expression shows clearly what he thinks of being interrupted in mid-conversation. "What is it, Gunner?"

She takes a deep breath. "Sir, I'm afraid I can't carry out my orders."

"What?" All noise on the bridge stops. Eyes go to her, to Kassov. With the clarity that strikes in mid-disaster, Irina sees Rur roll his eyes and turn his head. There is no returning now.

"I'd like to state on record that I morally cannot follow orders to attack innocent bystanders."

"Gunner, do you know what you're saying?"

"Da, Sir, I think I do. I'm going to be court-martialed, aren't I? I imagine I'll finish this tour of duty in the brig." And what will she do? There are people who help those like her...that ancient sect, the Brandixians, don't they specialize in defending moral causes?

"Do you know," puter translates an Ebettor remark, "What *we* do to our people who do not follow orders?"

"I really don't care." How can she be finding the courage to say all this? But now that it's begun, she finds it much easier to keep going. "I know what's done on my world, and I know that I will be given a fair trial." And maybe, just maybe, they'll begin to question what we did here, and maybe someone will take a closer look at our policies.

I doubt it. But maybe, she thinks. The hope will have to be enough.

A uniformed man with the red Security sash claps manacles around her wrists, and she allows herself to be led off the bridge.

She thinks she sees admiration in Rur's eyes just before the bridge door slide shut.

❀

T'to Yachim is unhelpful. "I don't know enough technology," he tells Jedrek. "Somewhere, on Nephestal I think, there are people who build ships and make weapons—but I don't know how to do it and I don't know who could help you in time."

"Blast. I feel so discouraged. I can't do a thing to help."

"You are doing things. You're doing the best you can."

Jedrek looks around the Relay's control room. It is a large space, about twenty meters across; freestanding consoles jut from every available surface, each with its own complex control panel. On one wall an open access hatch shows a corridor that leads into the very guts of the Relay, the black boxes that are now so useless. Data moves in Jedrek's mind, his fingers unconsciously twitch—he could fix those black boxes.

"I thought I had stopped a war, T'to. Now I find it's going to happen no matter what I do."

T'to Yachim leans sideways in the Human-shaped chair;

how uncomfortable must it be for a Dorascan? "A long time ago, oh, a few hundred Galactic Revolutions of Nephestal, the Iaranori thought they had stopped war. They had an Empire, very like yours except that it didn't control the entire Galaxy. Their colonization hadn't gotten that far. Fewer planets were fit to support life then. Anyway, the stories say that there was a long period of peace, a Pax Iaranori I suppose you would call it. They built a lot of good buildings, and made some pretty decoration and stumbled on some pretty nice music. And their biologists made efforts to breed aggressiveness out of their race.

"Well, this Empire lasted a good long time, but it didn't get much larger, and the Iaranor didn't respond when the hostile Core cultures made some forays into the Scattered Worlds. Soon their Empire began to crumble around the edges, simply from entropy.

"Finally the Emperor—an Iaranori named Takonnen—took action. He undid what the biologists had done, reintroduced aggressive tendencies, bred a whole planetload of atavistic Iaranori."

"There's a lesson in here somewhere, isn't there?"

"Does a Galactic Rider ever tell a story without a lesson? Just listen. Under their chieftain, Batydded, these new Iaranori supernovaed forth and, in a generation of bloody war, doubled the size of the Empire until it embraced every Iaranori in the Galaxy. Batydded herself led expeditions against the Core Worlds, toppled their structure of government, and removed Core military influence for millions of years." T'to twists and, apparently more comfortable, continues. "That generation of Iaranori produced works of visual arts, symphonies, plays and literature that have dazzled all subsequent civilizations. Ismallia, Batydded's capital, is still one of the most impressive worlds in the Galaxy."

"What happened next?"

"Their Empire, like yours, fell apart into warring factions. The Iaranori live longer than your people, but they do not live slower—Batydded survived to see her Empire fall apart and the Iaranori went through hundreds of generations of ignoble strife before they finally reached true racial maturity."

"So what's the lesson, T'to?"

"I don't know, friend. I wish I did. Maybe it would make living in this universe a whole lot more bearable."

"Thanks a lot."

"Everyone wants to find the solution to the problem of war. Your race is only one of many that's had their chance. And there are indications that you are started on the road to racial maturity." T'to sighs. "Every race that's been through the chaos necessary for maturity looks back on their youth, when things were cruder, when there was war and passion and furies that moved the stars, and universally we sigh and wish that somehow it could be that way again. I tell you truthfully, it isn't particularly pleasant to contemplate Human boots walking on worlds that Dorasc first settled, or Human ships using tachyon vesicles that we first found in space and used in our own engines."

For a moment Jedrek is conscious of the winds of time and the currents of the Galaxy moving about him. It's a consciousness he sometimes experiences when contemplating the full sweep of records in the Library. Without quite knowing why, he puts a hand on the Dorascan's skin. "I'm sorry, T'to."

"No matter. Change is the rule of the universe, and I have known pleasures that you cannot begin to imagine."

"You said that my race was on the way to maturity. What did you mean?" He gestures at the various viewscreens that show *Maria Theresa's* habitats and the ships that might destroy them. "We don't seem to be doing a very good job right here."

"The Elders on Nephestal know more than I do. I think the key to your peoples' maturity lies in what you call space settlements. Pocket environments, like the ones here. Where a large but manageable number of people have to deal together with a fragile environment. Your troublemakers, your malcontents, your destructive individuals who cannot handle their aggressive instincts...they are slowly being bred out as more and more of your people reside in settlements. There is no place there for a person who could endanger the whole community by one reckless act."

"You think settlements are taming us?" Jedrek laughs. "Sting was born on a settlement, and I'd like to see you make the suggestion to him."

"He is violent, yes, and aggressive—but I have not seen him be self-destructive, nor destructive of others without cause." T'to shrugs. "I am no mathematician, and the sociology of your people is said to be among the most difficult. So maybe I am not competent to say. I do know that the most successful Human Galactic Riders were born of settlement stock. I think that the future of your people lies with those of the settlements."

"You think the rest of us planetbounds are going to kill one another off, is that it?"

The Rider does not reply.

"That's all very wonderful, but it doesn't help us here and now."

"Agreed. You certainly do not have five hundred generations to wait for your people to become mature. Our whole situation here would be rather academic."

"So what do we do now, T'to?"

The Rider claps him on the shoulder. "We do what we must, Jedrek—as always. We do what we must. And we hope that's enough."

❁

from The *Rise of Culture*
in the First Human Galactic Interregnum
by Maarten Travesh; Nephestal, 26,500 H.E.

...Terran Empire techs and engineers designed and built their infrastructure for the very long term. Unfortunately for succeeding civilizations, they built *too* well.

Imperial technology, especially tech involved with vital infrastructure, was constructed to be durable, failsafe, and self-repairing. A rule of thumb among Imperial engineers was that machinery should be designed for at least a thousand-year operational lifespan; in many cases, machinery continued to function long beyond that range. Even after ten millennia, it was common to find abandoned or depopulated First Empire ships or settlements in perfect working order.

The most fragile tech was that involving the Ultrawave Effect—antigrav, tachyon phase, ultrawave, and defense screens. All based on the one item that the Empire could neither create nor manufacture, but only find naturally occurring in deep space: the delicate tachyon vesicle. And even so, tachyon vesicles in operation under minimal strain could easily last millennia.

It's obvious why the Empire would be so careful with vital infrastructure; however, the very longevity of Imperial technology proved to be a drag on the development of civilizations during the eight-millennia-long Interregnum. Rather than innovate and develop their own standards and solutions, societies tended to stick with established Imperial tech, maintaining the vast installed base of functioning equipment.

Not until midway in the eighth millennium CE, when enough Imperial infrastructure had broken down, did science and technology begin once more to move ahead in the Galaxy.

❖

31
Question
[TERRA]
6484 CE

The sight that meets Drisana's eyes is not a pretty one. Death never is.

She is still not quite awake. Sukoji's call pulled her out of a dream...no, more of a memory...a walk in the park with the Circle, back on Terra when they were all younger and Jedrek had not soured things.

Jedrek—!

"How did it happen?" She tones down the brightness of her cabin's viewscreen. What was the rock and ice of Styriin is now a blazing mass of fusion flame, and looking into it is like staring at the surface of a star.

She wonders if many of the Theresans were looking at it, and if they are blind now. It doesn't really matter.

"*Painbird* and *Deathcry* took up tight orbits around Styriin and kept up a laser barrage until the defense screen failed. They might have left it at that." Cilehe's voice is bitter. "They would have died soon enough when the atmosphere escaped. I guess Kassov wanted dramatic pictures to show back home. Those were worldcracker fusion bombs."

Drisana scales down the brightness once again. "Why doesn't it fade?"

"Pressure screens. They launched pressure screen generators. I suppose they want to make sure none of the Theresans miss the sight."

Well, *that's* hardly likely. Light from Styriin fills Theresan space like the emanations of a pocket sun. Be the first in your system, she thinks, to have your own private dwarf star. Plasma will dance at your command.

She switches off the viewscreen. "Thanks for telling me. I'm going back to sleep."

"Aren't you at all curious? Don't you want to know if

Jedrek was caught in that?"

Drisana's body betrays her; she bites her pillow and hopes Cilehe doesn't hear her gasp. A deep breath. "I don't give a crap, really."

"Well, he's all right. He was with the Galactic Rider when it happened. No thanks to you."

Drisana shuts off the intercom and settles down in her bunk. She thumbs the lights off, but still there is no darkness. From somewhere behind her eyeballs, the hot white light of what was Styriin burns through her skull. Six million people.

So, it isn't nice. Cosmos, no one wants millions to die. (Are any of them among the crowd she saw that day on Teerell? The woman with the allergic child, are her atoms swimming around stripped of their electrons? The man with business problems, did his troubles end in a wind of flame?) It is a sad fact of life that war means casualties, and if one starts to shed tears for all the innocents who died, one would be at it from now until the last calorie of heat warmed the last pinch of cosmic dust.

What of all the millions—billions—who died in the Empire's Formation Wars? Did the survivors complain, years later when they were guaranteed regular and healthy food shipments, instant communication, and a standard of living that had never been matched in the Galaxy? What of the billions who died on Karphos and in all the other defeats of a shrinking Empire at war with its rebellious daughter states? Did anyone shed tears for them when their lives bought a few extra years of Imperial rule, a few more lives of happiness?

Student of history as she is, Drisana knows that no corpse ever complained of its manner of death, and its survivors, no matter how grief-stricken, somehow managed to live on and even, eventually, to laugh again.

Jedrek is okay. She shouldn't care, she realizes. Everyone thinks she doesn't. No...maybe Sting knows. But Sting is avoiding her, avoiding everyone in the Circle, staying away from the ship and from all company. She is going to lose

Sting, after this is all over. Very well, let him go. Terra is full of young men and women who would be proud to take on Library work.

Sting is a good Librarian, devoted to his work and even more devoted to his boss—but she is never completely comfortable with him. She will feel better, actually, with him gone.

No, that's silly. Sting's company took her through awful years. Sting kept her alive that terrible morning when she discovered that the Library was not receiving a signal from Eironea, that they were finally and irrevocably off the air. His loss would be a terrible blow, and she would miss him dreadfully.

He spent too much time with Jedrek. Come to think of it, Jedrek probably poisoned Sting's mind, told the boy lies about her, made him—

Fusion light blares from behind her eyes, and Drisana twists on her bunk and gnaws her pillow helplessly. Jedrek, oh Jedrek! How did I lose you? How can I get you back?

And he probably doesn't even think about her, probably hadn't given her a single passing thought in all his years with the Independent Traders and then on Borshall.

She dials up the lights, opens her trunk. There at the top is her prize possession, given her by her own Head Librarian: a true paper book, a copy of some obscure religious document bound in supple priceless leather, the pages yellowed but still readable. Tireless nanos constantly work to preserve and repair the volume, so it has remained intact across the millennia. In the back of the book, where there were many blank pages, each Head Librarian had written his or her name with stylus and ink...her own flowing "Drisana Hardel," practiced for weeks before the actual signing, is the two hundred eighteenth.

She flips the pages, the book falls open. Pressed between its pages, its fragrance still clinging and reminiscent of the day she'd pressed it, is a Terran rosebud. The flower is now wrinkled and brown, and feels much drier than the brittle pages around it.

Jedrek....

There is a way...but she will never do it, never give up this book and the trust it implies. If billions of lives are nothing compared to the existence of a Galactic Empire, if millions of lives are nothing to two great star-spanning societies—then what is *one* life when measured against the legacy of the Human race?

She is Drisana Hardel, Head Librarian of the Terran Grand Library, and she will never forget it.

She puts the book away lovingly, turns out the lights, and drifts into a sleep peopled by ghosts of happier times.

❖

32
Union?
[CREDIX 5]
CI 4331

All links are in place. Somewhere, in an audience chamber on Credix, a telepath faces the Imperator and all His gathered ministers. That telepath relays what he witnesses to *Outbound's* mindreader; and here, in the privacy of the Captain's cabin, the old woman shows Gerda what she sees and hears.

Gerda never had an audience with the Imperator, never saw Him as anything but a face on the holoscreen and a distant figure at parades. This isn't the same as a face-to-face meeting—but it's the nearest thing she's ever likely to have.

Telepath straightens her neck, the lines of her face seem to smooth a bit, and her eyes open wide and serious. Gerda knows she is looking into the reflected face of her Imperator, and she bows. "Your Majesty."

"Put yourself at ease, Captain Lübchen," Telepath sys in a voice an octave too deep. "You must feel completely free to speak your mind. This is not a hearing, nor a formal session of the Cabinet. We are here merely to determine our course of action in your unique circumstances, and you are the one best able to tell us what your conditions are."

"Thank you, Lord and Master."

"Very good." Telepath turns, and Gerda has the strange feeling that she surveys a room much larger than the tiny cabin. Her eyes settle on a point that, in *Outbound*, would be three meters beyond the wall in the middle of the First Officer's cabin. "Councilor von Keimer, please tell Captain Lübchen what you've learned."

Telepath's face twists; Gerda gets the impression that she is trying to gain thirty kilos. Her voice is now somewhat higher.

"In the absence of the Ultrawave Relay we have other ways to keep in touch with outlying stations. The telepathic relay system. Our ships carry messages between worlds. Let me give you some of the facts our intelligence agents have observed in areas of tangential concern to the Imperium."

Telepath riffles imaginary datapads. "The Duchy of Elendan reports border skirmishes with Kellia. Our Kellian agents tell us that Kellia is suffering raids from someplace called Zinnberg, which is in the Geledi sphere of influence. Another example: troops of Neordan, under the pressure of Gotlanian attacks, have started inspecting trade vessels from nearby states friendly to the Imperium. Agents in Gotlan report that the government has taken this action following several attacks from Lathyros—again a state under Geledi influence—and Bosip. So far we have no word from Bosip, but I think when it arrives it will show that Bosip, too, is under pressure from an ally of Geled."

Back to the Imperator. "Councilor von Keimer is too wordy. The conclusion of all these examples is that your entire sector of the Galaxy is suddenly in turmoil, both military and political."

"The government of Ordes has fallen and been replaced by a new one hostile to the Imperium," von Keimer says.

Gerda leans forward, fascinated despite her anxiety at being a part of the innermost debates. "Obviously you think Geled is deliberately causing all this upset."

"Puter simulations, based on the scanty data we have, indicate a high probability that the Geledi war machine has been engaged, and that these skirmishes throughout the region will only grow worse. Many of the governments in the affected sector are strong and well able to resist Geledi might at first, but in the long range we may face trouble. Five hundred, a thousand years from now, will be too late for the Imperium to make contact with a strong Geled in command of a quarter of the Galaxy."

Telepath's face shifts again, and Gerda feels the gaze of some unidentified minister. "At all costs the Imperium must maintain a buffer zone of friendly states around our borders.

It is the only way to ensure our survival in a war-stricken Galaxy."

The present Buffer Zone, Gerda knows, is almost seven kiloparsecs deep, and has served to protect and isolate Credix since the last days of the old Empire. How much more do they want?

But it's a big Galaxy, filled with big people carrying big weapons. Who knows when some strong state from across the Galaxy would come sweeping through allies and try to conquer Credix itself?

"Forgive me for being so blunt, Lord and Master. I am only a Captain, and we are short of manpower here; I have a lot of other business to attend to. We *are* on a war footing, if you remember." Gerda does her best to keep impertinence out of her voice.

The Imperator smiles. "Quite right. How we need a voice like yours at these sessions, Captain." Telepath moves her head a fraction of a centimeter closer. "We've come up with several conclusions, which are borne out by our puter sims. First, if Geled continues making war, the dissatisfaction will only spread until it reaches our Buffer Zone and ties the Zone up in knots. Second, Geled knows where we are and has already tested our strength in confrontation with your ship—they are apt to perceive us as a threat and make it their goal to wipe us out." Telepath closes her eyes, reopens them. "Thus we have developed the following recommendations. One: Be it resolved and enacted that friendship with Geled is considered of vital importance to the security of the Imperium. Two: In order to carry out this policy, all declarations of war against Geled and the agents of Geled are now unilaterally revoked."

"Your Highness—"

"Three: A diplomatic task force is being assembled here on Credix to deal with Geled in consideration of a future Union between our two powers."

"But...." A look from the Telepath silences her; she is, after all, only a Captain.

"Four: In order to foster communication between our civilizations despite the vast and hostile gulf between them, you are ordered to see to it that Relay Alpha is repaired as soon as possible. This matter is assigned highest priority."

"What about the Theresans?"

"We will, of course, expect you to minimize the risk of civilian casualties.'"

"With all due respect, Highness, millions are already dead. No matter what *we* do, the Geledis do not adhere to the same moral principles. I do not see how I can possibly carry out those orders."

"The Credixian Imperium does not, of course, wish to see lesser cultures endangered. However, when the choice is between the survival of a lesser culture and the survival of the Imperium, there can be no other decision."

Gerda feels herself losing her temper. That will never do. "For Ancestors' sakes, it is nineteen kiloparsecs from Credix to Geled. For thousands of years neither one knew that the other even existed. How can you seriously believe that they are a threat to us, when they cannot even fight their way past less than a billion people in a converted pleasure cruiser?"

"Captain Lübchen, it is not your place to question the policies or decisions of your superiors." Telepath's face goes neutral for a moment, then lights up with the Imperator's countenance again. "I think it best if we send you a tactician. Fleet Headquarters will arrange a link through your telepath to Admiral Grau. If anyone can bring this action to a successful conclusion, it is she."

"Your Highness, I would like to state for the record that I do not approve of this meddling with my command."

"It is so recorded."

She feels all anger draining from her. They think they are doing right. Ancestors, maybe they are. How is she to know? And yet....

"One more question, Lord and Master. I cannot speak with my parents right now, and tradition says that you are the Father of us all. I need advice."

"I will do my best. The rest of the staff is dismissed."

"Lord and Master, what am I to tell the child? How am I to explain to him that we are making nice with the people who abused him? Father, you have not seen his tears, have not seen how he pulls back from even the most loving gesture. *I* have taken vows of command and I can understand that one must follow orders that may be personally distasteful—but Dal is young, and in his position I do not think the welfare of the Imperium a thousand years in the future matters much to him. Lord and Master, I fear that you will lose a subject and a son if he is not handled gently. *What am I to tell him?*"

Gerda wishes they were a kiloparsec closer, within range of Credix's Relay Zeta, so she could have a visual image. Only then could she be sure that she sees pain reflected on Telepath's face.

"Captain, do you suppose it would make things easier if I had a talk with the child?"

"With all respect, Majesty, I do not. In any case, he will not tolerate the presence of our ship's Telepath, so the question is academic." The Imperator has two children of His own, one a boy only a few years older than Dal.

"You will have to handle the lad on your own, Captain. I understand that you are an old family friend; I think you are in the best position to help him until he can be put into the care of our psych-techs here."

Gerda shakes her head. I have tried, she wants to cry out, tried to reach him and all I have run into is the awful memory that makes him quiver and turn away from me.

It is no use. She should have known better than to bring up the question. She bows her head. "I will do your bidding, your Highness."

The Telepath closes her eyes and folds in upon herself, signalling that the interview is over.

And why, Gerda asks herself, do I feel as if I have just put a knife through Dal's heart?

✿

33
Sanctuary
[MARIA THERESA/CREDIX]
Day 515 of the reign of Her Magnificence,
Olympia Marvelous VII
CI 4331

Ferdinand, Jedrek decides, is their best hope. The largest and most powerful of *Maria Theresa's* companion ships, it had all the equipment of a Terran Empire ship of the line, with a few extras thrown in. In its time *Ferdinand* was a shuttle for passengers, a Captain's Yacht for chartered side trips, and always protection for the mother ship. Now it will be the flagship of a navy.

Entering *Ferdinand* is like stepping back four thousand years to the High Days of the Empire. To Jedrek, the ship is surprisingly familiar—autoservants and mechs made sure that the battleship is as fresh today as it was when *Maria Theresa* set out on her final voyage. Food-synths are stocked, reactors in perfect repair and producing energy to their capacity, and all parts gleam.

In the engine room, Jedrek wrestles with an inspection plate, wrenches it off and shines his light into the cavity beyond. Coils and dark nodes, arching supports...and in the very center, an iridescent soap bubble aglow with its own inner light, sits one of the tachyon vesicles that power the ship.

He hates to do this—but it's necessary, and *Ferdinand* can function perfectly well with five antigravs rather than six. Alerting the ship's puter, he cuts power and feels the antigrav go dead as the vesicle's light fades.

He can build a gravity warp, he can install it as a weapon in *Ferdinand*—but it takes a tachyon vesicle. The only vesicles large enough are those in the antigravs that maintain the six—no, five now—habitats, and those in the ships. So it has to be the ship.

It is a truism that the limit to a Galactic society's size is the number and size of the ships that carry supplies from world to world. Hidden in *that* limit was the final check on Human expansion—the number of tachyon vesicles that could be found in cometary shells and pressed into service in antigravs, in defense screens, in ultrawave sets and tachyon converters.

He's come smack up against that check. Unless he wants to send ships out to prospect for vesicles...but no, prospecting is a full-time job.

He reaches in with gloved hands and carefully undogs the latches that hold the vesicle secure, then lifts the vesicle itself and hands it to a waiting autoservant. An iridescent bubble of unphased strange matter and frozen tachyons, totally inert—but when hit by coherent radiation of the right frequency, it can distort gravity, produce an ultrawave tone that could be modified to send instantaneous signals, and create in surrounding space lines of force that, put into motion around the proper axis, can generate a defense screen.

Zap it with the wrong laser frequency, pass it through too many shifting gravitational fields, and it will evaporate in an instant. How powerful and how fragile this thing upon which the hopes of *Maria Theresa* rest.

The autoservants are a huge help. They are, in their way, better than the barely-adequate Theresan techs. *Ferdinand's* puter controls repair functions of the servs and mechs, and the puter has four thousand years of experience with *Ferdinand*. It is not a sapient puter, nothing like the big Norns, Muspels or Lichtalfs of Borshall—but still it's smart and Jedrek has only to give it a few instructions before it is dragging parts out of forgotten storage lockers, almost anticipating his needs.

It's only later, during a meal break, while mechs work about him, that Jedrek has time to question.

Sure, he can build a gravity warp. And it might just be the secret weapon that would turn the tide in *Maria Theresa's* favor. If only it's used properly. Who will fly the ship, who will fire the warp at the appropriate instant? There are some pilots among the Theresans—Jedrek privately classes them with himself in ability. No ship under *Maria Theresa's* command has gone tripping between the stars for millennia, and their crews can't compete with experienced starhopping enemies.

"Someone at the primary airlock to see you, sir," an autoservant tells him.

Who...? Jedrek is alone in *Ferdinand*; he chased the ship's crew out during his refitting. Ah, well, any number of people might want to see him. Olympia, Dileene, any of the techs at work on his projects....

He wipes grease from his hands and hops a dropshaft to the level of the main airlock. The inner hatch stand open; inside the lock is a blank-eyed Dalbert.

"Dal, what's wrong?" Jedrek kneels before the boy and puts hands on Dal's shoulders. There are traces of tears on the lad's cheeks.

"I-I ran away."

"I can see that. Why?"

"Someone from home has taken over our ship. Telepath is doing all the talking, but it's some great tactician and Gerda has to follow her orders." He sniffs. "They brought *them* back, the Ebettor, and they're planning to attack Teerell next. With bio weapons." Sniff. "I couldn't stay. Not with th-the Ebettor aboard. Especially the way they looked at me. Ancestors forgive me, I just couldn't stay there."

"Hush." He holds the boy close; Dal breaks into sobs. "I can't say I blame you. A man can only take so much, Dal." So now it's *two* runaways, he thinks. Why not?

"Herr Jedrek, can I stay with you? Please? I have to stay with somebody, I'm not old enough and I don't know anyone. And I can't think of anybody else who would have me."

"Of course you can stay. I have a guest cabin aboard *Maria Theresa*, but I'm spending most of my time here. You're welcome to stay in either ship." He draws back and tousles the boy's hair. "I could use another pair of trained and willing hands."

"What are you doing? Everyone on *Outbound* has been wondering. You're driving that tactician from home into a spin—she doesn't know what to expect and Gerda told her you can do anything."

"I'm building a little of this and a little of that, and I hope to have this ship made over into a destroyer before long." How optimistic *that* sounds. "When have they scheduled the attack on Teerell?"

"No time set. They want to make maximum psychological impact, I heard them say. Geled wants to strike now."

Enough business talk. "Dal, does Gerda know where you are?"

The boy sticks out his lower lip. "No. I didn't tell her."

"Don't you think she should know?"

"She doesn't love me any more. She let those...she let *them* on the ship. She doesn't care."

Ah, what a simple thing are the hurt feelings of a child. If only he could be sure that his *own* feelings aren't equally simple. "She's worried about you, I know. I'm going to call her and tell her that you're safe with me."

Dal shrugs. "If you think that's best."

"I do. Now get your things and I'll have an autoservant show you where to stow them. Then come up to the bridge and be prepared to work."

Jedrek watches Dal vanish into the airlock, then turns to the bridge.

Why isn't there someone for *him* to run to?

●

Gerda is relieved. "You will send him back, will you not?"

Jedrek frowns. "I don't think he wants to go back. All due respect, and you know the boy better than I do, but right now I think he needs someone to trust. Someone that he knows he can put his faith in. Due to your circumstances and your duty, he feels somewhat betrayed by you."

"I could not—"

"Of course you couldn't do anything else. Asking a twelve-year-old to understand that is more difficult. I think its best for Dal if he stays here for a while."

"It is not safe."

"Nowhere within a parsec *is* safe." Jedrek sighs. "Tell you what I'll do, if you're that concerned about his safety, I'll turn him over to T'to Yachim. Surely you can't believe that a Galactic Rider would let a child come to harm?"

"No. Keep him yourself." She flushes. "I am sorry, Jedrek, I am under a lot of strain and I am not myself. I trust you...Ancestors know why, but I do. Take care of him—you will probably do a better job than I can."

Tension lines her face. She looks ten years older. It couldn't be easy, having your command taken out from under you and seeing terrible things done, things that went against your every—

"Gerda, how would you like a job?"

"What?"

"Can you scramble your circuit for privacy?"

"Scrambling." There is a break in the signal, Gerda's image dissolves into a billion little colored dots while *Ferdinand's* puter translates the scrambled signal.

"Gerda, I need a pilot and commander with experience. The ship isn't as powerful as *Outbound*, but I think it packs a few surprises you'd be happy with. How would you like to command the flagship of the *Maria Theresa* fleet?"

"Do you know what you are asking me to do? Resign my commission, say goodbye to home forever...I have a family, I have..." she trails off and looks straight into Jedrek's eyes. "You are serious, aren't you?"

"Totally."

She glances from side to side. "I promise, Jedrek, I will think about it. Seriously, I think."

"Make your decision soon, Captain. Or there may not be

anyone to welcome you when you get here." He frowns. "I don't suppose you can tell me when the attack on Teerell is scheduled?"

"I cannot."

He shrugs. Worth a try. "Listen, Gerda...I need a few more days. Can you have it postponed beyond that? For Dal's sake?"

"That is treason. You are presuming on a friendship. I *am* a Captain of the Imperium, after all." She closes her eyes. "How many days do you need?"

Jedrek thinks of the antigrav lying in tatters three decks below, of the many hours of serv and mech time necessary to build a gravity warp, of the sleepless nights..."Three?"

"I cannot promise. Signing off."

"Thanks, Gerda."

"Ancestors be with you." The screen goes dead.

Jedrek heaves a sigh, then starts tapping orders to the puter. There is still a lot to do.

❖

34
Persuasion
[TERRA/GELED]
6484 CE; GY 3216

In a vase near Sukoji's bunk are the remains of the rose Drisana sent her. Such a short time ago, can it all be true? From time to time as she works, Sukoji glances at the rose and frowns.

Displayed on her terminal are all the data she could gather about the Ultrawave Effect and Ultrawave Relays. Somewhere in this mass of numbers and symbols, Jedrek found the key to repairing Alpha. But where?

No use asking Sting if he'd given her all the information he gave Jedrek...she's questioned the lad three times already, and each time his answers are a little more abusive. She must assume that she knows everything Jedrek does.

Except...except whatever information Jedrek put into his data marble on Borshall. That has to be it. Looking at the equations, she can almost sense the shapes of missing pieces, where a few bits of data would show the way to a breakthrough.

Sukoji leans back in her chair and rubs her eyes. If anyone can reconstruct Jedrek's findings, it has to be he...she's the only one of the Circle with the requisite technical knowledge to even understand the equations.

Why? How many times has she asked herself why? Each time, the rose gives her a reason to go on. Drisana needs her. Drisana wants the Relay fixed, and Drisana's desire is like an eldritch energy that sets all space aflame. Sukoji has never really believed in anything, and she is sure she would never have the persistence to continue this task if it were only for herself...but in the presence of Drisana Hardel, one does not consider giving up.

With a shrug she turns back to her term. Maybe she can deduce the missing Borshallan pieces of the puzzle. Some kind of energy field is certainly involved, something that prevents large numbers of tachyon vesicles from interfering with one another. Say the words "Borshall" and "energy field" in the same sentence, and what comes to mind but the L-type pressure screens refined on Borshall in Imperial times. Is there anything in the pressure screen equations, something that would give her a clue when looked at the right way?

She knows she's on the right track—certain parts of those data were removed from the Library by the Empire for their blighted security reasons.

The intercom lights up with Drisana's face. "Sukoji, I'm sorry to disturb you but there's a boat here from the Geledi ships and they have requested to speak with all of us."

Sigh. "I'll be there right away. I'm not getting anywhere with this." She preserves all her work, then wipes the terminal and shut it off.

❂

The Geledi visitor is Kassov, the corpulent commander of *Deathcry*. A few stern-looking troops with wicked laser weapons accompany him. Sukoji is the last one into the dining room; as soon as she takes her seat between Drisana and Cilehe, Kassov begins.

"I would like to begin by expressing my sorrow that my ship has been the cause of misunderstanding in your ranks." He waves a hand. "You know how it is in war, things happen that sometimes one wishes would not."

Drisana puts her elbows on the table and leans across it toward Kassov. "No need to apologize, Commodore. You had virtually nothing to do with the incident."

"In any case, we *are* sorry." He wipes his brow; Sukoji notices that Cilehe has set the temperature a bit high in the dining room. Tumblers of ice water sit before the members of the Circle; there are none on Kassov's side of the table.

"Commodore Kassov, let's skip the chitchat and get to

business. You wouldn't leave your ship and come here in person without a good reason—tell us your reason and we'll tell you whether we agree."

"I can see that Terra has lost none of her legendary skill in diplomacy. I admire that, to be able to cut through all the extraneous—"

"Four tendays ago you never heard of Terra. Get on with it."

"Yes. My task force, which now includes the Credixian ship under independent command, has a goal that I believe you share. All other matters aside, we are here to repair Relay Alpha. I understand that this is *your* goal as well."

"Go on."

"We are certain that within the next few days we will be able to put a repair crew aboard the Relay. The operation goes well, and we think the Theresans will soon surrender."

"Kassov, say what you mean. They will all be dead soon. This will go much quicker once you realize that I never evade and do not cloud issues."

He smiled. "Forgive me. A starship captain sometimes has to learn—"

"I'm far more interested in your offer...which you have not yet made."

"Let me make it short, then. We are unable to fix the Relay. The Credixians do not have the necessary knowledge either."

"No surprise. Credix owns Relay Zeta and has not been able to repair it from minor damage a thousand years ago. That's why Zeta can't work up the signal strength to beam a message to Alpha."

"An interesting bit of data."

"Glad you enjoy it. Go on."

"Even our Ebettor friends do not have all the information they need to understand the Relay." He spreads his hands. "You possess the greatest store of data known to humanity. The scuttlebutt, indeed, says that one of your number has solved the problem of the Relay."

"Jedrek nor Talin is no longer with us. I'm sorry, I wish I could offer you his services."

"Nevertheless, you can still help us. Your Library has information that we can get no other way. If we all work together I am sure we could reconstruct the method of repair. All I ask is that one of you come with me to *Painbird*, where our techs are working closely with the Credixians." He narrows his eyes a bit. "Frankly, you are our only hope."

"You'll excuse us while we talk?" Drisana doesn't wait for an answer. She touches a stud on the arm of her chair and a privacy curtain shields their side of the table. The field allowed no sound to pass, and she covers her mouth with a hand in case any of the Geledis are lip readers.

"Sukoji? If it's to be any of us, it will be you."

Sukoji lowers her eyes. "I'm not getting anywhere on my own. Who knows what their techs have come up with? Of course I'll go."

Sting slaps the table. "I don't think it's a good idea."

Drisana locks eyes with the boy. "Good idea or not, it's the only way to get the Relay fixed."

He shrugs. "Do what you want. I'm only giving my opinion."

"Kedar, have *you* an opinion?"

"Eh? Send her. Go along, Sukoji, and luck be with you." He gives her a half-hearted smile. "I want to get this over with and get home."

Drisana nods, and drops the privacy curtain. "Sukoji will accompany you," she says.

Sting leaves the table.

❀

It is a short trip by gig to the Geledi ship *Painbird*. All the way Sukoji fingers her data marble. She dumped into it all the information she'd been studying before—she hopes it's enough. Well, if she needs anything she can always call

Worldsaver and have them feed her data directly from the Library.

The gig fits snugly into its berth, and the airlock opens. A number of uniformed crewmembers and two of the Ebettor wait beyond. She follows Kassov out of the gig, looking around curiously. Then, something trips her and she plunges forward into the arms of an Ebettor. It holds her tightly.

"Excuse me," she says. "Ouch. Let me go, please."

Kassov faces her with a smile. "Do you know how to repair the Ultrawave Relay?"

"No. I thought that's why I'm here." She struggles, but the Ebettor does not release her.

"And your associate, Jedrek nor Talin, *does* know how?"

"He says he does."

Kassov's smile broadens. "Good. Good."

"This isn't funny, you know."

"Of course not. Who said it would be?"

❀

Drisana paces. Four hours, and no word from Sukoji. It is not like her, to not report at least once.

She shakes her head. Anxious, that's all. After the Relay is fixed, she can put Library stations on Credix and Geled. Soon she'll need a larger staff, and after a while the Grand Library building will once more be filled with life. Maybe she can even start bringing people from other planets into the business.

Where is Sting? She hopes he isn't becoming like Jedrek. If there are going to be new staff members to train and supervise, she will need the lad's help.

Cilehe leans back in her couch (does the woman never sleep?) and announces, "Gig coming this way from *Painbird*, Drisana."

"Good. Lock it on."

"No, wait. They're just dropping a cargo pod. I'll send an

autoservant to pick it up." In minutes the serv is aboard with a meter-long cargo pod bearing the insignia of Geled. Kedar takes it from the autoservant and sets it on an empty couch.

The comm signals for attention. Cilehe answers, and an image of Kassov appears.

"Have you received our little gift yet?"

"We have not opened it, Commodore," Drisana answers.

"Do so, please. I'll wait."

Drisana nods, and Kedar opens the pod. It peels back automatically, and Kedar screams.

The pod contains a dismembered Human right arm. The lifeless palm is scribed with silver tracings....

"Sukoji." Drisana feels her stomach twist, quiets it with an effort. She turns back to Kassov, anger bursting in her gut. "What have you—?"

"She is still alive. In pain, but alive. She will remain that way until you send us Jedrek nor Talin to repair the Relay. We have run out of time, Sayyid Hardel, and we are not in the mood for further delay. Even as we speak our ships commence the final attack against the Theresans...when that attack is concluded and they have given up the Relay, we want nor Talin there to fix it. Deliver him and we will put Sukoji Boratte out of her...considerable misery."

Drisana can reply with nothing more than a cry of rage.

●

35
Reunion
[CIRCLE]
6484 CE

"Yeee'Haaa!"

The keening warcry cuts across all ultrawave circuits for kiloparsecs about. Six of *Worldsaver's* display screens light up with holos of a young Human male with very short dark hair crowned by a shapeless pseudoleather cap. Sting—his face split by a wide smile of sheer joy.

"What—?" Kassov turns away and the view shows what must be *Painbird's* bridge. The chubby Commodore goes white.

Drisana thumbs into the circuit. "Sting, what is going on here?"

"Look at your screens, Drisana."

She looks. Incredibly, unbelievably, *Deathcry* is accelerating away from the other two ships, moving in a wide circle that looks for all the world like the textbook plot of an ideal attack dive....

"Blast, he actually did it," Cilehe says. "He stole their ship."

Kassov faces Drisana with eyes ready to spring from their sockets. *"Give us back our ship!"*

With a smile Drisana closes the comm circuit, and Kassov's image fades.

❀

And yet another audience with the Imperator. The universe is so inside-out that Gerda is prepared to believe anything. The Imperator found out that she tried to delay the attack on Teerell, and she is being tried in absentia. They want Dal back to take punishment for jumping ship. Or...and this one worries Gerda most...in a fit of pique the Imperator has withdrawn the childbearing license for Margrethe and Lars, and their Union is off. She doesn't think the Imperator could with a stroke wipe out two families as long-standing as Lübchen and Ritter...but she's learned that in war all things are possible.

She looks at the orderly who brought the news, considers telling him that she cannot leave the bridge. It is a plausible excuse. Now that the Geledis dropped their blackmail bombshell, followed so closely by the Terran lad's capture of *Deathcry*, she needs to be alert and available. Anything could happen.

No, a summons from the Imperator cannot be ignored even in the face of death. Gerda smoothes her hair back and follows the orderly.

Telepath wears her Imperator face.

"Lord and Mas—"

"Don't bother with that, Captain Lübchen. You stand in the presence of the Inner Cabinet. We are assembled for emergency decisions following new developments in your situation. At the moment your role is simply to answer questions. Our telepaths will assure that you are telling the truth."

"I am ready to do your bidding, your Highness."

"True or untrue: Geledi forces kidnapped one of the Terrans and hold her hostage to force their will on the others?"

"True." Despite His position at the head of the vast Credixian bureaucracy, the Imperator is capable of fast movement and swift decisions when the occasion demands. All procedure, Gerda gathers, is now swept aside in a frantic search for the truth.

"So Admiral Grau told me. I did not want to believe her." Telepath strokes her chin and Gerda can see the face of the Imperator in that familiar gesture. "I understand that the Geledis are distracted at the moment."

"They are trying to recover one of their ships, which has

been hijacked by a Terran. What has become of its crew I cannot say. I would suspect mutiny."

Silence. Then Telepath speaks in a booming voice that Gerda knows is only a pale echo of the Imperator's tone. Still, even that echo makes Gerda straighten her back and sit up. This voice belongs to the ruler of three thousand inhabited planetary systems, giving orders that will stand as policy.

"The Credixian Imperium does not condone and has never condoned the use of terror as a military weapon. The Charter of the Imperium, which bears my signature along with those of all my predecessors, specifically mandates us to fight terrorism wherever we find it, within or without our borders." Telepath raises her hands. "What Geled has done, Geled will do again... . . . next time, some citizen of Credix may be put in danger. Therefore I immediately dissolve all agreements and treaties made between the Credixian Imperium and the government of Geled. Thus we immediately withdraw recognition of the government of Geled as a legitimate expression of its peoples' sovereignty. And thus I rule that there will be enmity between Credix and Geled for all the future." Telepath lowers her arms and makes a half-turn, then the mantle of the Imperator falls away and she was nothing but an old woman again. "The Imperator will be back in contact with you momentarily," she croaks.

Gerda is not dismissed; she can do nothing but wait and watch her viewscreens. Sting seems to have given up trying to fight *Painbird*; he is now leading the Geledi ship on a merry chase throughout the volume.

Telepath comes alive once more. "Captain Lübchen?"

"I am here, your Highness."

"I hope you were pleased by my announcement. Sorry I had to be so abrupt, the holo cameras were rolling and it is going into the archives."

"I am pleased, your Highness. I am not exactly sure why the change, but—"

"There are many reasons. We can't afford to trust Geled,

that's major. And also the fact that I wouldn't want our people to learn that we are supporting a government that does what *they* did to the Terrans. There are always rival claimants to the Throne, and enough supporters in high places can always be found."

"I understand. I think."

"There is another reason, Captain Lübchen: you, yourself. The day I last talked with you, I made seven hundred fifty-four separate decisions on matters brought before me. The puters tell me that those decisions affected the lives of upwards of twenty billion people. And of all those decisions, of all the pleas I heard and all the arguments and facts brought before me—the only thing I remember from that day is your question to me: what should you tell the child? It actually kept me awake that night. I've been thinking ever since, and I don't see why a person with your compassion and your sense, coupled with such loyalty, should be squelched. This latest incident was the trigger, but I have been building to this decision for a while. Captain, you have your command back. Do as you see fit."

Gerda bows. "Thank you, Lord and Master."

"And when you return to Credix, bring the boy to me. I will apologize to him in person."

"Thank you...Father."

❖

Jedrek can't help smiling. There's a fair amount to smile at, despite the fact that Sukoji is very probably in mortal agony. Sting came through at the last minute, in a rescue surely dramatic enough to satisfy the lad for a while. And now, with the Credixian government's turnover (did they have no consistent foreign policy?), Geled's short-lived attack fleet is reduced to one ship frantically chasing after another while the system laughs.

And Dal is going home. That's something else to smile

about. Gerda made up to the boy with a simple, "Dal, please come back," and Dal answered with a happy nod of assent.

Jedrek catches sight of a datascreen and frowns. *Worldsaver* is on a rendezvous course with *Ferdinand*. The matter is not yet over, will not be over for a while.

He stifles a yawn. Not enough sleep lately. The last thing he wants to deal with is a hysterical Drisana.

Ah well, no use putting it off. And there *is* Sukoji. He has no doubt that the Geledis turned her over to the Ebettor. He doesn't want to think about that.

When *Worldsaver* docks, Jedrek sighs and directs autoservants to conduct its crew to the bridge.

They walk in, looking eery bit as haggard as he feels. Kedar is first, his face lined and drawn. How can she have brought him along on this trip—doesn't she know what it cost him? Maybe when he returns to his home he will recover.

He glimpses *Painbird*, careening on the viewscreen. *If* he returns.

Cilehe looks like...Cilehe. The set of her jaw is no different than it was when he first saw her on board *Worldsaver*. But something in her eyes is reminiscent of ice melting on a hot day.

Last comes Drisana. Her face is frozen, and she walks like one asleep. For a second Jedrek thinks she's returned to her cocoon of indifference, then he sees her eyes. This time, Drisana's silence is born of grief and anguish.

Kedar starts at once. "Jedrek, I know you have your principles and I'll be blasted if I can understand them, but it's Sukoji's *life*."

Jedrek spins in the command chair. "I'm not going to repair that Relay. Kedar, I'm prepared to give *my* life to prevent it from being fixed."

"Does that mean you can also give Sukoji's?"

"Sukoji is dead. All we can do now is spare her a little pain. You have to be realistic about this. Blast it man, I was prepared to fight to the death of a civilization," he waves about him at the bridge. "Do you think I'm going to stop because of one woman, even if she does happen to be one of the most important people in my life?"

Kedar tilts his head. "Now you sound like everything fanatical about Drisana that you criticize."

That stops him. Jedrek opens his mouth, then closes it. Kedar is right...he *does* sound like Drisana. He looks at the Head Librarian, her head bowed but her back still straight, and gives her a bittersweet smile. "And now I finally understand you, Drisana. It's come too late, perhaps, but I understand."

"You don't," she mouths. "Not if you think blind fanaticism is all there is to me."

"I'm sorry, but I still can't repair the Relay. Understanding or no, Sukoji or no, I still cannot do it."

Drisana says nothing.

Cilehe pushes past Kedar. "Jedrek...*Worldsaver* is yours. Let us fight with you." She holds out a hand, and he takes it. "Come onto *Worldsaver* with us and we'll show them a thing or two yet."

He nods. In mid-gesture the viewscreen flickers. *Painbird* launches a smaller ship—puter identifies it as a long-range starboat. After a second or two it winks into tachyon phase, leaving an indistinct blue glow that dissipates rapidly. "Look, Geled has sent for reinforcements. We're going to need everything on our side now, Cilehe."

All occasion for smiling seems long gone, as he follows the remnants of the Circle onto *Worldsaver*.

❖

36
Loner
[TERRA]
6484 CE

A dried and flattened rose before her, Drisana closes her eyes and tries to forget. It is difficult—her entire life has been a struggle to remember, to connect, and now she wants desperately to disconnect.

Sukoji....

She remembers Sukoji in Terran sunlight, the most amazing red highlights standing out in her short dark hair. She remembers the curve of Sukoji's fingers over a terminal, the rapid movement of slender digits when she was struck by an idea, the slow, absent-minded tapping of the keys when Sukoji's mind was gone far away in thought. She remembers one wild hilarious night in New York when they were much younger and the entire Library Circle got higher than high on every happy-drug she knew, and they wandered the ancient streets searching for a place that would serve them real old-fashioned Terran eggrolls.

Sukoji....

This is grief. Drisana knows that. Images springing to mind of themselves, no way to avoid them or shut them off. Even the most minor recollection brings a lump in the throat, tears.

Drisana has been through grief before. There was Liset Tchien, whose death left Drisana Head Librarian before she was ready. They all grieved for Liset, and for tendays afterward there was weeping at the strangest times.

And there was the grief she felt over the Circle, after Jedrek went away and everyone else left her. *That* was impossible. Everywhere she turned provoked memories. The Grand Library building, the city of Alexandria, the Mediterranean Sea, the whole of the planet Earth—each triggered memories of what the Circle did, what the Circle said, what the Circle dreamed.

Drisana touches the rose and closes her book on it. Grief passes. Grief wanted to be killing, wanted you to rush out and embrace the oblivion you were so afraid of. But grief is ultimately not strong enough. Ignore it when possible, give in to it when necessary, and sooner or later it passed.

At least, she vows, Sukoji's torment and death will not be in vain.

Deep into sleep period, Drisana puts her book away and switches off the light. Around her, the ship is alive in a hundred million ways. She wanders the corridors of *Worldsaver* feeling like a holoimage, something not quite real. This is the domain of the servs and cybs and mechs and the puters that supervise them all. In a very old story book from a long time ago she encountered a children's story of nursery toys that came alive and played by themselves after midnight when the child was fast asleep. How amazed would the writer of that story be, to know that this fantasy is commonplace on every civilized world and settlement in the Galaxy?

Everywhere she walks, she catches just the tail-end glimpse of mechs scurrying away, autoservants dashing into access holes too small for a Human, suddenly-frozen patterns of winking lights on a control panel. Here is an entire universe of motion and purpose that Humans seldom saw, a world filled with humanity's servants going about their tasks of maintenance out of the sight of their masters.

The night belong to humanity's creations, not to humanity.

She finds herself at Jedrek's door, knocks. The door opens and they are face to face. In her strange ghostly awareness, she wonders what details about Jedrek will spur her grief when he is dead. The pale blue of his eyes, she decides; he carries a little of Terran skies with him wherever he goes.

He is half-asleep, his hair a bit flattened on one side. On his left hand he wears a metal ring...why did she never notice it before? Other than that, he is nude.

"Oh, Drisana, can't you let me get some sleep?"

She lowers her eyes. "Jedrek...don't shut me out. Please.

I'm not here as your adversary. I'm here because you're strong, and right now I need to be reminded that there is such a thing as strength." She rubs her eyes. "It's the middle of the night and it's dark and I'm lonely and afraid. Can't I come in and talk?"

Eyes dropping, he gives her a sleepy half-smile. "Come in."

In the dark, in his bunk, they nestle together as they have not done for eleven years. Drisana holds him tight, and he holds her. She tries to give back as much comfort as he gives her. This is not a time for antagonism or struggle—it is a time of truce, when they face one another as Human to Human and, for a moment, forget about the rest of the universe.

"I killed her," Drisana says at last.

She feels Jedrek's finger on her lips. "No. Not alone. I had my part in it. We all did."

"I'm sorry I brought you all here."

"Are you?"

Is she? "No, I don't think so." She forces a smile. "It sounded good."

For a long while neither says anything. Drisana wonders if he's gone to sleep, knows he hasn't. Then, finally, he whispers, "I haven't slept with a woman since I left you."

She doesn't quite believe that, but she lets it pass.

"No, I'm telling the truth. Men, and Denys, and Sting of course—but not another woman."

She suppresses a shiver. "Sting...I could never...."

"That's what he told me. He almost killed me for even suggesting it, I think."

She pulls back from him. "Jedrek, how did we get to where we are today? We had everything, everything, and now...."

"Don't sound like a cliché, Drisana. You know how we got here. A little of this, a little of that, and some strong personalities that had to wind up in conflict sooner or later."

After a while she remembers a point that's bothered her. "Why did you answer my summons? Why didn't you ignore it and stay on Borshall?"

"I don't know. Maybe...maybe because things weren't finished yet, and I knew that. When I left Terra so many years ago, I thought it was all over. Then I saw your rose, and I knew it wasn't."

"Is it going to all be over soon?"

He says nothing for a time, simply traces fingers through her hair. Then at last, "T'to says it won't be over for a long time to come. He says it all started billions of years ago, and we're still dealing with the same problem. Batydded, Aemallana, the Galactic Riders—they're all fighting the same battle and we're all part of the same story. It might go on forever."

"That's not what I meant."

"I know. It's late, Drisana, and tomorrow morning we have to go back to hating each other. Can't we forget about it for just a little bit longer?"

She smiles, and they say nothing more.

❖

Drisana lies awake in the dark as images race through her mind like dreams gone mad. Sukoji, Jedrek, Kedar, Cilehe, Sting...and in the middle of it all, like a star in the middle of a planetary system, giving light and energy and animating all about it, the datasphere of the Grand Library.

Sukoji's torment and death must not be in vain.

She fumbles in the dark, then smiles. Leaving the bunk gently to avoid waking Jedrek, she pulls on her clothes and leaves, padding swiftly down silent corridors toward the hangar deck.

❖

37
Savior
[RIDER]
Galactic Revolution 561.19775508

Jedrek wakes and doesn't know why. He fumbles for a moment in the darkness, feels the bunk next to him...Drisana? She is gone.

He lays back and closes his eyes. Oh, well, it was nice talking with her. Almost the way things used to be, he thinks. Silly girl, imagining she could bring back former days. As long as neither of them change, there can be no return to what was. Why can't she see that?

Sleep eludes him. It is almost as if he's too tired to sleep. He lets his eyes rest lightly closed, slows his breathing and lays perfectly still. Maybe he can convince his body that it wants to go to sleep. The trick works sometimes.

There are always sleepy-pills, but he wants to be fresh for tomorrow. There's still a lot to do.

With Cilehe's help and some of *Worldsaver's* spare parts, it will be much easier to complete *Ferdinand's* gravity warp. He'll put Sting in command of that ship, he decides. And the crewmembers of *Deathcry* who'd joined Sting's mutiny would serve to crew the hijacked ship, with some trustworthy Theresans to help out. There is the gunner, Irina Something-or-other, and her friend with the cyberharp, and various others he didn't know. Kassov made a lot of enemies on that ship. The other Geledis, as well as one Ebettor left from the three who were aboard the ship when Sting took it—they will remain in detention on a cold rock orbiting just inside the Teerell atmosphere curtain.

Twitching his fingers, he counts ships. *Worldsaver, Ferdinand, Deathcry.* And *Outbound*, or course. The three other Theresan ships—*Maximillian Francis, Mary Christine,* and *Maria Antoinette*—are afterthoughts. Seven ships to face—how many? How many ships will Geled send when that starboat gets within ultrawave range? Just how much opposition will Olympia's fledgling fleet have to face?

Well, the two gravity warps will take up a lot of slack. The limiting factor is energy. Maybe, Jedrek thinks, he should send the Theresan ships off to skim hydrogen to fuel reactors. Blast, the Relays were set up in pockets of space conspicuously low in stars and planets as well as interstellar gas and dust—to help them function, no doubt, and he has to admit it was a good idea. Moving grav fields would be a danger to the delicate circuits of the Relay, circuits just barely stabilized by Imperial science stretched to its limit. The presence of *Maria Theresa* and her habitats went a long way toward reducing Relay Alpha's effective lifetime.

His mind is drifting. Back to fuel. There must be a gas giant or a large, none-too-hot star within not to many tens of parsecs. Or would it be easier to just skim the interstellar medium, ramscoop-like?

He can do the calculation tomorrow. He turns on his side and feels himself slipping into sleep at last—

He jerks awake, curses. Well, it was a good try. He might as well do the calculations right now, he might forget them in the morning and he will never get to sleep with that preying on his mind.

He needs raw data—maps of the volume nearby, and the density of the interstellar medium. He reaches in the dark for his data marble and his term.

His fingers close on something that doesn't feel right, a permaplastic sphere a little larger than his marble, with a chain attached....

He closes his palm over it and receives a shock. Only one person has a data marble containing the complete archives of all the Head Librarians back to Imperial times.

"Drisana?" No answer. He switches on the lights. The cabin is empty. His own marble is not at bedside where he puts it every night, in case he wants to do some midnight reading.

He smiles. Tomorrow they'll exchange marbles and laugh at her mistake, and that will be it.

Mistake?

One thing is certain about Drisana Hardel: she does nothing by mistake. Her plans might go agley, but she is never ever without plans and contingency plans.

Why does she want his data marble?

He's fully awake now, awake and dreading. It fits too well, fits her impulsive character and her dedication. She's going to attempt to repair the Relay.

He has to stop this growing panic. Think it through, Jedrek. With the information in that marble, can Drisana succeed in fixing Alpha?

…Yes.

For all that she tries to pretend to be a mechanical incompetent, Drisana can handle machines and can program a mechs to effect certain repairs. Nothing difficult about that. She might not have the training to interpret equations and come up with real-world answers for them…but she wouldn't need to. Jedrek's notes, his conclusions, even his speculations on the things that might be possible from the new technology—all were in the marble.

She could do it.

By this time he's dressed and, remembering his knife, he runs out of his cabin toward the hangar deck. If all the boats are in place and Drisana asleep in her cabin, he's going to feel silly….

Boat number one is gone. As quickly as he could, he activates the launch cycle for number two. No telling how much time she's had with the Relay already. He doesn't know how long it would take to repair it—that really depends on what the damage is.

Boat Two launches, and for a while Jedrek is busy with the controls. He's the first to admit that he's no one's pilot—but there's no time to wake the others and have someone fly for him. Luckily the autopilot can handle most of the trip. Good thing tachyon phase isn't involved, or he'd wind up parsecs from his destination with no idea of how to get back.

On the viewscreens Relay Alpha glitters in starlight like a Santamas tree deprived of its framework and crowning star. But what is that odd shape on the side of the Relay?

Jedrek smiles, weak with relief. The strange protrusion is T'to Yachim's ship. He might have forgotten, might have slipped up and allowed her through—but the Galactic Rider is on the job, and T'to will never let Drisana in to do her repairs. All that remains is to collect Drisana and bring her back, a little shamefaced and probably defiant, but still without a working Relay.

As he docks the boat he is almost in good humor. He hangs Drisana's marble around his neck, and waits patiently as all airlocks cycle...then he follows the only possible route to the Relay's control center.

Everything is as it was before, except that the hatch to the inner workings of Alpha is closed. T'to Yachim stands at one of the consoles, facing Jedrek. The Rider gestures a greeting.

Where is Drisana? Her boat is docked outside; she must be here.

"Greetings, Jedrek nor Talin."

"Greetings, T'to Yachim."

"If I am any judge of Human expression, you are puzzled."

"You are, T'to. I came in search of my friend Drisana. Has she been here?"

"She has."

"Is she gone?"

"No."

Suspicion enters Jedrek's mind. There are no signs of a fight, but....

"Did you kill her?"

"By the sacred name of Aemallana, no! Do you think me capable of such an act? No, Drisana is within." The Rider gestures to the access hatch and the heart of the Relay.

"You let her in?"

"It was her desire. I cannot stand between anyone and her destiny."

"Do you know what she's doing in there?" He can't believe T'to let her pass.

"She is waiting for you. She does not know it herself, but she is."

"How long has she been here?"

"But a few minutes."

He steps to the access hatch, pauses and looks back at the Dorascan. "T'to, why?"

"We do not force, Jedrek nor Talin. You know that. The only way I could have stopped her from passing that hatch was by using force. I could not do that, or I would have been no better than Geled and the Ebettor."

"You're strange, T'to Yachim. Very strange." The hatch is secured by conventional latches; he undogs it.

"Jedrek—your weapon?"

He looks at his knife, unclips it from his belt and tosses it across the room to T'to. "Here. I usually don't remember it." The last latch comes undone.

"All the gods go with you, Jedrek."

He says nothing, merely pulls himself through the hatch.

✸

Welcome to Imperial Centcom
Today is Solday, 11 November TE 268

Imperial Centcom is a cooperative effort between the Departments of <u>Technology</u> and <u>Commerce</u>. Our mission is to oversee communications throughout the Empire and beyond.

Your Account
- <u>Citizen Accounts</u>
- <u>Business Accounts</u>
- <u>Government Accounts</u>
- <u>Set Up a New Account</u>

Place Calls
- <u>Local</u>
- <u>Ultrawave</u>

Mail

Government Services
- <u>Grand Library</u>
- <u>Court of the Empress</u>
- <u>Imperial Council</u>
- <u>High Court</u>
- <u>Provincial Governments</u>
- <u>Planetary Governments</u>

- <u>Bureaucratic Corps</u>
- <u>Dept of Colonization</u>
- <u>Dept of Commerce</u>
- <u>Dept of Technology</u>
- <u>Diplomatic Corps</u>
- <u>Imperial Navy</u>

News & Features
- <u>Today's *State of the Empire* Report</u>
- <u>Entertainment</u>
- <u>Life</u>
- <u>Shopping</u>
- <u>Travel</u>

- <u>Sports</u>
- <u>Financial</u>
- <u>Local</u>
- <u>Personals</u>

<u>Contact Us</u> | <u>Careers</u> | <u>Terms & Conditions</u> | <u>Store</u> | <u>Help</u>

38
The Touch of Hands
[CIRCLE]
6484 CE

The access tunnel is about a meter and a half wide; there is no grav, but handholds are set into the wall between black permaplast boxes. The machinery that makes the Relay possible surrounds Jedrek—field coils and recorders and the receptors that turn feeble starlight into power. Generators and governors and a million different circuits, each with its own purpose and each engineered to last forever. The problem with the Relay is not in this outlying section; these units are eternal, self-repairing.

He passes one, then two bulkheads with inspection hatches, each closed and dogged; he unfastens each as quickly as he can and continues moving. About twenty meters down the shaft he arrives at the last hatch.

He unlocks its closures and pulls the hatch open. It swings in his direction, revealing the pale glow of a worklight.

He drifts in.

The central room is small, a sphere perhaps three meters in diameter. The walls are crowded with the same black boxes that line the way in. There are no more hatches; this is the only entrance.

Off-center in the room, a collection of tachyon vesicles takes up much of the available space. Large and small and every size in between, they are tightly-packed in an intricate geometry. At first glance, Jedrek discerns dozens—but the longer he looks, the more he sees, an infinity of iridescent spheres. Their skins merge, interpenetrate, blur into one another, until they are one unitary structure. Struts of gleaming dellsite hold the entire mass stationary.

This, Jedrek realizes, is what it *must* look like. This is inevitably the result of all the pages of equations stored in his marble. Had he seen this earlier, with nothing else to work on, he would have known that the principle of the Relay involved a great departure from conventional technology.

Drisana floats motionless before the crystals. In her left hand she clutches Jedrek's data marble; at her right, floating free, is a toolbox attended by two ten-centimeter mechs.

"Do you know what you're going to do?" Jedrek asks. She turns at his voice; her face shows no emotion. Not the set determination he expected, nor the pained guilt he witnessed...how many hours earlier? No, her face is a clean slate. The mass of vesicles is reflected in her eyes.

"I'm about to repair the Relay. I know what's wrong, Jedrek, and I know how to fix it. Look, it's only a matter of replacing some Radigan units, and patching a few contacts in the linear transducer. I'll have to add a new assembly for stabilizing the field to the seventh power, but that won't be hard—most of the parts are here and with your plans I could build it blindfolded."

"That's not what I mean. I realize that you know *how* to repair it—do you know what happens afterward?"

"The Library goes back on the air."

"Right." If not for his respect for fine machinery, he would spit. "And with it, the Relay makes communication easier throughout this sector of the Galaxy. Geled gets into closer touch with the Ebettor, and soon instead of six there are thousands and millions. Do you think anyone in the Galaxy can stand against an army of Ebettor? With Geled as a starting point, they'll take over every civilization in the Galaxy. What good will the Library be then?"

"People always need information."

"Blast it, Drisana, stop living in a fantasy universe. The Ebettor aren't the type to allow free flow of information. That goes against everything they stand for. The Library is going to be shut down just as soon as they make it to Terra—and they'll make it their business to get to Terra soon."

At last the look of determination comes onto her features. "I lived through eleven years of hell for this. I abased myself and called for help. I lived through wars, and kidnappings, and I sacrificed one of the people most dear to me, all that I could be here with this equipment and get it repaired. I don't care about anything else, Jedrek."

"And you know what's going to happen to the Galaxy after the Ebettor have their way. Get T'to to tell you about societies in the Core sometime. If you think what happened to Dal and Sukoji is bad, that's just the beginning. It will be rape and murder, robbery and terrorism, on a scale vaster than anything you're capable of imagining."

"I don't care!" Tears on her cheeks match those on his.

"And it won't stop with just Humans. We'll be bred, bred like the ancestors of the Ebettor were, and soon we'll be nothing but another regiment of shock troop—just like they are. And still it won't stop. Humans, Ebettor...they're both the same thing, you know...will be turned against the Galactic Riders, against the remaining free societies of the Scattered Worlds, against Nephestal. And when it ends, there will be nothing at all left, only a Galaxy denuded of life and a few scattered things that were once Human, waiting for orders from their masters to turn their fury upon themselves. Pitiful creatures, hating life and wishing they could die. Is that what you want?"

"I...don't...care."

"Drisana, for the sake of everything that's decent in the universe, listen to me."

She turns away, fumbles at the toolbox. A micro-manipulator slips from her shaking grip; then she turns and reaches out a hand to him.

"Jedrek, help me."

He touches her hand, clasps it, palm pressing into palm in a grip as strong as life itself.

Jedrek.

Drisana.

He feels her palm, feels the tracing of every silver line as they match up to his. Datafeed implants, long silver artificial neurons that stretch from brain to palm, palm to brain...and now they are in direct contact. Born of pain and fear and the passion of essential loneliness, their minds leap toward one another across silver threads and for a few fleeting instants they are linked more intimately than their bodies could ever approach.

Jedrek, help me, I'm so alone ....

I'm here.

It's you I want, not the Library. Oh, why didn't I see it sooner? I was hiding myself behind the datasphere. Don't you see, all this time I was jealous of you...jealous of you and Cilehe and Kedar and Sukoji.

Jealous?

Yes! You had lives outside the Library, you had friends and hobbies and things you cared about. You were capable of loving and being loved, of being interested in others beside the Library. It was you, Jedrek, that I hated most. You went off to Borshall, you were a success and you lived with a man you loved and you did everything that I was afraid to do. Everything I could never let myself try. And then you came when I called, but it was still the same. You made friends with the Theresans, you took Sting away, you helped the Credixian boy...and all the time I was unable to go one step beyond myself and my need for the Library.

Keeping their palms in contact as though the fate of the Galaxy depends upon it, he pulls her closer and holds her tightly. *Drisana, love.*

I—I hated you, I hated everyone. And so I allied myself with the Geledis, without even knowing what I was doing. It was like you said, I hated life and wished I could die, so I transferred all my feelings to the Library, hoping that would make me real.

As if the intimacy is too much for her, she pulls her palm back, but keeps holding Jedrek tightly. "Cosmos, Jedrek, how do I get back from this awful place?"

He strokes her hair and kisses her forehead. "You've taken

the first step. What you've done, that was hardest. Now the rest of it will be easier."

"How?" There is no hysteria...maybe she's too tired for that, maybe she just doesn't want to surrender for fear of losing herself under the screams.

"One step at a time, one day after another. I'll help. It begins...it begins with a cry for help, an admission that you need others." He pulls the toolbox to him, fishes until he finds a high-power laser cutter. He hands it to her. "It begins with freeing yourself from what you *think* you need. *Then* you decide what to do with your freedom."

She takes the cutter, stares at it dumbly for a moment, then raises it. It is a variable-frequency laser; it takes her only seconds to dial through all possible frequencies at max power.

A brief discord of every note sounded at once—then the tachyon vesicles destabilize, like a million bubbles popping all at once. Relay Alpha is finally and irrevocably dead.

Hand-in-hand and palm-to-palm, Jedrek and Drisana go to greet the Galactic Rider.

❋

Dedication Speech for Ultrawave Relays
by Jane Elendan, Secretary-General of the Imperial Council
Year Day TE 70

Mesayyid of the Imperial Council; Citizens of the Empire: Human Beings across the Galaxy: Welcome. It is my great pleasure, and my even greater honor, to dedicate this network of Ultrawave Relays under the auspices of Imperial Centcom.

This is an historic moment. For the first time, the entire Galaxy is knit together by instantaneous Ultrawave. I stand here in the Imperial Council chambers on Terra—but my words and image appear simultaneously on all of the 252 worlds and countless settlements inhabited by Humans. From Lathyros to the Patalan Cluster and from Amny to distant Wakmarrel...no planet, no settlement, is isolated now.

Please join with me in thanking the thousands of engineers, techs, and others who labored so hard and so long to bring this gift to Humanity.

While these Ultrawave Relays are a project of the Terran Empire, but I must stress that their use is not limited to Imperial worlds. No planet, settlement, or person will be required to join the Empire in order to utilize this marvelous communications network. Imperial Centcom operates as a business, free of political influence, and will accept any and all customers. We want this boon available to the whole family of Humanity.

Better communications can only lead to better understanding among peoples. Better communications can only allow us to know each other better, to reduce fear, hostility, and misunderstanding. Better communications can only increase peace.

This is my hope, and the hope of the Imperial Council.

❂

39
The Decision of the Imperium
[CREDIX]
CI 4331

Jedrek stands behind Sting on the bridge of *Ferdinand*. It is, he decides, his place...especially with Queen Olympia Marvelous beside him, counting on his work to save her people.

One ship at a time, the Geledi war fleet winked into being.

Geled still doesn't know that the Relay is inoperative and likely to remain so forever. Jedrek hopes this display will convince them. He waits until the last of the Geledi ships—twenty-five in all—appears, waits until they form into a globe around *Painbird*. Then he smiles and nods to Sting.

For this occasion, *Ferdinand's* crew is carefully chosen to be completely representative: Credixians, Theresans, Geledis, Terrans...Jedrek is sorry T'to declined their offer to be aboard. This once, and this once only, a kind of galactic Union comes about.

Sting's hands play over the controls, and the ship moves. A few abortive shots by the Geled fleet, stopped easily by *Ferdinand's* defense screen...then they are between the Relay and the Geledi fleet. A kilometer away, Alpha looks much the same as it has since the day it was constructed. Jedrek looks for, and finds, the Spiral-and-Triangle of the Imperial Ultrawave Authority, the seal of Imperial Centcom. As an historic relic, this Relay is valuable—as a symbol of the future, it is priceless.

"Fire when ready, gunner," Jedrek orders.

Irina Lerenko answers with a smile. Her uniform is not new, only the insignia of *Maria Theresa* is—but she looks like a new woman. She bends her head to her gun console, punches a few keys, then stabs a button with a proud finger. Accuracy of aim is not, after all, that important—but from the control screens Jedrek sees that she hit the exact geometrical center of the Relay with an error measured in millimeters.

Indicators surge, there is a flash of nova-light, and Relay Alpha collapses upon itself under a thousand-gee grav field.

All attack from the Geled fleet ceases. Then, ponderously, the ships begin to change position.

"I don't believe it." Cilehe's words sound from the speaker. *Worldsaver* lies half a kilometer off the port side. "They're moving into attack formation. They're going to try to fight with us."

"*Worldsaver* and *Ferdinand* will engage their heavy destroyers," come Gerda's orders from *Outbound*. "*Deathcry*, hold back and grapple with their smaller ships. Theresan guard, keep the habitats safe. I want *Painbird* for myself."

The attack begins.

✸

An hour later Jedrek knows why he never became involved in a war. Six Geledi ships destroyed, five by gravity warp and one blasted with a lucky shot from *Deathcry*. Now the Geledis have discovered *Maria Theresa's* weak spots, and Jedrek's fleet is kept busy trying to protect the habitats and the mother ship herself.

Only once did Geled make the mistake of trying to attack the apparently-defenseless Needz and its dome containing the Hlutr. They found out in short order that a Galactic Rider is fully capable of force when necessary.

"This isn't going well," Jedrek announces. The four ships of his fleet are linked by scrambled ultrawave circuits; he doubts that the Geledis can pick up and decode their signals.

"I hate to say it, but you are right," Gerda says. "Jedrek, on your next pass I think you should come over to *Outbound*; with your help we might get out of this after all."

Outbound sends a gig to pick him up. Jedrek admires the pilot; with the way ships are dashing about, protecting four volumes among four ships—the three Theresan ships were been early casualties, but their crews are safe—it's a wonder that the pilot doesn't lose control and go sailing off into interstellar space. Jedrek sighs with relief when he reaches Gerda's ship.

Gerda and Dal await him in the Captain's cabin; the ship's Telepath is also there. Disagreeable-looking woman, he thinks.

"What's up, Gerda?"

"Telepath can put us in contact with Fleet Headquarters at home. I have been trying to explain to them that our position is desperate—I do not think they really believe me. There is a long tradition of Credixian commanders asking for more than they need."

"Let me talk with them."

Gerda nods, and Telepath changes her expression. "I am Fleet Admiral Theis. What is it this time, Captain Lübchen?"

"I am Jedrek nor Talin of Terra, interim commander of the *Maria Theresa* battle fleet. I suppose my rank is somewhat equivalent to yours, Admiral, so the Captain asked me to talk with you." Jedrek frowns. "Do you realize that we are outnumbered more than three-to-one by those Geledis?"

"Our studies have shown that one Credixian ship...."

"I don't care abut your studies and I don't care about your bureaucracy and I don't really care about what you think of the matter. Have you heard the directive that your own Imperator issued on this situation?"

"Ja, Certainly."

"Then you know that Captain Lübchen is in complete command. She needs enough ships to even up the sides—at least—and she needs them as soon as you can get them here. They should have been sent days ago; as it is we'll have to keep battling until they arrive."

He catches a faint telepathic echo: *...damned upstart Outsiders...* Then Theis speaks evenly. "I have explained to Captain Lübchen time and again...."

"Get me the Imperator."

"What did you say?" The tone is exactly that of a very

short man whose authority has just been questioned.

"I am an agent of a friendly foreign power and I demand to talk with your Imperator...or someone who can speak for him. Now are you going to get him?"

"I will see if any of the Privy Secretaries can spare a moment for you."

For a second Jedrek considers unleashing Drisana—or even Sting—on the Privy Secretaries. But not over a telepathic circuit; he is best retaining control of the situation himself.

"I asked to see the Imperator a while ago, Jedrek. It is not going to do any good."

"I represent a foreign power, as I said. They can't put me off the way they can with you. Let's see what happens."

Telepath croaks, "Ambassador Reinhardt of the Diplomatic Corps." Her face softens and Ambassador Reinhardt's voice takes over. "What can I do for you, er...Admiral nor Talin?"

"I have been trying to convince your Fleet Admiral to send more ships here. A few days ago you decided that Geled was your worst enemy in the Galaxy, and now we're about to be tromped by them and no one will lift a finger."

The Telepath gives them a smile possibly meant to be comforting. "I assure you, we realize the nature of your plight, and action has been taken—by direct order of the Imperator himself, I might add. This matter is too important to leave to the Navy; it was turned over to my department and the churches."

"*What* action has been taken?"

The smile again. "Ever since the Imperator's policy was announced, we have been pressuring our allies. Credix is larger than Geled, you see, and we have a good many more allies. We can stir up trouble for them just as they were able to trouble us. Our simulations say that within two days Geled will have so many border skirmishes and revolts close to home that they will recall their fleet from the area of the Relay—especially since you have demonstrated that the Relay is of no more use to them. They will be unable to deal with

Maria Theresa for quite a long time, don't you see?"

"And what about the Relay? They can always try to build a new one, or construct a string of local Relays. That's what we're fighting this war for—to keep them from getting Relay power."

"Don't try to fool an old diplomat. Wars are fought for many purposes." The Telepath strokes a nonexistent mustache. "They lack the technical know-how to build a new Relay, I believe. They will also be so bothered in the future with minor wars that they'll have no economic base to build Relays. Do not be concerned, Admiral nor Talin, we will make sure that we keep an eye on what Geled is doing."

"Well, you'd better be right, or I know a young lad who would like very much to visit Credix and settle a score with you."

The Ambassador laughs. "Very well, then. You will see that I am right. And Admiral...next time you try to get something done, please save yourself the trouble of dealing with the military. Theis is a bit hidebound at times, and while I don't want to say anything against a fellow servant of the Imperium...."

"I understand. Thank you."

The Telepath relaxes, and Gerda shakes her head. "Now what?"

"Now, I suppose, we wait."

"And after that?"

"We'll see."

❃

Thirty-two hours later, the Geledi fleet breaks up. Gerda wants to chase *Painbird* into tachyon phase and destroy it; Jedrek stops her. "Let it alone. Kassov will get his punishment when he returns home...and I'm sure the Ebettor will deal with *their* people in ways we can't even comprehend."

"What about Sukoji?" Kedar has still not stopped grieving,

nor hoping she could be rescued.

"We'll never know, I suppose."

"But they still have her data marble, and whatever conclusions she was able to make from the Library's data and what the Credixians gave her. Do you think they'll be able to figure out how to build a Relay?"

Sting turns around in *Ferdinand's* command chair. "It's not a problem." He smiles an evil smile. "T'to Yachim snuck me onto their ship. Sukoji's safe in our sickbay, recovering nicely. And while I was retrieving her, I took care of the Ebettor at the same time." He holds up a data marble, then licks his finger. Jedrek doesn't want to ask any more.

"And what now?" Gerda asks.

"Time it is for a celebration, think I," Olympia answers.

There is no argument.

❁

40
Librarian
[CIRCLE/RIDER]
6484 CE; Galactic Revolution 561.19775508

Celebrations end, and finally it is time for farewells.

Everyone gathers in *Maria Theresa's* spacious docking bay, while four ships wait just outside the atmosphere curtain.

Queen Olympia, resplendent in magnificent furred robes, gives a short speech of thanks. "Wish I, that we friends remain will. Wish I, that you free will feel, to *Maria Theresa* to return." She kisses each one of them regally.

"Thank you," Kedar says with a nod. "We may be back...but we're all agreed that we're not going to tell others how to find you. *Maria Theresa* and her folk will be left alone."

"Thank I you, Sayyid Yavam. Thank I, all of you." A most un-royal tear trickles down her cheek; she turns abruptly, and is gone.

Gerda and Dal bid farewell next. Both are in their best uniforms, the colors of Credix bright and their faces shining. "We will be home in time for Margrethe and Lars to get married. And who knows," the Credixian Captain says, "the Imperator might even grant each of us breeding rights for this." She tousles Dal's hair. "It would be nice to raise a family, I think." Dal wrinkles his nose, and Gerda laughs.

Dal steps forward and Jedrek kneels before him. "I want to thank you, Jedrek," the boy says, "for everything you did for me. And I've decided that I don't want to be a starship captain when I grow up—I want to be a tech and design space settlements."

Jedrek hugs the lad. "Be a captain. It's a lot less frustrating."

Irina and Rur are next. Jedrek presses both their hands warmly. "Are you sure you're going to be all right in the Credixian Imperium?"

"Better than Geled, for a while at least, I think. Who knows, we might go back sometime."

"Good luck."

When *Outbound* flies away and blinks into tachyon phase, Jedrek is surprised to find tears in his eyes. He holds Drisana's hand more tightly, and thinks how nice the bittersweet pain of separation feels, in contrast to *no* feelings at all. She smiles as though she's received his message.

Outwardly, Sting hasn't changed much since Jedrek first saw him in Eisenhower Spaceport. The boy is perhaps a fraction of a centimeter taller, maybe a little less cheeky...but still undeniably and uniquely Sting.

"You can still have *Ferdinand* if you want it," Jedrek offers.

"Are you kidding? I've made the best choice." He stands next to Cilehe, gives her a friendly kiss. "Thank you, Sayyid Cilehe. I'll take care of your ship. Are you sure you want to give it to me?"

"No...but I'd hate to have to fight you for it. Take it, Sting, with my blessing."

He hugs and kisses Kedar and Sukoji, then approaches Jedrek and Drisana. "Thank you," he says, giving each of them a kiss.

"Where are you going?" Drisana asks.

"I don't know. There are a lot of little settlements and worlds out there, places where a fellow can have fun and live forever if he plays it right. Don't worry, I'll be back—I'll find you, if only for a visit every now and again."

"Take care of yourself," Jedrek finds it difficult to talk.

"I always do."

"Sting?"

"Yes, Sayyid Drisana?"

"Here." From her pouch, Drisana produces the Library datasphere. "Take it, it's yours. Put it to good use."

Tears show in the lad's eyes. He hugs Drisana again, and for just a second Jedrek catches sight of the Sting ordinarily visible only in sleep, the little boy who doesn't really want to leave home.

Without another word Sting boards *Worldsaver*, and goes directly into tachyon phase without even setting up a vector. "The kid is a born pilot," Cilehe says. "Don't ever tell him I said so."

"Are you sure you can fly *Deathcry*?" Kedar asks her.

"If Sting could do it, do you think I'll have trouble? And as soon as I'm back, I'll have a duplicate of *Worldsaver* constructed."

Together Kedar, Sukoji, and Cilehe board *Deathcry*. At the edge of the atmosphere curtain Cilehe turns back and shouts, "Jedrek, whenever you're read—" then vacuum cuts off her words.

"Sure, in a bit."

T'to Yachim approaches him. Jedrek claps the Dorascan on what could loosely be described as the shoulders. "It's been good knowing you, T'to."

"Here is your knife, Jedrek."

"Right, I don't want to forget *that*."

"You will return to Borshall now, I suppose?"

"Right. Come see me some time. You know how to get there."

"I can find out." T'to turns his large eyes on Drisana. "Sayyid Drisana, what will you do?"

"I don't know. I want to return to Terra, and make sure the Library is in good shape. I want to verify that all those data packages are still in their proper places, just in case they're needed later. And I have a book to turn over to my successor. Then," she squeezes Jedrek's hand, "I'm off to Borshall with Jedrek. Should be an interesting trip."

"I have been in contact with the Elders on Nephestal."

"What do they think of all this?"

"With the Elders, it is difficult to tell. They seem happy that the Core has suffered defeat again."

"But it hasn't," Jedrek interjects. "Geled is under their influence. The Ebettor have done their damage."

"No," T'to answers with authority. "The people of Geled are of good, freedom-loving stock. We will send more Galactic Riders, and we hope they will listen to us. Nothing and no one is ever lost, my friend, while there is light and song and happiness left in the Galaxy."

Jedrek looks from T'to to Drisana. "Touché."

T'to continues. "The real reason I brought up the Elders, Sayyid Drisana, is that they have an offer for you. How would you like the post of Director of the Humanity section of the Grandest Library of all, the Museum of Worlds on Nephestal, which serves the Galactic Riders and the whole community of the Scattered Worlds?"

"You're serious?"

"They are. Your information, they feel, is too important to ever be lost. Humans are as vital to the Grand Scheme as any other race—they feel it is time that a Human managed Human knowledge."

"When do they want me?"

"The Elders are relaxed about these things. No doubt they have seen you arrive in dreamtime, and they will know when to expect you. Two years, ten, fifty—time doesn't mean that much to them."

"Then you may tell them that I will be there. But first," she takes Jedrek's arm and meets his eyes, "I have things to do and people to meet."

He holds her closer, and knows that everything is finally right.

❂

The tale is told in the Scattered Worlds that the Guardians of Human Knowledge served faithfully for scores of Galactic Revolutions. Here ends the story of the first of them, and the Terran Grand Library's last Circle.

Timeline

2153 CE - Terran Empire founded

2223 CE (TE 70) - Ultrawave Relays begin operation

2386 CE (TE 233) - Starcruiser *Maria Theresa* lost

2464 CE - Terran Empire falls

c. 2750 CE - Independent Traders begin to gain influence

4723 CE - Relay Delta fails

5378 CE - Relay Beta destroyed during Geled-Natal War

5739 CE - Relay Zeta fails

6473 CE - Grand Library Circle breaks up

6484 CE - Relay Alpha fails

The Milky Way Galaxy

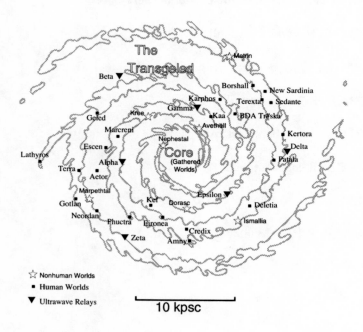

Scattered Worlds Chronological Sequence

Sequence	Era	Events & Stories
0.0	before 2.4 billion BCE	Sapient life in the Gathered Worlds
1.0	c. 2.4 billion BCE	The Pylistroph Seed Vessels launched
2.0	c. 1.2 billion BCE	Gergathan proclaims Mertorthar Flight of the Daamin Schism of the Hlutr Empires of the Scattered Worlds
3.0	c.100,000 BCE	Pre-Imperial Terra
3.75	2042 CE	*Dance for the Ivory Madonna*
3.85	2068 CE	*Hunt for the Dymalon Cygnet*
3.962	2103 CE	"Gamester"
3.968	2103 CE	"Big Improvement"
4.0	2153 CE (TE 0)	First Terran Empire
4.55	TE 219	*Weaving the Web of Days*
4.852	TE 361	"Candelabra and Diamonds"
4.882	TE 403	*A Voice in Every Wind*
5.0	2624 CE	Interregnum
5.38	6484 CE	*A Rose From Old Terra*
6.0	12,488 HE	Federation of Families
7.0	20,724 HE	Second Terran Empire
8.0	24,356 HE	Post-Imperial Humanity
8.5	c.30,000 HE	*The Leaves of October*
9.0	c.3 million HE	Endtime

If you enjoyed this book,
please spread the word
by telling some friends.

s

To read in-progress books and
to learn how you can support quality sf,
visit
www.supportSF.com

s

For official Scattered Worlds gear,
information, and e-text editions,
visit the Scattered Worlds website at
www.scatteredworlds.com.

GET FREE BOOKS

For every ten Speed-of-C books you buy,
we'll send you another one free.

You can buy ten different titles,
ten copies of one title, or any combination.

In each of our books,
you'll find a barcode and number
in the bottom right corner of the last page.
Cut out the original barcodes from
ten Speed-of-C books, and send them
to us along with your name, mailing address,
and email address.

When our next book is released,
you'll receive a free copy.
It's as simple as that.

Speed-of-C Productions
PO Box 265
Linthicum, MD 21090-0265

Books from Speed-of-C Productions

The Curse of the Zwilling
by Don Sakers
0-9716147-2-5 • 384 pages • $19.99

It's Hogwarts meets Buffy at Patapsco University: a small, cozy liberal arts college like so many others – except for the Department of Comparative Religion, where age-old spells are taught and magic is practiced. When a favorite teacher is found dead under mysterious circumstances, grad student David Galvin finds that a malevolent evil has awakened. And now David, along with four novice undergrads, must defeat this ancient, malignant terror.

The SF Book of Days
by Don Sakers
0-9716147-6-8 • 184 pages • $14.99

Drawn from the pages of classic sf literature, here is a science fiction/fantasy event for every day of the year...and for quite a few days that aren't part of the year. From Doc Brown's arrival in Hill Valley (January 1, 1885) to the launch of the Bellerophon *(Sextor 7, 2351), this datebook is truly out of this world.*

PsiScouts #1: At Risk
by Phil Meade
0-9716147-3-3 • 132 pages • $9.99

In the 26th century, psi-powered teenagers from all over the Myriad Worlds join together as the heroic PsiScouts.

Act Well Your Part
by Don Sakers
0-9716147-7-6 • 189 pages • $14.99

A classic gay young adult romance, back in print for its adult fans as well as a new generation of teens. At first Keith Graff dislikes his new school. He misses his old friends, and despairs of ever fitting in. Then he joins the school's drama club, and meets the boyishly cute Bran Davenport....

Order through your favorite bookstore, online retailers such as Amazon.com, via our website (*www.scatteredworlds.com*), or mail orders to Speed-of-C Productions, PO Box 265, Linthicum, MD 21090-0265. For mail orders, please include $4 per book for shipping & handling.

The Scattered Worlds universe of Don Sakers

Dance for the Ivory Madonna
a romance of psiberspace
by Don Sakers
0-9716147-1-7 • 460 pages • $19.99
Spectrum Award finalist; 56 Hugo nominations
*"Imagine a **Stand on Zanzibar** written by a left-wing Robert Heinlein, and infused with the most exciting possibilities of the new cyber-technology." -*
*Melissa Scott, author of **Dreaming Metal, The Jazz***

A Voice in Every Wind
two tales of the Scattered Worlds
by Don Sakers
0-9716147-5-X • 108 pages • $7.50
On a world where meaning lives in every rock and stream, and every breeze brings a new voice, one human explorer stands on the threshold of discoveries that could alter the future of Humanity.

Weaving the Web of Days
a tale of the Scattered Worlds
by Don Sakers
0-9716147-0-9 • 113 pages • $7.99

Maj Thovold has led the Galaxy for three decades, a Golden Age of peace and prosperity. She is weary and ready to resign, but tshe faces one last battle: a battle on the strangest battlefield known: a web of living tendrils that stretches across interstellar space. A web where Maj's enemies wait, like spiders, for their prey....

The Leaves of October
a novel of the Scattered Worlds
by Don Sakers
0-9716147-4-1 • 304 pages • $17.50
Compton Crook Award finalist
The Hlutr: Immensely old, terribly wise...and utterly alien. When mankind went out into the stars, he found the Hlutr waiting for him. Waiting to observe, to converse, to help. Waiting to judge...and, if necessary, to destroy.

Order through your favorite bookstore, online retailers such as Amazon.com, via our website (*www.scatteredworlds.com*), or mail orders to Speed-of-C Productions, PO Box 265, Linthicum, MD 21090-0265. For mail orders, please include $4 per book for shipping & handling.

Printed in the United States
83075LV00004B/4-27/A

9 780971 614796